Second Chance
Ranch

LIZ ISAACSON

"For thou, Lord, art good, and ready to forgive; and plenteous in mercy unto all them that call upon thee."
~Psalms 86:5

Chapter One

The walls in Kelly Russell's life had never seemed so close. Of course, they hadn't been this putrid shade of yellow for a long time, either. Her parents lived with the motto of "use it up, wear it out, make it do, or do without," and kitchen wall paint was no exception.

But if Kelly could ace this morning's job interview, she had a chance of getting her own walls again. Soon. And she'd paint them. Maybe blue, or purple, or green. Something cool. Anything but the stark white she'd had in California—or this dark yellow.

"I have to drive out to the ranch." She straightened her jacket as she glanced toward her mom and son, who sat at the kitchen table eating breakfast. She'd sailed through her college admissions interview in this jacket. She'd been hired for her first real job in this jacket. She'd also worn this jacket in divorce court and been granted full custody of her son, Finn.

She hoped the turquoise number would work its magic today. She tugged down the hemline, wondering when her black skirt had gotten a smidge too small.

Probably while you were sitting on the beach these past five years. She knew there'd be no sitting at Three Rivers Ranch, though she hoped the accountant would at least have an office.

"It's about twenty-five miles on that old, dirt road," she continued, knowing her four-year-old son wasn't listening, but hoping her mother was. "So I'll be gone for, I don't know, at least two hours. Maybe three."

"We'll be fine," her mom said. "I've taken care of children before."

"I know." Kelly pressed her lips together and determined that she did not need another layer of lipstick. She'd slick on clear gloss just before the interview. "But it's been a long time."

It had been twenty-four years, to be exact, since Kelly had been four. And her mother didn't seem as sharp as she once had.

Her dad grumped his way into the kitchen, but Kelly knew his frowny face was an act. "Hey, Finny," he said. "Want to go throw the pigskin?"

"Just a second, Daddy." Kelly crouched down and drew her son into a hug. "Love you, baby. Be good for Grandma and Grandpa."

She stood, and a sliver of nervous energy ran through her as she thought about returning to the ranch she'd loved as a teenager. She could practically smell the dust, hear the horses whinnying, and picture her best friend waving from the front porch, though Chelsea lived in Dallas now.

"Three Rivers needs a new financial controller," her mom said as she walked with Kelly to the front door. "You're qualified, and Frank knows you. He'd have to be dead not to hire you."

"Didn't you say he was going to be retiring soon?" Kelly worried the inside of her bottom lip with her teeth.

"That's what Glenda said." Mom put both hands on Kelly's shoulders as Kelly pictured the ladies down at the hair salon gossiping about everything from the price of beef to who'd moved in over the weekend. "You've got this." Her mom nodded and released her.

A rush of appreciation lifted Kelly's lips into a smile. "Thanks, Mom."

As she drove away from her childhood home, she made a mental list of things she could thank her parents for. Giving her a fabulous childhood under the wide, Texas sky. Paying for fifteen years of dance classes, which had provided her with a skill she'd used to fund her college education. Teaching her how to laugh.

Allowing her and Finn to take over their basement after her divorce.

She thought of her work at the local grocer as she pointed her pathetic excuse for a car toward the ranch. She'd been back in Three Rivers for several weeks, and she'd taken the first job she could get. But ringing up milk didn't pay well enough for her to buy her own house and raise a child. And the nearest dance studio was in Amarillo, fifty miles away. The investment of time and money to get there and back didn't make teaching ballet a viable option.

Kelly's fingers tightened on the steering wheel. "I've got this," she repeated. The gently rolling hills calmed her, as they always had. She'd spent countless hours out here with nothing but her thoughts, the wind, and her friends. The open, blue sky further anchored her. She'd loved lying on her back in Chelsea's backyard,

7

creating stories from the clouds that rolled by. And the summer storms—she and Chelsea had made up their own songs, their own lyrics, their own choreography, all to the sound of thunder.

By the time she turned down the dirt driveway that led to the homestead, a sense of peace filled her. This ranch had been her second home growing up, and coming back to it now felt *right*. If she could get this job, it would be the first step toward getting her whole life back.

The nerves returned. She took a deep breath at the sight of the familiar house, imposing the first time you saw it. But Kelly knew better. She'd been in every room, felt the love and warmth from the family pictures hanging on the walls.

Kelly laughed at the memory at the same time her chest squeezed. Working at Three Rivers would provide a little safety at a time when Kelly had none. No pressure or anything.

She noted the American flag flying in the front yard of the ranch-style home. She'd kept in touch with Chelsea over the years and knew her younger brother, Squire, had joined the Army. His mother was obviously proud.

Kelly wondered if she'd get to see Heidi today, maybe experience one of her powder-scented hugs. A nostalgic smile played at her lips. She hoped so.

She left the house behind as she drove to the edge of the homestead, passing the barns, stables, and grain towers. Three industrial trailers edged the property before it gave way to the bull yards, and Kelly parked next to a row of dirty trucks, her little sedan a miniature vehicle among the bulky ranch equipment.

She glanced around as she walked through the packed-dirt parking lot, noticing that not much had changed. The clucking of chickens and the lowing of cattle met her ears, attributes that indicated this was indeed a working ranch. Kelly sidestepped a particularly large stone in the path. She'd have dust all the way to her knees by the time she made it inside. Everything about her spoke of a city businesswoman entering a whole new world, but she'd had to wear her heels. This was an *interview*.

Unfortunately, the metal steps and ramp were grated, creating a veritable gauntlet for her Jimmy Choo's. She supposed the heels, though fashionable and absolutely the perfect statement for this outfit, weren't exactly ranch attire.

She shifted her weight onto the balls of her feet and made it up four steps before her right heel sank through the metal. She set down her purse and tried to wrench the shoe free as she balanced on her toes. The Texas heat caused a trickle of sweat to form on her forehead. She did not want to enter the interview dusty, heelless, and now sticky.

She swung her hair over her shoulder, the movement throwing her off-balance. She gripped the railing to steady herself and prepared to make another attempt at freeing her shoe.

"You know, most ranch hands wear boots," a man said behind her.

Kelly's heart tripped as a strangled sound came out of her throat. She straightened, her hand smoothing down the back of her skirt, where a high slit was located. Had he seen anything?

She pressed her eyes closed. She'd never felt out of place on this ranch, and she wasn't going to start now. "Yes, I can see why," she agreed. "However, I didn't get the memo." Kelly opened her eyes and twisted to see who she'd need to avoid on the ranch. Because she was going to get this job, sweaty, mismatched, and dirty notwithstanding. She expected to see a cowboy—preferably one with a multi-purpose tool he could use to cut her free.

But this man, standing over six feet tall, didn't wear the regular stonewashed jeans and long-sleeved shirt. No siree. Not a boot or a belt buckle was in sight. Instead his pressed khakis and black polo accentuated his athletic body. Biceps strained against the sleeves of his shirt, a clear testament that ranching did a body good. Maybe he drank a gallon of milk everyday too. The only two indicators that he belonged in Texas were the cowboy hat perched naturally on his head and the panting dog at his side.

Kelly's reasons for wanting the position suddenly shifted to a completely new level. She gave herself a mental shake—she needed a job, not a boyfriend.

"Ma'am." He took off his hat and ran his fingers through his thick, brown hair. She couldn't tell from his sly smile and the amused sparkle in his eye if he was secretly laughing at her predicament or if he'd seen way more leg than she'd intended. She found herself returning his devilish smirk. Why was her stomach doing that floaty thing? She suppressed it and smoothed her hand over the back of her skirt again.

As he settled his hat back on his head, Kelly twisted and slid her feet out of the toes of her shoes. She turned around carefully so as to avoid touching the jagged metal, and placed her feet back on her shoes. Good thing she'd taken all those dance lessons. Still, her calf muscles hadn't been used this way for a long time.

As she took in his form again, she recognized his cobalt blue eyes still sparking with mischief, his straight, long nose, and his square jaw where that smile remained.

"Squire?" She wobbled a little as she spoke.

He seemed startled at the use of his name, his smile fading. Squire studied her for a moment, thunderclouds darkening his eyes into a shade of gray that reminded Kelly of the churning ocean. "I don't think we've met," he said.

Oh, they had. He just possessed a lot more to admire now than he had in high school, including a pair of unforgettable dimples that appeared as his grin returned. "Are you going to clue me in?" he asked. "Or just stare at me until your name appears in my mind?" He folded his arms across his broad chest and quirked his eyebrows.

She blinked rapidly, embarrassed that she'd been caught gawking. "I'm Kelly Russell." She shook her head, wishing she could shake away the words just as easily. "I mean Armstrong. Kelly Armstrong."

"Like, Bond. James Bond?" His throaty laugh tickled her ears. "Sorry. Doesn't ring a bell."

He shrugged like it was no big deal that he didn't remember her. Kelly couldn't understand how he could've forgotten. She'd practically lived down the hall in his sister's room.

"Yeah," she said, still balancing backward in her shoes, the heel still jammed into the metal steps. "Remember, I was on the cheer squad with Chelsea? I slept over here all the time?" She peered at him, but his face remained impassive, stoic.

"Chelsea had a lot of friends," he said. "Were you one of the gigglers?"

"No!" Kelly blew her hair out of her eyes, but it stuck to her forehead. She gave up hope of going into the interview without a bucket of sweat dripping from her face. "Remember how we used to choreograph dances and make you judge us?" Kelly emitted a nervous giggle before she could quell the sound.

"You just wanted to watch football, and we'd drag you into the backyard and make you watch us do our high kicks." She attempted the move now, realizing too late that her skirt was too tight for such things. Her foot barely made it above her knee and that slit allowed a blast of air to go up her skirt.

Squire's eyes closed briefly as she pressed down her clothes once more. The dog whined, somehow sensing her stupidity and warning her to *stop now!*

She'd lost her mind. *So this is what it feels like*, she thought. She'd let Squire completely undo her composure. Still, it bothered her that he didn't remember her. She took a deep breath, trying to refocus on the impending interview.

"Okay, well, whatever. Maybe you can help me get out of this mess." She pointed at her shoe and tried for a carefree chuckle. It sounded more like a strangled cat. At least it wasn't a giggle.

Squire joined her on the fourth step, steadying her as she turned around and stepped back into her shoes properly. "Why don't you just take off the shoe and then yank it out?" He released her and continued up the stairs while his dog slipped past them to lie in the shade. "In fact, I would've removed my shoes first, climbed the steps and then put them back on. At least shoes like that." He gave her a flirtatious wink, and her memory stumbled. Maybe this man wasn't Squire Ackerman. Kelly had certainly never seen him with more muscles in his body than stars in the sky. And he'd never flirted with her.

"I'd like to see you wear shoes like this," she muttered, her gaze murderous as she glared at him.

"I would *rock* shoes like that, darlin'," he said. "And Kelly? I remember your high kick being much...higher."

Her heart cartwheeled through her chest. He did know who she was! That little snake.

Before she could formulate an answer, he entered the building and let the door crash closed behind him.

"Take the shoe off, *darlin'*," she mimicked, but she did what Squire had suggested. The metal was just as hot and ragged as it looked. She balanced on the ball of her foot, trying to do as little damage as possible, this time to her skin. Her heel came free, and thankfully, it had only suffered a few minor scrapes.

"Is he always like that?" she asked his border collie, but he simply looked at her with a pleading expression, as if to say, *Please don't attempt that high kick again.* She vaguely recognized the animal, but she couldn't recall his name. She did remember that Squire had always loved his dogs. "Bet he'd help you if you got stuck."

She removed her other shoe and scampered up the rest of the steps barefoot. As she slipped back into her heels on the safety of the rubber mat outside the door, Kelly wiped her brow, sent a prayer heavenward that she could ace this interview, and took a deep breath. Then she pushed open the door.

Squire Ackerman winced at the sound of the door banging closed behind him, the metal on metal reminding him of being trapped in the tank. Immediately, the smell of hot gears and diesel fuel assaulted him, though the more accurate scent in the administration trailer would be men who worked with horses.

He took a moment to center himself, grateful he'd managed to navigate the stairs and enter the building without Kelly seeing his limp. As he strode down the aisle toward the ranch hands, he wasn't as successful. He'd been back at Three Rivers long enough for them to get used to his somewhat stunted gait, and they all busied themselves as they sensed his approaching fury.

"Where's Ethan?" he growled at Tom Lovell, the only cowboy who hadn't found a pretended task upon Squire's arrival.

"Sent him out to the north fence, Boss." Tom's gum snapped as he chewed it. "You said it had popped its rungs."

"How long's he been gone?"

"He left about seven." Tom stared steadily back at Squire, something the Army major appreciated. *Tom would make a good general controller*, Squire thought. But Clark sat at the front desk, and he'd run the operations on the ranch for almost as long as Squire had been alive.

Squire grunted his acceptance of Tom's answer and hurried

around the short, semi-permanent partition. The shoulder-height wall separated the front area of the trailer, where the cowboys met and received their assignments, from the row of permanent offices he'd built into the back.

His father's door was the first on the left, Squire's second, and their accountant occupied the last office.

He might as well start thinking of it as Kelly's. Squire knew his father had already hired her in his mind. The interview was simply a formality.

Squire's phone buzzed in his front pocket, but he waited until he'd made it inside his office, shut the door, and flipped the lock. Only then did he remove his phone, already knowing who had texted. Squire sighed, wishing he'd never taught his mother how to use technology.

Has Kelly arrived?

Like she didn't have her nose pressed against the front windows, watching and waiting for Kelly's car, simply so she could text him about it. She'd also sent message after message last night, each asking if Squire could handle seeing Kelly again. Her last one had said, *Forget about last time. This is your second chance.*

He'd ignored all her messages until that one. Then he'd sent back, *There was no last time, and there is no this time. Mom, stop!*

He definitely wanted there to be a *last* time. His invitation to her senior prom proved that. Her rejection screamed through him as loudly now as it had a decade ago. There would definitely *not* be a *this time.*

He leaned against the locked door and closed his eyes.

She hadn't driven the forty minutes to the ranch to find a new husband, he knew that for certain. He couldn't let the lines between them blur like they had last time.

At least he'd assigned Ethan a task in a remote quarter of the ranch. A calculated move, since Squire knew Ethan was the best looking cowboy employed at the ranch, with the biggest ego. He would've hit on Kelly before she even made it into his father's office. Squire had sent him away to protect her from Ethan—not because he was jealous or worried about the competition. Definitely not because of that.

Squire knew the moment Kelly entered the building, and not only from the way the walls vibrated as the door slammed shut. That sound would never become familiar, and Squire blinked away the blinding images of smoke rising from a mangled heap of metal that used to be a tank. The one driven by Lou.

Though dangerous, he focused on what he could remember about Kelly to help drive away the memories of his last deployment. The scent of her perfume had stuck with him through the years. As he'd passed her on the stairs, he'd caught the same whiff of cocoa butter and honeysuckle he'd always associated with her.

Kelly's voice floated through the thin walls of his office. "Thank you, Tom." Squire stuffed away the twinge of guilt that he'd caused her embarrassment. *He* hadn't worn impractical footwear to the ranch.

The walls shook again, Squire's signal that his dad had arrived. He'd expect Squire in the interview, though he'd already decided to hire Kelly. Squire didn't understand the point of the interview if he was going to hire the first person who walked through the door.

She's the only *person*, he reminded himself. Still, she'd barely made it *through* the door, what with those ridiculous shoes. He'd had to employ his military training to keep his face blank while he'd spoken to her.

Pretending he didn't know her may have been childish. Crossing his arms made him appear imposing and big, and he knew it. He'd done both on purpose to keep her at arm's length. He hated that she turned him to mush with a tropical scent and a smattering of freckles.

He took a cleansing breath, praying for the strength he lacked. He'd experienced plenty of frustrating situations during his dual deployments overseas. He could weather this too, especially since Kelly Armstrong had made her interest clear years ago. Nothing between them had changed. He was still Chelsea's little brother, someone Kelly had overlooked so often Squire had felt so completely invisible he'd sometimes startled when she spoke to him.

His phone buzzed again, but he chucked it on his desk before yanking open the door and heading toward his father's office, taking careful seconds to make sure his left leg didn't outpace his right.

Squire studied Kelly from a distance before he entered the room. Her turquoise blazer gave her a feminine figure, with a white blouse barely visible underneath. She wore those four-inch black heels and just the right amount of makeup to be professional. Her sandy hair fell halfway down her back; her light green eyes were as magnetic now as they'd been ten years ago.

He crossed his arms. A stampede of raging bulls did not scare Squire Ackerman. Bad weather could not deter him. Women did not affect him.

Major Squire Ackerman had complete control over himself, his emotions, and what he let other people see.

Especially Kelly.

"I am fearless," he heard her say as he stepped closer to the doorway. "Who else would leave their cheating husband in California, trek halfway across the country with their four-year-old son, and attempt to start over?" She tried for a carefree chuckle, but her eyes caught his as he moved into the office. The sound stalled in her throat. She crossed her legs and gave him a pointed stare, but her gaze didn't flicker to his injured leg.

"Sorry I'm late." He settled on the corner of his dad's desk, ignoring Kelly completely though his fingers curled into fists, needing to corner and interrogate the man who'd cheated on her. "What did I miss?"

His father glanced up at Squire. "Miss Kelly said she can get Three Rivers back in the black."

Squire snorted. "How did *Miss Kelly* say she'd do that?" He reached down and opened a drawer in the desk. He pulled out a thick stack of file folders. "Because our last guy left us in a mess of trouble." He dropped the files, which were incomplete financial records, on the desk. They made a deafening bang.

Kelly flinched. She swallowed, a nervous movement that drew

his attention to the slender column of her neck. Frustration frothed inside his chest, filling and fighting and overflowing until he felt choked with longing for a future that could never come to fruition. He wished he could go back in time and stop himself from asking her to the prom. Maybe then he'd have his dignity. Maybe then he could look her in the eye. Maybe then he'd be glad she'd applied for this job.

"I'd need to see the files in order to articulate a proper plan," she said, only a slight tremor in her voice.

His dad nudged the stack forward. "Take 'em."

Kelly eyed the paperwork, which probably weighed more than she did. She stood and dragged the folders toward the edge of the desk, staying a healthy distance from Squire. "I can come back tomorrow with a proposal."

"No need," his dad said, and Squire knew what was coming next. He stood up and put his hands in his pockets in an attempt to look bored.

Sure enough, his dad said, "You're our only applicant. If you think you can do this, the job is yours."

Kelly stared at him, unblinking.

A shiver squirreled down Squire's back at the same time his stomach clenched. "Dad, let's not be hasty." He glared at Kelly like she'd somehow bewitched his father into offering her the job. He knew she hadn't, just like he knew it was easier to act like a jerk to put distance between them. If she didn't like him, then she'd avoid him. The very thought made his heart tumble to his shoes, but he needed the distance.

He turned away from her and leaned closer to his father. "We can't afford another disaster."

"I won't let you down," she said.

Squire's blood squirmed in his veins at the assurance in her voice. He couldn't believe her. She'd let him down before and didn't even have the decency to admit it. He gave her another sweeping glare as his father clapped his shoulder.

"Show her to her office, son." He tipped his head her way. "Clark out front will give you the paperwork you need."

"Thank you." Kelly smiled and shook his father's hand, but he pulled her into a hug.

"It's good to see you back in Three Rivers, Miss Kelly."

Squire wished he didn't think so too. The fresh ink on her divorce papers felt like a shield he should wield.

"Thank you, Frank." She turned to Squire, almost like she would shake his hand too. He stepped back, a clear message for her to keep her handshakes to herself.

"This way." He led her down the hall, past his office, and into the last one in the back corner of the trailer. It was where he'd discovered the discrepancies between his father's bank accounts and the quarterly reports.

He'd never been so angry. So frustrated. So helpless. Not even when his tank platoon had been targeted in Kandahar and he'd lost four men in his company, been injured himself, and witnessed the more horrific things that fire did to human flesh. No, this betrayal ran deep, and it meant his parents couldn't afford to retire anytime soon.

Squire had never felt the love of ranching the way his father had, and his father's father before him. The ranch needed to stay in the family if his parents had any chance at surviving financially, which made it disappointing that Squire didn't have an older brother.

But he understood duty, always had. Even though he wanted a different life, somewhere else, if his dad wanted to retire, Squire would do whatever he could to make the transition easier.

Kelly flipped on the light and entered her office. She'd lugged the files with her, and Squire considered taking them from her. *What could it hurt?*

But he knew what it would hurt. He'd worked too hard for too long to build those walls around his heart.

"Let me take those," he said anyway, his voice much softer now that he was alone with her. She had to stretch up while he bent down, his forearm cradling hers, as she transferred the load to him.

She stumbled, her shoulder crashing into his ribcage. A grunt escaped his mouth, and she gasped. "I'm sorry." She stepped back and tugged on the bottom of her jacket.

"It's fine." He moved to the desk, a definite limp in his step and a flush rising through his neck. He watched as she inspected the built-in filing cabinets, ran her finger along the blinds covering the single window, and tested out the chair behind her desk.

She finally looked at him. "I like it."

"Great," he said dryly. "It's not like we'd change it if you didn't."

She gave him a withering look. "Come on. It's me, *Kelly*." She tried a smile, and he allowed himself to return it halfway.

He knew who she was. She was the girl who danced with his sister. Who slept over on the weekends. Who'd bewitched him so completely he'd convinced himself a senior would go to her prom with a sophomore. If she'd gone with someone else, he might've understood.

He shoved the sourness down his throat where it belonged.

While he hadn't been this close to Kelly in years, the real prize she offered was solving the ranch's financial problems. He couldn't forget that.

He'd moved on with his life. So had she. She'd gone to college, gotten married, had a kid. And now a divorce.

He allowed himself to fully smile. Maybe she wasn't out of his league anymore. *She most definitely is*, he corrected himself as he stepped closer to where she sat. "You still know any of your dance moves? Besides that pathetic high kick, of course."

She threw her head back and laughed. "I'm sure I could choreograph something for you. Remember when I used to do that?"

"Yeah. You and Chelsea were so annoying."

"I'm sure we were." The glint in her eye spelled *mischievous*. "So do you make it a habit to leave helpless women trapped in your stairs?"

"You're hardly helpless, darlin'." Squire sat in the chair opposite of her desk with his arms crossed.

She busied herself with the files, shifting them around without really changing anything. "I also don't remember you being such a scoundrel." Though she'd moved away from Three Rivers, her

Texas twang remained. He liked it, and wanted to hear her say his name in her pretty little voice.

"I don't remember you wearing such high heels," he shot back.

The silence lengthened between them, until Kelly asked, "How's your mother?"

She hadn't forgotten her Texas manners while she'd been gone. Squire would give her that. "She's good. She's given new definition to the word overbearing now that she knows how to text. But she's good."

Kelly leaned forward, and Squire caught a glimpse of her younger self, the girl he'd crushed on so long ago. "You don't like your mother texting you? Why? It cramps your style while you're out digging ditches?"

Squire could've sworn she was flirting with him, but the idea was ridiculous. She was coming off a messy divorce and had moved in with her parents. He'd heard what she'd said about moving halfway across the country alone. She wasn't looking for a relationship, especially with her new boss.

"As a matter of fact," he said. "It does. Digging ditches requires a lot of concentration. Texting is distracting."

"Don't dig and text." The flirtatious sound of her voice wormed its way straight into his heart. He'd remembered a lot about her, but her voice had faded quickly. He realized now how much he liked listening to her talk. "That is so you."

His pulse galloped, slowing to a trot as he leaned forward, like they might share something meaningful if they got just a little closer to each other.

Her phone chimed, and she jumped up. "That's my alarm. I need to get back." The playfulness and hope drained from her voice and face. She glanced up and smiled, but it had lost its savor. Squire watched the weight of real life descend on her, clouding the girl he'd once known.

"Can you help me get these to my car?" She indicated the folders.

"You don't need to look at them tonight," he said. "You start tomorrow. Look at them then."

She blinked a couple of times, confusion racing through those beautiful eyes. "I'll just take a couple folders." She picked them up and stepped toward the door just as Squire did.

Close enough to feel the gentle heat from her skin, Squire found a flicker of fear in her expression. He wanted to reach out and comfort her, ask her what her ex had done to her to make her so nervous, demand to know how he could have changed her into someone other than the Kelly she'd been.

Instead, he said, "You really don't need to take those. The ranch'll still need your help tomorrow." He moved into the hall ahead of her.

"Is it really that bad?" She joined him, her purse swinging between them.

"Just about." Squire noticed the silence in the front of the trailer. The cowhands had gone out on their assignments for the day, leaving Clark alone at the controller's desk.

"Miss Kelly," Clark said, heavy on the cowboy accent as he handed her a manila folder. "If you fill these out and bring 'em back tomorrow, I'll get y'all on the payroll."

Kelly grinned, tucked the folder into her purse along with the others, and thanked him. Clark barely acknowledged Squire, something he was used to. Clark knew everything about the ranch, from how to run it to how to let it run itself. If Squire was being honest, Clark should've taken over as foreman.

They both knew it, and it seemed like every other cowboy on the ranch did too. He had his work cut out for him to win over the staff and figure out how to manage something as vast as a cattle ranch. He'd tried some of the tactics he'd learned in the Army about taking over a company when the commander had been killed in action. But cowhands weren't soldiers, and they hadn't quite warmed to him the way his comrades in Afghanistan had. Squire had learned that men would trust him when he showed them they could.

He needed to do that at Three Rivers, but he hadn't quite figured out how.

Kelly didn't know any of his failures on the ranch, and she didn't need to. He wouldn't burden her with his unrealized dreams, permanent physical injuries, and financial troubles.

She removed her heels before stepping out of the admin building, and he had a momentary flash of him sweeping her off her feet and carrying her down the steps.

Longing lashed his internal organs like a whip. Thoughts like that were why he needed to put so much distance between them, why he needed to constantly remind himself of the duties he'd taken upon himself as ranch foreman. He had to find the missing money before he could even think about anything but the ranch.

"See you tomorrow."

Squire focused, the fantasy of him and Kelly dissolving as he realized she'd already made her way down the stairs and to her car. She waved, and he watched her climb into her sedan and drive down the road, kicking up dust as she went.

He frowned at himself, needing a cattle gate on his emotions to keep them contained. He glanced toward the stables, wondering how he could possibly endure day after day with Kelly so close.

Chapter Two

Squire went to the house instead of returning to his father's office. He just couldn't muster the energy to learn about fencing issues, the location of aquifers, or the schedule of selling and shipping the herd. He'd helped out on the ranch growing up, but only tending to the horses, riding the fence line, and weeding his mother's massive vegetable garden.

When he'd gotten old enough to learn the business of ranching, he'd gone off to school and then the Army.

He found his mother in the kitchen, bent over a recipe. Squire couldn't name how many times he'd seen her in that exact position. If she wasn't cooking, she was gardening, cleaning, or sewing. He and Chelsea each had at least fifteen quilts to "start them off right" should either of them ever get married.

Thoughts of marriage blasted bitterness through his bloodstream—because thoughts of marriage conjured never-to-be images of him in a black tux while Kelly clutched his arm and wore a white dress.

"Squire," his mom said, her voice sounding faint and far away. "You okay?"

He blinked his way out of the Kelly-induced fog. "Hmm? Yeah."

"How'd the interview go?"

"Dad hired her." He sat on a barstool to watch his mother cook. "You're not surprised, are you?"

Peace wafted over him whenever he sat at this counter and spoke with his mom. He smiled at her when she glanced up. "Kelly was the only applicant, and she does have a master's degree in accounting."

His mother pulled open the fridge and retrieved a package of ground beef and two green bell peppers. "You don't sound happy about hiring her."

"She has no experience," Squire said, removing his cowboy hat and running his fingers through his hair. "She might be worse than Hector."

His mother wielded her knife with precision as she split an onion in half. "That would be impossible." She lit the stove and put a cast iron pan over the flame, her gaze sliding over Squire in that assessing way all mothers had. He knew she was looking for something, he just didn't know if she'd found it.

"She's…different," he said, a well of unease pooling where his oxygen should be.

"So are you," she pointed out. "Maybe it will work out this time."

"Mom." Exasperation roared and reared over his previous contentment. "There was no *last* time."

She chopped and diced, drizzled olive oil into the hot skillet, and tossed all the vegetables in. They sizzled and jumped while she added the seasonings. "I know."

Squire didn't think she did. "I'm her boss. I can't go, I don't know, getting involved with my accountant."

"Good point," she said. "You couldn't get involved with your sister's best friend either. But sometimes God has a way of putting people right where they need to be, right when they need to be there." She brandished her wooden spoon at him to enunciate her point.

"Sure, Mom." Squire stood up before she splattered him with sautéed vegetables. He'd gone to church with his parents until he'd left for college. Then Sunday had become the only day to sleep in or get caught up on homework. His faith hadn't dwindled, just his outward manifestation of it.

During his deployments, he'd attended services whenever he could. There was nothing like war to make a man question what he believed. Especially about where he might go after this life. Squire had given a fair amount of thought to the subject, and his belief that God was merciful and kind had been strengthened.

Squire returned to his cabin and changed into his workout clothes. Maybe God could make sure his weight training drove Kelly from his mind completely, though all of his previous pleas to this same end had gone unanswered.

Kelly burst through the front door of her parent's house, her heart tumbling up her throat. "I got the job!" She dropped her purse as her mom jumped up from the couch in the living room.

"You got the job?"

"I got the job!" She grabbed her mom in a hug, laughing and spinning her around. "I was the only applicant, but I got the job."

The back door slammed and Finn raced through the mudroom and into Kelly's arms. "Mom, guess what?"

"What, baby?"

"Grampa says I threw the ball fifteen yards."

"That's great, Finny." She ruffled his hair, knowing a four-year-old couldn't throw a ball that far. "Guess what? I got a job that will help us get a house of our own." She beamed down at her son, basically a miniature of Taylor. His dark hair; his strong, square face; his unending energy.

Finn's eyes weren't quite as dark as her ex's, but they hovered between green and brown in a beautiful hazel color. The only mark of herself she could see in him.

"I don't want to get a house," Finn said, squirming out of her hug. "Grampa says he's gonna build a new chicken coop, and I can help." He ran through the house to the backyard.

Kelly stood, a sigh escaping her lips. She couldn't live with her parents forever, but having her dad in Finn's life had brought her son's smile back. He rarely left her father's side, and as hammer blows came from the backyard, warmth radiated in Kelly's core.

She moved to the back door and looked through the window. Twenty yards away, out by the shed, her dad bent over several pieces of cut wood, nails clenched in his hand. Finn stood in front of him, a hammer at the ready. She'd never seen Taylor do anything similar with Finn, and as she watched, her mind wandered to Squire. She could definitely see him working and playing with his kids.

"You can stay as long as you need to," her mom said, and Kelly's thoughts about her new boss scattered.

"I know, Mom. But we can't live here forever, even if he wants to." She kicked off her heels and left them by the back door before she moved into the kitchen. "I have a little bit more to go before I pay off the divorce lawyer. Taylor and I agreed to split everything regarding Finn right down the middle. I could probably save enough to put a down payment on a house and move out in a couple of months."

Her mom nodded, tucking a stray strand of Kelly's hair behind her ear. "Where will you go?"

"Somewhere in town." She began to make lunch. Her shift at the grocery store began at two, and while she'd gotten the position at the ranch, she couldn't blow off Vince. She'd give her two-week notice today and hope Vince would let her work on the weekends.

"Maybe over by Crystal," her mom said, watching her set water to boil for the pasta. "There are newer houses on the west side of town."

"Maybe," Kelly said, content as she thought about Finn playing with Crystal's boys. Kelly would like to be close to her cousin too. She thought about taking Finn out to the ranch. The idea of him running free—riding horses, feeding calves, playing in the dirt— made her heart expand by double. Finn would absolutely adore the ranch, the way she had as a child.

And there were a lot of men out there. But Finn just needed one man in his life, someone who loved him and wanted him around. Taylor wouldn't be that man, and again Squire stole into Kelly's mind. She shook him away, stirring her thoughts into the pasta pot until hot water sloshed over the sides.

"Once I have enough saved, I'll look around." Kelly put the wooden spoon down and flashed her mom a smile. Planning more than a day or two out brought a sense of accomplishment Kelly hadn't experienced in months.

Her mom turned the conversation to the weather, a safer topic that gave Kelly some relief from the heavier matters weighing on her mind. It had been an exceptionally dry spring, and her mom worried about the possibility of not having the traditional fireworks show at the upcoming Fourth of July celebration. But Kelly's mind wandered back to the ranch. Nerves crowded her stomach as she thought about going to work tomorrow, of seeing Squire. If only she had a few weeks to review everything she'd learned in five years of college so she could put together a proposal that would impress him.

Finn and her father banged into the house, asking about lunch. Kelly forced away her confusing thoughts about Squire and fearful worries about being inadequate at her new job, painted on a grin, and opened a can of spaghetti sauce.

The next morning, Kelly stirred before the sun rose. Not because of nerves or bad dreams, but because Finn was whimpering. Suddenly wide-awake, she pushed the folders off the edge of the bed where she'd discarded them last night and hurried out of her bedroom. Theirs were the only two bedrooms in the basement, situated right next door to each other, so she arrived at his bedside in seconds.

She stroked Finn's hair off his forehead, and he calmed. "You're feverish. Did Grandpa give you chocolate after dinner?"

Finn moaned, which Kelly took as a yes. She went into the small bathroom in the hall. She had a plethora of children's medications, and she selected one that would bring down Finn's fever quickly. She filled a cup with water and took it in with the pain reliever.

She woke him and made him drink the medicine and a sip of water. He settled right back to sleep, looking angelic in the soft light coming from the bathroom. She carefully lay down beside him on the double-wide bed and closed her eyes. She needed to be up in a couple of hours to get ready for work, but she could hope for a few minutes of rest.

She startled awake at the sound of her mother calling her name. "You'll be late on your first day. Are you ready?"

Adrenaline swamped her, forcing her pulse to drum against her tongue. Kelly took a few seconds to gather her bearings. The spot next to her—in Finn's bed—was empty.

She hustled into her bedroom, but her phone alarm had been silenced. "Finn!" she called as she realized she didn't have time to shower.

"Yeah, Mom?" Finn came bounding into the room, already wearing an adult-sized tool belt held tight by the masterful use of a bungee cord.

"Did you turn off my alarm?" She wasn't surprised at his miraculous recovery. He often ate too many sweets, experienced a low fever and stomach pain in the night, and woke up good as new.

"Yup. You were tired."

"Finn, I have to go to work this morning. Remember Mommy got a new job?" She flung hangers around in her closet, searching for the right outfit to wear.

Finn watched her, and she finally sent him back upstairs. She couldn't blame him for turning off her alarm. He'd done it many times since they'd moved here.

She sucked in a deep breath. She could only imagine what Squire would say if she showed up late.

She hurriedly stepped into a pair of purple corduroys, matching them with a flowery silk top. She slipped on a more ranch-practical pair of black boots and moved into the bathroom.

A groan escaped as she took in her appearance. She turned on the water and ran wet fingers through her hair to get it to lie down. With a hot cloth, she washed her face. After whipping out the hairdryer and doing a quick fluff, she did a half-decent job on her makeup, and practically sprinted upstairs.

"Breakfast?" her mom asked from the kitchen.

The clock read eight thirty-two. "No time," Kelly panted. "I'll be fine." She kissed Finn, grabbed her purse, and ran out the front door.

She parked next to the ranch trucks at nine o'clock sharp, thanks to some pedal-to-the-metal driving. The shocks on her sedan might never recover, but Kelly would take car repairs over being late.

Squire's dog was already snoozing in the shade as she climbed the stairs and banged her way into the administration building. She glanced around surreptitiously for him, but didn't see Squire in the open area to her left. She handed her folder of paperwork to Clark just as a blond cowboy stood and whistled.

"Well, who is this sweet drink of water?" he asked, swaggering toward her.

Kelly almost laughed out loud, but managed to keep her face placid. Clark answered for her without looking up from her paperwork. "That there's Ethan," he told Kelly. "He's good for almost nothin'."

"I'm good for everything, sweetheart," Ethan corrected as he moved closer. Too close. He smelled halfway between showered and mucking out the horse stalls.

Kelly straightened her shoulders and looked up at him. "Is that so?" She itched to take a step away but held her ground. "Got anyone to vouch for that?"

Ethan settled his arm across her shoulders. "You will be soon, little lady."

"Ethan," a man barked.

Kelly jumped, her hands automatically coming up to cover her spasming heart. Ethan dropped his arm like she'd spontaneously combusted. His second reaction took several seconds longer, but he eventually turned toward Squire.

"Boss." He didn't look ashamed, didn't tip his hat.

Squire steamed like he was four seconds from going into

Tasmanian devil mode. His eyes stormed; the muscle in his jaw twitched, and he folded those bulging arms across his chest.

Kelly pressed her lips together to keep her smile contained. She definitely wasn't trying to make sure her lipstick was as fresh as possible.

"Did you get those bulls moved to yard three?" Squire asked.

"Didn't know I was supposed to," Ethan responded.

"I put it on the board for today." Squire hooked his thumb toward a white board behind him in the open area of the trailer where the cowboys had been hanging out yesterday. Kelly only saw two or three there now and assumed the rest were out tending to their assignments.

"Well, then I'll get right on it," Ethan said. "And I'll get back to you later, pretty lady." He tipped his hat to her and with a final glance in Squire's direction, left the trailer.

Kelly noticed Squire's grimace as the door slammed. His teeth clenched and his eyes pressed closed against something only he could see.

"You're all set," Clark said as if he hadn't been present for the showdown that had just taken place. "Here's the password for the computer."

Kelly took the slip of paper and stepped with confidence toward her office. When she reached Squire, she had the strangest urge to reach up and smooth the tension from his shoulders.

"Good morning," she said, focusing on stepping past him without touching him. He smelled like wood smoke and musk, and she silently took the deepest breath she could manage.

"Morning." He followed her through the trailer to her office and sat in the chair across from her desk.

She suppressed her sigh, sat down, and pulled the files from her purse like they could shield her from his presence. "These were pretty messed up." She glanced at him. "What do you know about them?"

"About what you just said. They're messed up." He stared back at her, and again she noticed that he didn't wear normal ranch attire. Today he was wearing jeans, but it was obvious they hadn't spent any time outside in the sun. No belt. Clean, new hiking boots. He wore a short-sleeved button-up shirt in lilac. She didn't think an Army man would be caught dead in purple, but on Squire, the light color served to enhance his muscles.

His cowboy hat sat in place, covering his dark hair, and his striking eyes reminded her that he was dangerous to her health. Everything about him seemed vibrant, while she felt pieced together in yesterday's clothing.

When she realized she was staring, she pulled her attention back to the file. "Why'd you say you didn't recognize me yesterday?" She kept her eyes down. "I mean, you obviously did."

"From what I remember, you like doing things by yourself." His mouth seemed painted in a level line. His arms couldn't clench any tighter across his chest. His tension bled into her, which made her stomach squirm in a wobbly dance.

She flipped open the file, unsure of what he meant by such a comment. She knew she didn't need him in her office, all up in her business, as she studied their financial records. "I'll let you know when I find something, or when I have a plan for what we should do."

"Great." He stood, reached into his pocket, and extracted his phone. He leaned over her desk to see what papers she had. "I wouldn't start there."

"It was the one on the top," she said, a vein of annoyance working its way into her voice.

"Doesn't mean that's where you should start."

Her stomach chose that moment to emit the loudest growl that had been heard this side of the Mississippi.

He chuckled. "My mother usually serves breakfast at seven," he said. "She might have something leftover. You want me to go get it for you?"

"No," she said quickly. She certainly didn't need Squire bringing her food. She ran her fingers through her limp hair, cringing at the somewhat greasy texture. "I'm fine. I just skipped breakfast this morning. Wasn't feeling well."

He lifted his eyebrows, but not in surprise. More like a challenge.

"Not feeling well?" he repeated. "Nervous?"

"About this job?" She forced a laugh. "No. I've got this. It was something I ate at work last night."

"You have another job?" The eyebrows went down, but she didn't like the compassionate tone in his voice either.

"No," she said. "Well, I do for a couple more weeks. But just on weekends."

"What do you do?"

She really wanted him to leave. Maybe then she could crawl under her desk and bask in the shame of her situation. "I, uh, work at Vince's."

"The grocery store?"

"Don't tell me you've forgotten about them, too." She gave him a look that could melt steel and returned her attention to the files. "Maybe you need to see a specialist about your memory loss." As soon as she said the words, she regretted them. Maybe he'd been injured on one of his deployments. She knew better than anyone that not all wounds were visible.

His low chuckle prompted her to look up, but she refused to give in to the grin tugging against her lips. Her sweet tooth would have to be satisfied with cookies, not Squire's tasty laugh. At the thought of food, her stomach rumbled again.

He flipped through the stack of files and plucked a thick one from the middle. "Start here." He plunked the folder on top of the one she'd been reading, turned, and left her office. She watched him go, noticing that he favored his right leg. Only a slight hiccup in his stride, but present nonetheless.

So he *had* been hurt overseas. Even as she wondered what had happened, relief that he'd left her office flowed through her strong enough to anchor her to why she was there. And it most definitely wasn't to find a cowboy.

Chapter Three

"Squire?" Kelly's voice came from the doorway of his office just before lunch. He turned from the window, where he'd been standing, staring into the openness of the ranch and wishing he could be out there instead of in here. His right leg almost gave out from the shift in weight, and he clenched his teeth against the pain shooting through his hip and into his back.

"What happened to Hector Ford?" She didn't enter the office.

Squire wasn't surprised at the question. He'd want to know about the person who'd made the mess he now had to clean up.

"He died," he said, drinking in the compassion in her eyes. Could she care about the ranch after only a few hours of work? "About four months ago."

Kelly's mouth opened in a round O. "And you're just now replacing him?"

Squire shifted his weight to his good leg and folded his arms, determined to remain passive despite her presence.

"It took a while to go through his disjointed system," he said. "I studied the files, but it took me several weeks to figure out the discrepancies between my dad's finances and the reports Hector provided."

"Where's the money that's missing?"

Squire abandoned his post at the window as he shushed her. He waved her into the office, glancing toward the cowhand's space—he saw no one—before he closed the door behind him. "No one knows about the missing money except for me. Even my dad doesn't know. It needs to stay that way."

"Okay," Kelly said, her eyebrows puckering together in a pinch that Squire felt in his gut. "But your dad knows something's wrong."

Squire scrubbed a hand along the back of his neck. "Yeah, I told him his savings weren't as much as he'd thought. That he wouldn't be able to retire as soon as we'd hoped." He exhaled. "I don't know where the money is. Hector doesn't have it where I can find it. His widow moved to Dallas after his death. She's living with their daughter. If she has access to the money, she doesn't spend it."

Kelly chewed her thumbnail as concern radiated from her expression. Anger fumed beneath Squire's skin. He didn't need her pity now, just like he hadn't needed it in high school. Somehow, even with her staring right at him, he felt as see-through as freshly Windexed glass.

"How do you know all that?" she asked.

"I hired a private investigator," he said. "There's a lot of money missing. I don't think it's been spent, and I want to find it if possible. Naturally."

"Naturally," she repeated. She worried her bottom lip between her teeth, drawing Squire's attention to her mouth. He turned away from her in favor of the window.

"Okay, thanks." She moved to leave.

"Wait," Squire said, facing her.

"Yes?" She cocked one hip, her expression full of challenge.

Familiar bitterness coated his mouth, making it difficult to swallow. So she didn't like being in a position of non-power. Too bad.

"What have you found?" he asked.

"I'm only about a third of the way through the files."

Squire squinted at her. "I have more for you in my office at home. So you're not as far as you think."

"Do you live here on the ranch?" she asked. "Can we go get them now?"

"I live in one of the cowhand cabins, but the files are in my office at the house. We can go get them if you'd like." He shrugged. He was having a hard time caring about the ranch today. More than usual.

"I wore boots." She glanced down at her feet, and Squire followed her gaze. "I can go myself."

He almost groaned at the sight of her knee-high, thick-heeled boots. What was with this woman and heels? "I'll help you carry them."

She moved down the hallway and out the door, Squire behind her. She navigated the stairs successfully, even if she did grip the handrail like it was her life support.

He whistled at Benson as he descended the steps. The dog

bounded to his side, and pushed his nose into Squire's palm, somehow sensing that Squire needed to release some tension.

He had to walk slowly to stay by her side as they navigated their way to the house, which suited him fine because it allowed him to even out his stride. "Does every shoe you own have a heel?"

She rolled her eyes. "I needed something cute for my interview."

Squire paused and cleared his throat as embarrassment rose through his face. "I'm real sorry I didn't help you out of those steps yesterday, darlin'."

"Maybe you'll be able to make it up to me," she said.

Squire almost tripped over his own feet, his injured leg further complicating how quickly he could right his footing. "I'll try," he said when he found his voice. "Assuming you keep wearing shoes unfit for a ranch."

"Assumptions aren't nice," she said, an extra twang in her voice as she repeated something his mother—hers too, probably—had said countless times.

He'd made a lot of assumptions about her, especially after she'd ignored his invitation and gone to her prom alone. Even a rejection would've been better than the silence she'd given him.

He'd assumed she thought him too young. Too unpopular. Too inferior.

He wondered what her real reasons were, but the wounded pride lodged in his throat kept him from asking.

A gentle breeze brushed them as they walked, but it couldn't drive away the inadequacy cascading through Squire. He smelled lunch about a hundred yards away, and Kelly's stomach roared again.

"You should eat lunch with the cowhands." He really didn't want her eating with the boys, especially Ethan. He also didn't want her to know that he cared who she spent her time with.

"Right," she said. "And have them all make comments about my heels like you have? I don't think so."

He pulled his grin like he'd pull a punch, the way he did so his true emotion didn't seep out. But happiness trickled down to his fingertips that she didn't want to eat with the cowhands.

"I haven't told anyone about the whole step thing," he said. "Some of the boys would be downright devastated to know you couldn't even make it into the building."

She slugged him. "I can make it anywhere."

"Yeah, like to California and back." The words left his mouth before he could assess what kind of damage they'd do. He wanted to suck them back in, or have the wind wisp them into silence. But they hung there between them, the easy comfortableness they'd had now gone.

Spiders writhed in his gut, but he didn't know how to un-say something. He mentally kicked himself for a few steps as he frantically searched for something to smooth things over.

"I'm sorry," he said, wondering how many times he was going to have to apologize today. "I shouldn't have said that."

She waved her hand like it was no big deal, but Squire saw the heavy lump she swallowed and the reflective quality of her eyes before she focused on the row of cabins lining the backyard.

"Mom could make you up a plate, and you could eat in your

office," he said.

"I'll be fine. If I can handle you, I can handle a few cowboys." She didn't sound two shakes from crying, and relief sighed through him like sand over bare toes.

She tottered, her ankle twisting as she came down on a dust-covered rock, and Squire lunged for her. Her right arm flailed as he caught her left. Her ankle gave out, and suddenly he held all her weight by just her elbow. He managed to right her, and she leaned into him for a moment, her breath staggered. He wrapped both arms around her and took a deep drag of her cocoa butter scent. "You okay?" His voice betrayed him by coming out like he'd gargled with glass.

Good one, Major Obvious, he chastised himself. *Way to keep things neutral.*

He quickly released her, noting her nervous laugh and matching hers with one of his own.

"Maybe I'll need to invest in a whole new line of footwear." She frowned down at her boots like they were snakes.

Squire straightened his shirt and took a deep breath to steady his increased heart rate. He reminded himself that Kelly was his employee, someone he had once crushed on, someone who'd stomped on his soul. Nothing more. She had absolutely no experience in accounting. He had to keep an eye on her, not because he liked what he saw, but because he needed her to solve the financial problems of the ranch.

"You coming?"

He glanced up and found her several paces down the road. He

hurried to catch her, reminding himself of the way his heart had clenched like he'd tried to stuff it into a too-small boot when he'd taken Kelly's advice and asked someone to the prom. She'd encouraged him for weeks before he got up the nerve. He'd been walking and running and fighting in those too-tight boots ever since. At least with her.

"Hey, Ma," he said upon entering the house. She stood in the cavernous kitchen, the scent of baking bread and roasting meat filling the space. "You remember Kelly Armstrong?"

His mother put down her rubber spatula and came around the counter, her face beaming like the moon. "Kelly, of course. How are you, dear?"

Kelly laughed as she embraced his mother. "I'm great, Heidi. How are you? I can see that you haven't lost your touch in the kitchen." Her stomach gave another loud growl.

They chatted for a few minutes, while Squire watched. Kelly seemed more at ease in his mother's presence. She had a natural ability to make small talk; her smile was quick and her questions sincere. He didn't have to think very hard or go back very far to remember why he'd liked her so much.

Something new and strange flooded him. Something tipped with forgiveness, made of acceptance, and coated with confusion. Something like letting his heart out of the cage he'd locked it in.

He cleared his throat, much the same way he wished he could dislodge his thoughts. "The files are in my old bedroom." He motioned down the hall, and Kelly excused herself from her conversation. Even though Squire was a full-fledged adult, he still felt the laser gaze from his mother as he followed Kelly further into the house.

"You remember where it is?" he asked.

"Your bedroom?" She glanced over her shoulder. "Yeah, end of the hall, take the stairs up, turn right. You hated us coming in there."

His defenses rose. "You guys were always making fun of my posters."

"You liked weird stuff," she said. "Rugby or something."

"Cricket," he said. "My uncle went to Australia and brought me back all the equipment." He touched her arm to get her to stop. "And those posters might still be up. Try not to laugh."

He moved past her, went up the seven steps, turned right, and continued down the hall to his old bedroom. The door stood open, and he went inside. He'd transformed his room into a comfortable office with a long, leather sofa, more masculine paint color, and a professional desk.

But the cricket posters still covered the entire wall behind the couch. His dad had built a bookshelf where Squire displayed his football trophies and a few pictures from high school.

Squire didn't want to live in his parent's house, so he'd adopted a cowhand cabin. He kept his room here, though, and he sometimes slept in the house if he was feeling particularly lonely. Not that he felt that way very often. There was something about being alone that straightened the crooked thoughts in his head.

Alone, he could rely on himself. Trust himself, the way the Army had taught him.

Kelly took in the posters. "Fun," she said, but it didn't sound like she really thought so. "You could take them down, you know."

"Right." He opened the filing drawer in his desk. Several dozen files sat inside, and he hefted them out. "Like how you said I should ask someone to prom." His muscles turned into boards. His pulse slammed against the roof of his mouth. His own courage surprised him.

"You never did take my advice." She picked up a picture frame while Squire's fingers turned numb and he forgot to breathe or blink or blink or breathe.

He *had* taken her advice. He'd asked *her* to prom. Did she not remember? How was that possible?

"I've never seen this picture," Kelly said, drawing his attention from his stampeding thoughts.

He set down the files and joined her at the bookcase. She held a framed picture of Squire in between Chelsea and Kelly, both in their full dance performance make-up. Her light green eyes mesmerized him in this picture, and he remembered staring at it as he fell asleep at night. "That's from one of your competitions. You guys were seniors, I think."

She peered closer at it. "We're wearing a green costume. That was *Save Me.*"

"I can't believe you remember that," he said, especially if she couldn't recall a bedroom full of balloons—his name printed on a slip of paper in one of them.

"I can't either." She replaced the picture on the bookshelf and moved on to the next one. This one portrayed Squire and his father, their arms slung over each other's shoulders, before one of his football games. "I also didn't know you played football."

"I made varsity my junior year," he said. "Started all of my senior year."

"Oh, I'm sorry I missed all that." She shot him a rueful smile. "I would've liked to have seen you play."

A swell of pride inflated Squire's chest, but he simply clasped his hands behind his back. If she'd known he'd go on to varsity fame, would she have gone out with him?

"I don't play anymore," he said. "Not much use for football in Afghanistan, and the cowhands don't have time." He didn't mention that he couldn't run very well.

She ran her fingers down the golden football figure on one trophy. "Bet you could still throw the ball around, though."

Squire watched her fingers for a moment and moved back to his desk before he said or did something foolish. Acceptance of her rejection—or whatever that feeling in the kitchen had been—didn't erase everything between them.

He lifted the files and headed for the door just as the lunch bell rang. By the time he could lug the paperwork back to Kelly's office in the admin trailer and return to the house, the cowhands would be served and eating on the deck.

Perfect, he thought. He'd patterned his behavior after his father's, who often arrived late to lunch so as to avoid socializing in the kitchen. He'd noticed that his father did the same.

Kelly padded after him, but she didn't make it out of the kitchen. Squire's mother hooked her elbow through Kelly's and steered her toward the bar. "Come eat lunch with us," she said. "You too, Squire, after you drop those off."

Squire nodded and headed outside. With the administration trailer empty, Squire didn't encounter anyone as he limped into Kelly's office. He deposited the files on the corner of her desk and hesitated before leaving.

Kelly had been in this office for all of a few hours, and yet it smelled like her perfume. He breathed in deeply, allowing himself this moment to enjoy the scent in the air.

She'd placed a framed picture on her desk, and upon stepping around the corner, he examined it. Kelly smiled back at him, her hair lighter and her skin tanner in this picture than it was currently. She held a toddler on her lap, and Squire picked out the similarities and differences of Kelly in him. He had the tint of green in his eyes, like hers. But he sported a square face and a rounded nose, with a head full of nearly black hair that curled at the ends.

Squire knew Kelly's hair didn't curl. She'd complained about it enough to Chelsea for the whole county to know. He let his gaze wander along her desk, finding a list of things to do, all of them focused on her job. The files he'd brought from his father's office sat in two neat piles, one still taller than the other. A notebook lay in front of the piles, with notes scribbled in green pen.

The door to the trailer slammed, and Squire scampered out of her office with his head down, like another bomb had been dropped on him. He definitely didn't want to get caught somewhere he shouldn't be, moony-eyed and slack-jawed over a few pens and notebooks.

Because that was all this tide of unease in his stomach meant. She was organized and she'd help the ranch find the missing money. He needed that, and he also suddenly wanted time to get to know her again, find out what had happened in high school, discover if his white-dress-black-tux fantasies could come true.

Fear reared against his thoughts, as he'd never let them roam so freely—at least not where Kelly was concerned.

"Hey, girl." Squire ran his hand down the nose of Juniper, the black mare who'd taken a shine to him. She nickered and tossed her head gently, nudging his shoulder.

"I know," he said, the anxiety and helplessness draining from him with the presence of the horse. Juniper dropped her head, sniffing Squire's pockets for a treat. He pulled out the apple he'd grabbed from his office and offered it to her. She crunched through it, her long lashes half-closed over her enormous black eyes.

Hank ambled closer, a bay stallion that Squire's father had purchased two years ago. He lifted his head over the fence and snuffed at Squire.

"Yeah, me too," Squire said, not really sure what conversations he was having with the horses, only knowing that they eased the river of pain in his mind—and his leg.

The bay showed his teeth before pulling his head back over the fence. He wanted an apple too, but he was too proud to ask.

"I didn't forget about you, boy." Squire reached in his other pocket and produced a second apple. Hank nudged Squire's right leg, in the exact area where his femur had been crushed under the weight of the tank. No one had seen that bomb coming, but Squire had driven right into it.

Four men in Squire's company had died. Two more had burns over half their bodies. He pressed his eyes closed as the smell of fire and metal and blood flooded his nose. The pops of machine guns and flames and screams, the eerie quiet that followed. The brush of desert wind, carrying sand and moans and death.

Juniper whinnied, somehow knowing that Squire had disappeared into the memories. He yanked his eyes open to find himself thousands of miles from Kandahar. Touching the horse's neck, the sounds and smells from that fateful day evaporated.

Hank nudged his knee one last time before taking the apple. Though Squire's femur had been completely pulverized and the doctors couldn't repair it, he knew others had been sent home with complications he couldn't imagine, and still others had returned to their loved ones in boxes. Steel rods, pins, and plates kept his body together now, and sometimes the ache in his leg brought Squire's teeth together in agony.

"Yeah, still broken," he told Hank, though this time he wasn't sure if he meant his leg, his mind—or his heart.

Kelly enjoyed watching the cowhands bustle through the line, filling their plates with Heidi's delicious casserole and bread. They each thanked her with a tip of his hat and a "Thank you, ma'am."

They continued out the sliding doors to the deck, where they ate in the shade.

She watched for Squire to return, but he didn't come. She loaded a plate at Heidi's insistence and sat down with her and Frank in the kitchen. They told her stories about Chelsea, her job in Dallas, and the man she was dating.

Kelly listened and asked questions to keep the spotlight away from her. Surely the Ackerman's knew why she'd returned to Three Rivers.

Sure enough, Heidi finally put down her fork. "Tell us about your son, Kelly."

She swallowed the last bite of her garlic bread, which suddenly turned to sand in both taste and texture. She coughed to clear the crumbs. "Finn will turn five just before the Fourth," she said, her Texan drawl returning no matter how she tried to stop it. Something about the ranch brought out the cowgirl in her. "Right now my daddy is indoctrinating him to love football and wield a hammer." She grinned and took a sip of water, which only turned the bread to lead in her stomach.

"Does your mother watch him while you're at work?"

"Most of the time," she said. "My cousin helps too. We live with my parents right now, but with this job, I'm hoping to get a place of my own."

"In Three Rivers?" Heidi had a way of asking questions without seeming pushy. Kelly remembered this from high school, when she and Chelsea would try to get off the ranch for a party. In the end, Heidi always knew what was happening, even if she'd been lied to.

"Probably," Kelly hedged, though she was fairly confident she'd stay in town. "I'm still working on the details."

"Let us know," she said. "We'll have the cowhands come help y'all move."

"Mother," Squire said, entering the kitchen. "We can't just make them do anything we want." He washed his hands before he picked up a piece of bread and buttered it. "They have work on the ranch, not playing moving company." He shot his mother a tense look that Kelly suspected should've landed on her.

"We pay them to work for us," his mother said, seemingly unfazed by Squire's admonition. "We can have them do anything we want."

"No, we can't," he argued as he settled next to her at the table. "They have work to do. Our fences don't fix themselves, and those cows are dumber than posts. They'd starve if we didn't put the hay right in front of them." He glanced at Kelly. "No offense."

She held up her hands in surrender, marveling at the change in him. One second, he was kind and teasing and fun, the Squire she remembered from high school—with some grown up benefits. The next, he was moody and dark, throwing death glares left and right like horseshoes.

"I don't have much to move anyway," she said. "I managed just fine getting here from San Diego by myself. I'm sure I can move out of my mother's basement." She stood abruptly, needing to get away from Squire's heady scent and negative attitude.

"Thank you for lunch, Heidi. I should be getting back to work." She strode out of the kitchen. She heard Heidi say something to

Squire in a tone of disapproval, but she didn't care what.

She couldn't read him, and she couldn't keep up with what made him go from flirty and fun, to apathetic, to downright rude. As she squished through the dust back to her office, she determined that the best course of action would be to stay as far from him as possible.

Though Squire was dashing, she couldn't jeopardize her career by allowing herself even a taste of him. She'd only end up with a stomachache.

She hadn't noticed Squire much in high school—he'd always been Chelsea's little brother—but now she couldn't help taking note of his presence. His personality filled the room, his flirtations awakened something dormant inside her, and she found she wanted to learn more about him.

She squashed the flickering flame of attraction she'd felt, telling herself that she simply wouldn't enter his once-bedroom again, wouldn't think about the picture he'd kept for so long—whether he lived there or not—wouldn't try to reason through why out of only two pictures on his bookshelf, one was of her.

A jolt of realization struck her like lightning cleaving a tree. She felt frozen solid though the sun beat down with intense heat.

Like how you said I should ask someone to prom.

Squire had sounded so cynical, worn a look of anger and disapproval. She hadn't understood and had chosen to deflect his attention to the photos.

She understood now.

All those balloons.... She'd never been able to find a name on any of the confetti strips, so she hadn't known who had asked her, hadn't known who to answer.

"Squire." She spun back toward the house, her body made of hot, liquid lava.

No wonder he hadn't helped her out of the steps. No wonder he was so hot-cold, hot-cold.

She forced her steps toward the admin building, needing time to formulate an apology for never responding to his prom invitation.

As she settled behind her desk, she sent a prayer of thanks for the opportunity to be employed at Three Rivers. With a calm breath, she opened another file and pushed back thoughts of Squire and how safe she'd felt standing in his arms.

Chapter Four

By five o'clock, Kelly had a dozen pages of notes and the first stack of files read. Her head pounded like nothing she'd felt before, and her feet were freezing because the air conditioning was quite efficient at warding off summer as it tried to sneak inside.

She packed her notes and a few of the files and got up to leave. Two steps past his office, Squire called her name. She pressed her eyes closed and took a deep breath before turning. Would he see the guilt on her face?

She offered a silent plea for the same help now. "Yes?"

"Status report?" He leaned against the doorjamb and crossed his arms. His shirt pulled along his biceps, and Kelly had to consciously pull her eyes back to his.

"Excuse me?"

"You've been reading those files all day." He took one step closer, his hands falling to his sides. "What have you learned?"

Kelly couldn't make a plan of action in one day. The records Hector had kept were scattered and disorganized and many were simply missing.

Squire knew everything that was in those files, and she worked to tamp down her rising annoyance.

"You're missing one million, six hundred and thirty-seven thousand dollars," Kelly said, her voice low so as to not be overheard. "Hector had accounts for your parents for personal use, for the ranch, loans for land improvements, loans for acquiring more cattle. They all seem to be in order."

His eyes seemed to glow from beneath the brim of his cowboy hat. "I know all of that."

"I've had one day." She shook her purse toward him. "I'm taking these files home. When I find something worthwhile, I'll let you know." She turned away, her temper in danger of erupting. She was tired, and hungry, and she could not have this conversation right now.

She made it outside with her dignity intact. The door didn't bang closed, but she wasn't going to go back and fix it. She unlocked her car and found only more stifling heat. As she reached to close the door, she heard someone chuckling. She glanced back to the trailer to find the reason she hadn't heard the door close: Squire stood there, laughing.

"Good chat," he called, lifting his hand in a friendly wave.

"Yeah, yeah," she muttered as she slammed her door and put the car in reverse. The drive home gave her the time she needed to decompress.

She left her purse in the car and went inside to find Finn. Instead, she found her mother stirring something in the kitchen. "Where's Finn?"

"Daddy took him over to the corner store," she said, glancing up. "He earned a dollar by feeding the chickens, and he wanted some penny candy."

A blade of disappointment sliced through Kelly. She was glad her son was safe and happy, but she missed him. For the past four years, *she'd* been the one to provide his safety and happiness. Turning that over to her mom and dad had been hard.

She reached into the fridge for a bottle of water, pulling her phone out as she went. She sent a text to her cousin, Crystal, asking if she could come over tonight. Kelly got an enthusiastic response before she even opened her drink.

Come by tonight after nine! We can chat.

And by chat, Kelly knew her cousin meant *break out my stash of hidden Girl Scout cookies.* Kelly's whole body sighed in relief at the thought of Thin Mints and Crystal's strategies for dealing with Squire's moods. She still needed the words for a decade-too-late apology to fall into the correct order.

"Good first day?" Her mom pulled Kelly into a much-needed hug.

"Good enough," she said, making her voice strong. She stepped back and didn't meet her mom's eyes.

"Mom!" Finn burst through the backdoor, wrenching the exhaustion from Kelly's muscles. "Grampa let me drive the lawn mower today!" He jumped into her arms, one tiny fist clenching a brown paper sack. "And he paid me for feeding the chickens, and look, I got those red fish Daddy used to buy me."

Her heart simultaneously leapt for joy and withered in pain. Finn seemed so happy, even when talking about Taylor, the man who had lied about where he'd been and painted over everything with candy and roses.

"The lawn mower?" she asked, looking at her father.

"I was on it with him," he assured her. "But he did feed the chickens himself. My daddy used to give me a dollar for feedin' the chickens. Finn's a natural."

"Dad, it's throwing stuff. Anyone can do it." She gave him an affectionate peck on the cheek for adoring her son. "Thanks, Daddy."

"I can throw the football too, Mommy. Come watch!" Finn wiggled away from her, abandoned his sack of candy on the floor, and sprinted outside. She laughed and followed him, even though her sweats and the couch were calling her name.

"How was work?" her dad asked as they followed Finn into the backyard.

"Tiring."

"You'll get used to it," he said, putting his arm around her shoulders.

"I hope so," she said, though she knew she would. The job she could handle. But Squire.... She'd never get used to the sugary sight of him.

As Kelly crept through town on her way to her cousin's, contentment washed over her. Three Rivers hadn't changed much, with its long Main Street, where cheerful storefronts lined the sidewalks. The barber, the grocer, the various eateries and hot spots. She took comfort in knowing some things never changed.

She glanced to her left and saw the park where she'd grown up playing. A new jungle gym, updated swings, and a safer slide set had been installed, but the same tall oak trees stood sentinel. She heard herself laughing with her cousins while her mother and aunt chatted on the benches, and nostalgia twirled through her. She longed for easier, happier times.

She passed the bank, the post office, the government square with it's white brick exterior. It gleamed as it always had. Glenda's salon sat with another group of restaurants, doctor's offices, and the elementary school.

Kelly relaxed against the headrest in her car. Old as it was, she loved this town. With a peaceful sigh, she knew she'd been led to the decision to stay here and raise Finn. After driving through more shops, past another grocery store, and beyond the last gas station in town, she made it to her cousin's. No sooner had she killed the engine and stepped from the car did Crystal call her name.

"Get back here!" Crystal waved over the fence, causing Kelly to smile.

She bumped through the gate and entered the backyard, where Crystal waited with a platter of cookies and a hug. "Hey, girl. You look good."

"Thanks," Kelly said as she took a seat in the deck chair, the soft sunset reminding her that there was no place on earth quite like Texas. Everything moved slower here, even the breeze meandering through the trees and the way the sun took it's sweet time disappearing into the dusk.

She moaned as she took a bite of her cookie.

"So what's new?" Crystal asked, taking a handful of chocolate-dipped sweets.

"Started my job today at Three Rivers Ranch."

Crystal choked, a spray of crumbs flying from her mouth. "Did you see him?"

"See who?"

"Major Ackerman," she said, raising her eyebrows like she couldn't believe Kelly needed to ask.

Kelly laughed. "He's my new boss."

"You should take advantage of that." Crystal waggled her eyebrows up and down. "If you know what I mean."

Kelly shook her head and took another bite. "Not gonna happen, Crys. Been down that road. It's rocky, and leads you back to your parent's basement."

Crystal took a few moments to put the pieces together. "You mean, you and Taylor…?"

"He was my boss." Kelly picked up her bottle of water and swirled it, watching the liquid go round and round, her thoughts far away in a past boardroom in Dallas.

"Not going to do that again. Besides, I have Finn now, and he doesn't deserve anything but the best." Kelly appreciated the first stars as they began to wink in the darkening sky. She wondered if she'd ever marry again. Sure, it was her choice, but what choice did Finn have? She had to remember that she had more than herself to take care of now. She couldn't afford to go off her strict, male-free diet, even for a pair of dimples and the knowledge that she'd missed her opportunity to dance with Squire.

"Maybe it's like Scott said on Sunday," Crystal said. "Maybe you just need to take that first step before God can guide your feet."

Kelly studied her cousin, surprised that Crystal's words practically mirrored her own thought that God had guided her to Three Rivers. "I don't think he meant I needed to start anything with Squire."

"Maybe Scott didn't." Crystal's eyes rounded in innocence as she took a dainty sip of her milk.

"Why don't you ask him?" Kelly laughed, her nerves jumping as the sugar did its job.

Crystal giggled with her, but their joy dissolved into silence as they both contemplated the sky. "You know, God led me to Scott," Crystal finally said, her voice as serious as if she hadn't had an ounce of sugar.

"I know." Kelly remembered how perfect her cousin's love story had been. Handsome man. Young bride. They'd known they were meant for each other from the first date. Scott had just finished his ministry training, and Crystal had just finished high school. But true love couldn't be stopped, and they were married the January after her graduation.

They had a good life—the kind Kelly had experienced in San Diego. Well, until she discovered the cheating, lying husband bit.

She believed that if she took a step, God would direct her feet. The sweet peace she'd experienced over her decision to settle in Three Rivers proved it. But she worried that she'd already bypassed the path she was supposed to be on when it came to men. Maybe that road was miles away, on another plane. Maybe because she'd chosen the wrong man the first time, she didn't deserve a second chance.

"Remember all those balloons I got?" Kelly asked. "For my senior prom?"

"Yeah," Crystal said. "You never figured out who sent them. Went alone with me and Chelsea, hoping he'd be there and say something."

Kelly suddenly had to sniff and fight back tears. She nodded to buy herself some time. Her dress had been plum, her shoes silver. She remembered seeing Squire there, but he'd never approached her, instead sticking to the sidelines and shadows before leaving early.

"It was Squire," she said.

Even the crickets turned silent.

"No way," Crystal finally breathed. "How do you know?"

Kelly swiped an errant tear away. "I don't know for sure. But I'm pretty sure based on some things he's said and how he's acted."

"It's fate," Crystal declared, exhaling as she threw herself back in her deck chair. "How romantic."

"Crys," Kelly said. "It's not romantic." She leaned forward and grabbed her cousin's hand to pull her from her imagination.

"Help me come up with an apology."

"Yes, apologize. Then you can start dating him."

Kelly sighed in dramatic fashion, though her own mind now raced with fantasies, all of them featuring the striking Army cowboy.

She wasn't sure if he'd hurt her, steal her heart, or simply give her a sugar rush. No matter what, she had to apologize.

Squire couldn't stand another evening by himself in his empty cabin, or in the mansion where his parents lived. He turned away from the window, sourness coating his throat. He had a half a tank of gas, and as he headed outside, he wondered how far he could get before he ran out.

Not far enough, he thought as Benson barked.

"Yeah, we're going for a ride." The dog bounded ahead of him and leapt into the back of the truck. Squire started the engine and aimed himself north, instead of east the way he usually did. Once, with a full tank of gas, he'd made it all the way to Oklahoma City before turning around. His father had been livid, though Squire couldn't blame him. It *had* been a school night.

He drove until he saw the "Welcome to Oklahoma" sign. Squire had driven to the border many times when he needed to see the sky and figure out what to do. Here, he'd decided to join the Army. Here, he'd decided to go into pre-veterinarian studies. Here, he'd released his dreams to finish his medical degree and open a small veterinary clinic in town.

Here, he'd become the dutiful son who would inherit Three Rivers Ranch.

He got out of the cab and climbed in the back of the truck with Benson, already praying that he could find some solace. Darkness wouldn't fall for another couple of hours, and Squire wouldn't be missed until morning. Maybe not even then.

When he'd returned from his deployment last fall, his leg still cast and healing, his mind was filled with hurt and anger. This stretch of sky had helped, especially with Benson nearby. Then his father had told him he wanted to retire. A few months later, Hector died, and everything got tangled. If the ranch had the missing one-point-six million dollars, Squire could hire a foreman. Three Rivers would stay in the family, but Squire wouldn't have to live it, breathe it, take care of it.

He'd been the one to suggest hiring an accountant—one who had a degree and knew the law—who could help them out of their "financial predicament." Kelly had the piece of paper, but Squire still wasn't sure she could get the job done.

As soon as he thought of Kelly, his thoughts tangled again. The confusion on her face when he'd mentioned prom. The interest when she'd asked about the picture. He should've discarded it a long time ago. Just like the cricket posters. But they meant something to him, and when he'd cleaned out his teenage bedroom to make a space for himself as a man, he hadn't been able to throw them away.

He let his mind wander to more carefree times, when all he worried about was working out and playing football. He remembered Chelsea driving him to school, how they'd stop and get Kelly, how she'd have to sit so close to him in the truck.

He'd felt like he belonged to a group back then. First with Kelly and his sister. Then with the football team. With his Army buddies, his squad. Since he'd returned, he felt like he didn't belong anywhere, not with his parents, not at the ranch, and not with Kelly.

The next morning, Squire woke with hot Benson-slobber seeping through his pants. He nudged the dog, which scrambled to his feet. He yawned, and let his tongue hang out as he panted.

"Let's go home, boy." Squire jumped out of the truck and stretched, noting that the sky bled a shade barely lighter than dawn. He still had plenty of time to waste before Kelly showed up for work.

He made it the last five miles to the ranch on gasoline fumes, parked, and arrived in Kelly's office before she did. He drummed his fingers on her desk, though she wasn't late yet.

"Are you lost?" She entered the room with her purse slung over her forearm, the files she'd taken home gripped in her hand. "Isn't this my office?"

"Nice shoes," he said, taking in her flats. She also wore a pair of gray slacks and a frilly, pink blouse that matched the color of her lips.

"Thank you." She put her purse in a drawer and appraised him with some apprehension in her eyes. "Nice clothes you wore yesterday. What? You didn't go home last night?"

Squire scrubbed the back of his head, noting his need for a shower, unsure if he should be embarrassed or pleased that she noticed what he wore. "Uh, not exactly."

"Oh, a little sleepover somewhere?" She crossed her arms and cocked one hip, her mouth turned down in disapproval.

"Me, Benson, and the Oklahoma border." Squire gave her attitude right back to her. He swore she almost smiled. Almost.

"Yes, well. What can I help you with, Mr. Ackerman?" She settled at her desk, but didn't start working.

A snag of hopelessness hooked his heart. "Come on," he said, trying to smile in a way that would make her relax. "Don't be like that."

"Like what?" She flipped open a folder and looked at it. She wasn't reading though.

"All *Mr. Ackerman*. I'm not the boss."

"You're not?" She shot him a meaningful look through her eyelashes.

"Okay," he said, standing. "I just wanted to ask you to do the taxes first. I thought of it last night. We filed an extension because of Hector's death, but I think they need to get done."

"But if I don't know where the money is, how can I complete the taxes?"

Squire shrugged. "I'm not the accountant."

"Exactly," Kelly muttered under her breath, but when Squire turned back to her, she gave him a sugar-sweet smile. "I'll get right on it, Boss."

He left, his heart pounding as if he'd just completed a hefty set of weights. Half from frustration at her attitude and half in appreciation of it, he willed his pulse to slow as he entered his office. But he had nothing to do, and he ended up in the front half of the trailer where Clark was updating the white board.

Clark never wore anything but jeans, a flannel shirt, and brown cowboy boots. Squire suspected his hat had been sewn to his head, though the brown hair poking out from under the brim had just been cut.

"Only Tom's working today?" Squire asked when he saw that the board was mostly empty.

"Givin' the boys some time off before plantin'," Clark said. "Tom could probably use some help with the horses."

Squire had spent countless hours in the saddle of his horse, Lucy. But she'd died a few years ago, and he'd bonded with Juniper. "Sure, I'll head over to the stable now."

Anything was better than suffering here, only a thin wall separating him from Kelly.

"In that?" Clark swept his gaze from Squire's feet to his head. At least he had his cowboy hat on. "I think he's muckin' stalls, Boss."

"Thanks, Clark."

The controller removed his hat and scratched his right ear. "And then he's gonna be out in the fields, checkin' on the hay. Might want some sunscreen."

Squire thanked him and hurried to his cabin. He couldn't stand another day of watching Kelly work, of wishing she'd burst into his office with a miracle. She'd only been here one day, and his constant loitering obviously wasn't welcome. At least his plan to push her away was working, though it did little to cheer him.

Benson ran in circles around Squire's legs when he came out of his cabin dressed in his dirty jeans, crusty boots, and work gloves.

He yipped like he hadn't gone to work with Squire in months. And he hadn't.

Sadness sang through Squire, and he reached down and scratched the old dog's ears. "I know, boy. We get to work the horses today."

Benson licked his hands and face before tearing off toward the stables. Squire followed and found Tom in the thick of shoveling out the stalls. "Need a hand?"

"I knew you were comin'." He smiled. "Your dog can't keep a secret."

Benson barked, and Squire swore the dog wore a smile.

Hank whinnied. "Your horses either." Tom nodded toward Juniper and Hank, who had both wandered over to the fence.

"No treats this morning, guys." Squire stroked Juniper's nose and ran his hand down Hank's neck. The strength he gained from the animals made him bow his head in gratitude.

"You don't need to help," Tom said, breaking into Squire's prayer. "I'm almost done."

Squire picked up a shovel. "You think I'm too soft?"

Tom chuckled. "Nah." He scanned him from head to toe. "Just haven't seen you wear digs like those for a while."

Squire grunted in response. Maybe he'd be more successful in convincing himself—and everyone else—he wanted the ranch if he worked it more often. He lost himself in the feeding of the chickens, preparing the bottles for the calves, and brushing down the horses. By lunch, he could've passed for a real cowboy, but he didn't have to be happy about it.

Chapter Five

The following day, Squire left the ranch and headed into town. Ranching was an around-the-clock job, but the administrative items fell off on the weekends. He planned to grab lunch at his favorite pizza joint next to Vince's grocery store, and then head into Amarillo. For what, he didn't know. He just knew he couldn't loiter around the ranch today.

After he got his food, he crossed the street to the park and found an empty bench farther from the playground. He'd taken the first bite of his pizza when a woman said, "What are you doing here?"

Wiping his mouth, Squire squinted up. Kelly stood in front of him, her hands on her hips.

Warring emotions made his stomach seize. Apparently, excitement didn't mix well with disappointment. "Eating?"

"I can see that," she said. "Why are you eating *here*?"

He took a long drag of his soda. "Because it's a beautiful day in Texas." He smiled from under the brim of his hat. "And last time I checked, it was a free country." He paused as she huffed and checked over her shoulder. "If not, I don't know why I spent sixteen months in Kandahar."

Her expression softened and her gaze flickered to his right leg. Ah, so she'd seen the limp he'd tried so hard to hide. She wore black pants and a blue polo with Vince's embroidered on the left pocket.

"You just get off work?" he asked to get the topic away from his injury.

"Just going in," she responded, focusing again on the playground. "I brought Finn for lunch, and my mom is picking him up before my shift."

"So you *do* eat," Squire said. "Want to sit?"

She swung her attention back to him, her face an interesting mix of surprise and uncertainty.

"I don't bite," he said, picking up his pizza again. "Unless you're covered in cheese and pepperoni."

His words elicited a quick smile—*Victory!* he thought—and she sat way down on the other end of the bench. She placed two fast food bags between them, and they seemed very much like a barrier to Squire.

"Which one's Finn?" he asked.

"Red shirt." She pointed toward the slides, where a dark-haired boy bounced up and down while waiting for his turn.

Squire watched him for a couple of seconds before focusing on Kelly again. The creases along her mouth had softened; the edge from her eyes had melted. As she watched her son play, Squire could see and feel the love she had for him.

Squire knew he hadn't been in love with anyone yet, even Kelly.

He wasn't sure what that felt like, but if the light glinting in her eyes was any indication, Squire thought love was pretty fantastic.

If it could loosen the rubber band constricting his heart, even better.

If loving someone could dull the past decade, set him free, give him hope for the future, he'd take it.

"He's cute," he said.

"He looks like his father." She sucked in a breath. "I mean—"

"I see you in him too," Squire said as the boy slid down the slide with pure joy on his face. He began running toward them. "The smile, for sure. His chin."

"Mom!" The little boy arrived, full of energy and fun. "Did you see that?"

"Sure did. Sit down and eat."

The wiggling Finn sat and took the paper off his hamburger. "This has no cheese."

"That's because that one's mine." Kelly snatched the burger from him and handed him the one with yellow paper. "Try this one."

"You don't like cheese?" Squire asked.

"Depends on the situation," she said.

Finn peered at him. "Are you a good guy or a bad guy?"

"He's my boss," Kelly said.

The word clearly had no meaning to Finn, whose eyebrows puckered. "So we can talk to him, right?"

"Right," Kelly said, ruffling his hair.

"I'm a good guy," Squire said. "My name is Squire. What's

yours?"

Finn looked at Squire's extended hand and then to his mom. Kelly gave him an encouraging nod, and he shook Squire's hand. "Finnley Xavier Russell."

"Wow." Squire chuckled. "Can I call you Finn?"

"Yeah, sure," he said, picking up his juice box.

Kelly grinned down at him, and when she lifted her eyes to meet Squire's, the smile remained.

He suddenly realized this could be his life. Sitting in the park on Saturday afternoon, eating lunch with his family, watching children swing and play tag and throw baseballs.

His arm slung across Kelly's shoulders.

His throat tightened as a powerful sense of belonging washed over him.

But this wasn't real. He didn't *belong* to Kelly and Finn, and they certainly didn't belong to him. Other couples dotted the benches, called to children, threw Frisbees to their dogs.

Squire realized that what he'd been missing was a family.

He slid a glance to Kelly, but she was absorbed in talking to Finn and eating lunch. He likewise focused on his food, his heart hollowing as he realized his fantasy of sitting at this park every weekend with Kelly was not his reality. Never would be.

"Grandma's here," Kelly said, standing. "Be good, Finny. See you in the morning, okay?"

Squire got to his feet too. "Nice to meet you, Finn." He patted the little boy's head before Finn ran toward Kelly's mom. "Good to see you, Kel," he said, his tongue stumbling slightly over the once-familiar nickname. "Have fun at work."

"Oh, yeah," she deadpanned. "I just love checking people out on Saturday night."

"We used to check out a lot of people on the weekends."

She laughed, her eyes brightening as she did. He realized that the spark of life he'd loved in high school only appeared when she allowed herself an uninhibited laugh.

"I think I prefer that sort of checking out to this." She nodded toward the grocer. "But I can't be late." She took a few steps away and then turned back. "See you Monday."

He lifted his hand in farewell, his attention singular as she crossed the street and entered Vince's. He followed and aimed his truck southwest to the busy streets of Amarillo. But the city didn't hold what he needed—a distraction. He was afraid that nothing would be able to free his mind of Kelly Armstrong, past or present—except the woman herself.

Kelly exuded politeness for the customers. Made small talk about their Saturday night plans. Counted their change. But her thoughts revolved around sitting next to Squire and eating lunch.

Finn usually shied away from most men, but he'd plopped right down next to Squire, shook hands with him, talked to him. Kelly tried not to read too much into what had happened at the park. Squire was well dressed, handsome, with a kind smile. He practically screamed American hero from his very pores. He'd been wearing a new scent today, one Kelly knew she'd smelled before but couldn't quite place. She stewed about it as she weighed bananas, bagged cans, and handed over receipts.

By the end of her shift, she realized she'd spent the entire eight hours thinking about Squire Ackerman. She sat in her car for a few extra minutes once she'd pulled into her parents' driveway, trying to fence him from her mind before she went to bed. She couldn't stand dreaming about him too.

She didn't even know how he'd rooted himself so deeply in her subconscious, her newfound guilt notwithstanding. He hadn't been particularly nice to her at the ranch, instead hovering while she tried to work, then criticizing which task she chose to do.

But he *was* tall and handsome, and his cobalt eyes sucked her in like a strong vacuum. She didn't understand how someone could live life so fully, without regrets and heartaches. One thought of his limp, and she knew Squire had a past, and that it wasn't all roses and sunshine.

She smoothed back the wisps of hair that had escaped her ponytail and hurried into the house. Her dad snoozed in the armchair, Finn curled into his side. Her mom glanced up from under the halo of lamplight across the room, her needle flying through her cross-stitch. "Hey, baby."

Kelly managed a closed-lip smile. She wasn't sure why, but she felt like she needed to be alone so she could cry. And not the kind of crying because she'd just found out her husband was a cheater and a liar, or the kind where she had to now be a single mom, or the kind where she'd been hurt physically.

The lonely kind of crying. The slow weep of missing a part of your life you used to love. Of coming home and finding someone there to listen, to discuss your life with, to hold close.

"I'm going to bed." She scooped Finn out of her father's lap and lugged him down the stairs. She managed to tuck him in and press a kiss to his forehead before the first tear fell.

Crystal's husband Scott stood at the front of the congregation, his sermon beginning to pass the length of Kelly's attention. Cuddled next to her, Finn's soft breathing indicated that he'd fallen asleep. He sometimes did during church, especially after her father let him stay up late watching Discovery Channel.

Kelly stifled her own yawn. While she usually enjoyed the timbre of Scott's voice, and the messages of forgiveness or mercy, what she loved most about church was the peace she felt when she attended. Like all her cares existed somewhere, but she didn't have to think about them inside these walls.

She sighed and closed her eyes. Down the row sat Crystal and her three, boisterous boys. The only time Kelly saw them without dirty hands or yelling about something was at church. A smile sang through her soul, just about the same time the choir started the closing hymn.

The meeting ended and her dad lifted a still-sleeping Finn into his arms. Her parents moved down the aisle, speaking to their friends and neighbors.

Kelly leaned over and helped Crystal pick up the cereal her two-year-old had dropped during the sermon. Once they had all the sippy cups packed, all the shoes back on, and everyone turned toward the exit, the room had mostly cleared.

Scott stood in the back, shaking hands and hugging widows. Kelly followed Crystal and her nephews, taking a deep breath as she neared the exit. Out there, the real world waited.

"I don't know." Squire's voice froze her feet mid-step. Her heart kicked against her ribs, and she smoothed her blouse before she could tell herself not to.

He stood to her right, in the other aisle, near the exit on the opposite side. Her view of him was partially blocked by Susie Randall, one of the stylists at the salon. A young, blonde hairdresser with fake nails, fake eyelashes, and other fakeries.

Kelly ducked around Scott and took an eavesdropping position in the foyer. If Squire turned and took four steps through the doorway, he'd see her. But right now, the wall protected her and allowed her to overhear his conversation.

"It would be fun," Susie said, her voice set high on *flirtation.* "Word is y'all haven't been out with anyone since y'all got back."

"My dad's needed a lot of help out at the ranch," Squire said. Kelly detected a note of reluctance in his voice. Her insides performed a pirouette at his rejection of Susie. If he wasn't interested in such a petite, perfect woman, maybe Kelly had a chance.

Maybe just a taste of sugar wouldn't hurt....

Where did that come from? She startled away from the wall just as Crystal called her name. Thankful she didn't have time to psychoanalyze herself, she turned to leave.

"Miss Kelly," Squire said, suddenly at her side. His Texas twang shot sweetness right down to her toes.

She resisted the urge to appreciate the sight of him in a dark suit and pale yellow tie. Just because he smelled like pine trees and honey didn't mean she could afford a taste of him. Along with his perfectly tailored clothes, he wore a cowboy hat and a smile Kelly knew had attracted Susie Randall.

"Oh, hey," she said, a little breathlessly. She reminded herself that she didn't attend church to pick up a dessert. She wasn't back in Three Rivers to find a new husband.

Squire nodded toward the door, where Crystal stood gaping. "I think your cousin wants you."

"Did you want me?" she asked, realizing half a heartbeat late how her question sounded. Her mouth dropped open like her jaw muscles ceased to exist. "I mean—that's not—"

"Oh, I did." He leaned closer, his eyes sparking with blue lightning. He brushed his hand along her elbow. "Are you going to the picnic?"

She shook her head, but his words refused to be dislodged. "Finn fell asleep."

His expression remained neutral. Pure Switzerland. "Maybe you'd have time to walk me there?"

Kelly glanced toward Crystal, who stood in the doorway, her eyebrows high and her mouth open. Without any help from her cousin, Kelly looked back at Squire.

"Okay."

Squire gestured toward the door, an encouraging smile on his face, and they stepped past a still-gawking Crystal.

"Interesting sermon today," Squire said, his hands tucked neatly into his pockets.

Kelly had a hard time remembering what Scott had spoken of. "What did you find interesting?"

Squire peered up into the sky, taking a few moments before he spoke. "Do you believe God knows what He's doing?"

"Yes," Kelly said, still searching her memory for Scott's words. She noticed that Squire wasn't trying to hide his limp today. "Don't you?"

"I did." Squire spoke softly, pausing at the corner to check for traffic, though on a Sunday afternoon there was none.

"What changed your mind?"

Squire met her gaze, sheer intensity in his. "I watched four men in my company die. Two others get burned beyond recognition."

Kelly's stomach flipped and flopped, and she reached out and ran her fingers down Squire's arm to his hand, where she held on. "I'm so sorry."

He tapped his right leg. "All I got was a rod in my leg. Then I'm good as new." He clipped out the last few words as he stepped off the curb, taking her with him since their hands were still joined. "I guess I'm just wondering why I'm still here and countless other men aren't."

"God must need you here."

"One man who died had a wife and four kids." Squire dropped her hand, and a chill danced through Kelly. "Surely they needed him. Certainly more than anyone needs me." He spoke with a measure of bitterness Kelly couldn't quite understand.

The park came into view, and Kelly stalled. For some reason, she did not want to be seen arriving at the picnic with Squire.

"Thanks for walking with me. See you tomorrow." Squire stepped away from her, and she watched him join the festivities without looking back.

She worried for a moment that she'd upset him with her statement that God needed him here. Maybe he was just hurt she hadn't apologized about the prom yet.

She sagged against the lamppost behind her, unrest pirouetting through her bloodstream. She could not get involved with her boss. Not again.

But with every beat of her heart, another dose of desire for the sensitive Army cowboy spiraled through her body.

Monday morning found Kelly in her office, her computer open to the tax program she liked best, with an Internet window listing the current tax laws under that. The former accountant at Three Rivers had scattered the financial documents throughout multiple folders and filing drawers, making it hard to track down the papers she needed.

Kelly entered the itemized deductions into her program line by line, taking careful seconds to make sure she had double and triple-checked the figures before moving to the next step.

A light knock on the door drew her eyes from the files.

"Morning," Squire said, leaning in her doorway with his hands deep in his jeans pockets. He hadn't shaved since she'd seen him on Saturday, and the scruff on his face only added to his intrigue.

"Good morning." Kelly leaned away from her computer, her thoughts flying from coherent to crazy in under a second. "Are you sick?" She stood and moved around her desk to press her fingers to his forehead. She had to stand on tiptoe to do it.

A frown creased his eyebrows. "No. Why?"

"It's...." She checked her watch. "Almost eleven, and this is the first I've seen you today."

"Very funny," he said, stepping past her to the chair. He settled himself and looked at her, those eyes blazing with mischief from beneath his cowboy hat. "Don't let me interrupt."

"So you're going to watch me prepare taxes?" She sat down in her seat and pulled a file closer. "You need a new life."

He leaned forward. "You're doing the taxes?"

She shrugged like it was nothing. But she'd deliberately *not* started the taxes on Friday, simply because he'd suggested it. Today, though, something had shifted. Fine, something had tilted inside her when she realized he'd asked her out all those years ago. Something which had only been strengthened by the light touch of his hand in hers as they walked and talked after church.

"You're doing that weird thing again," he said. "Where you act like I can read your mind, but you should know I can't." He grinned at her, and she saw the life in Squire's face, but sadness lingered around him too.

"You told me to do the taxes," she pointed out.

"I *suggested*," he said.

She set down the folder. "You practically demanded."

A smile twitched against his lips. "I'm working on my delivery of my requests," he said. "I blame the Army for my commanding tone and what I've been told are 'murderous glares'."

Kelly laughed. "Why *did* you join the Army?"

"They paid for my schooling," he said. "I got a partial football scholarship at A&M, but I knew I wasn't going to be a great collegiate athlete. So I joined the Army reserve, and they paid for my pre-vet program."

She fiddled with a pen while she listened. "Do you want to be a veterinarian?"

A flicker of hope passed through his eyes. "One day," he said. "I only had time to finish my Bachelor's degree before I got deployed."

She considered him, remembering the horrific things he said he'd seen. "What do you do for the Army?"

"Infantry squadron leader," he said.

Her heart skipped a beat. "You fight?"

His eyes didn't lose an iota of their teasing sparkle. "It's not hand-to-hand combat, darlin'. We use guns, not swords."

"I know," she said, feeling a bit foolish. She *had* imagined him face-to-face with an enemy, trying to land the killing blow with a curved blade.

"Specifically, I man the Abrams."

Confusion puckered her features. "The Abrams?"

"I drive the tank."

"Oh," she said. "Impressive." He'd clearly adopted the workout

83

policies of the Army as a daily habit, and his calm demeanor likely came from his training to keep cool during difficult situations.

"Or at least I did."

Kelly's eyebrows rose. "Did?"

He tapped his right thigh. "They gave me an honorable discharge after losing my femur."

Compassion filled her, an uncomfortable sensation after trying to keep him at arm's length. "I'm sorry to hear that." She nodded toward his leg. "The leg, and the discharge."

He took a deep breath, his chest rising as his eyes closed. Kelly again had the impression he was reliving something she'd never understand.

His eyes opened and held hers. "I'm okay with both things now."

"Does your leg give you trouble?"

"Yes."

His simple answer sent a fierce rush of appreciation through her. Appreciation for him, and for all servicemen who had sacrificed to protect her freedoms.

"I'm sorry," she said again, finding the words inadequate but having nothing better. Why were they so easy to say in this conversation and so impossible in others? She needed to say something. Now.

Say something.

Say something!

"Squire—"

"A lot of things give me trouble these days." His expression darkened, bringing the moody, upset version of Squire Ackerman. "So you obviously finished your accounting degree."

She swallowed back the word vomit containing her apology. "Obviously." She tapped on her computer track pad to wake the machine, not wanting to talk about herself.

"What else have you been up to?"

"Not much," she said. "Being a mom. Cooking, and cleaning, and taking Finn to playgroups. We lived in San Diego before, or when...." She cleared her throat as she mentally berated herself. *Great, Kelly. Bring up your ex. Awesome way to win over a guy.*

She panicked as she realized she was trying to win over Squire Ackerman. Her best friend's younger brother, Squire! Of course she was. She owed him an explanation for her silence.

"Sometimes I miss California. The heat in Texas is much different." She wished her voice didn't sound so strangled.

Squire gave her a serious look, his head cocked to the side like he could hear more in her words than what she'd said. "You should feel the sun in Kandahar."

"Is that where you just returned from?"

"Sort of," he said. "I spent six months in the hospital in Germany before my discharge. But I served one deployment in Afghanistan and this last one in Kandahar."

She raised her left hand, which used to be bedazzled. "One divorce here." The smile she tried on felt stretched too far in some spots and sagged in others, like an ill-fitted swimming suit.

"He must not know what he's missing." His words settled into the silence, between the cracks in her heart, where they tried to burrow into the soft places.

He stood, sending his chair into the wall behind him. "I should go."

She nodded as he strode out of her office with the grace and power of a man who'd never seen a day inside a hospital. If she hadn't been looking for it, Kelly wouldn't have noticed his limp.

The words she should've said were still contained. *Oh, he knows. He just chose someone over me.*

Chapter Six

"Squire?" Kelly poked her head into his office a few minutes before quitting time. He wasn't there. She tried Frank's office, but she hadn't seen a light on all day. The rest of the trailer was likewise deserted, except for faithful Clark at the front desk. He moved like cured honey, slow and smooth, his hands weathered from years of outdoor work. His skin looked like tanned leather, and his face practically cracked when his expression changed.

"Have you seen Squire?" she asked him.

"Not since 'bout one," he said, his voice hard and rough. "He don't usually spend all day out here."

She looked over her shoulder, as if she could see through the solid metal door to the house. Kelly didn't really want to go traipsing all over the ranch looking for him, so she hurried back to her office for her purse and phone. Dictating a text as she retraced her steps, she told Squire she needed to meet with him over some missing documents. Important tax documents.

All the sales documents for the cattle at Three Rivers in the past five years.

She hit send as she climbed in her car. "I can't stay tonight," she continued, speaking slowly into her phone. "Let's meet at nine in my office tomorrow." She backed out and drove past the equipment buildings, the stables, and the calving stalls—which she'd learned from Tom were full thanks to a successful calving season that had ended just a few weeks ago.

The house sat on the end of the row, the sprawling garden in line with the ranch buildings. Beyond that, a row of about twelve cabins was spread. She wondered which one was Squire's and what she'd find inside. Five minutes down the road, he called.

"Hey," she said, still thinking about which pictures he'd have displayed in his cabin, and if he'd used one of hers for target practice.

"Missing documents? Clarify."

"Yes, sir, commander, sir," she said, barely refraining from rolling her eyes. "Is that what your squadron called you?"

"Major, actually."

"Okay, Major Ackerman." She smiled to herself. Teasing Squire was more fun than she remembered. She sobered quickly at his growl. "I don't have the income records for any cattle sales."

"None?"

"Nothing for the past five years. I don't know how Hector came up with the numbers for the taxes. I spent all afternoon digging through those files, and there's not a single document detailing any profit."

She turned from the bumpy ranch road onto the highway. "Three Rivers has been claiming a loss for five years, and without any income documentation, it's no wonder."

Squire coughed and then cleared his throat. "Well, I-I honestly don't know what any of that means."

She imagined him lounging on the leather couch in his old bedroom, the picture of her next to him on the bookcase. Her heart kicked out an extra beat. "It means, Major, that Hector has been filing a loss for the ranch." She spoke kindly, hoping she didn't sound condescending. "That means that, according to the IRS, you've been spending more money to run the ranch than the ranch actually makes. You get a break on taxes, because really, you're not making any money to be taxed on. So far, so good?"

"I think I'm with you," he said.

"The ranch has been selling cattle each year, hasn't it?"

Squire took an extra few seconds to answer. "I believe so. Kel, I'm foreman, but I know almost nothing about operating a cattle ranch." His low voice held twinges of embarrassment and sorrow. "My dad's been teaching me, day by day. So I know we just finished calving season, and we got about two thousand new calves. We'll only keep half of those. The cow-calves are selling for a lot this year, too."

Kelly's suspicions about Squire being hesitant to run the ranch intensified. She wondered why he was at Three Rivers when he didn't want to be. Duty? Loyalty? Necessity?

"We'll also sell off a couple hundred of our breeding heifers, and we have four bulls that are done siring." He paused. "So we'll replace our heifers with some of our calves that are several years old, and sometimes we purchase some. We'll use several younger bulls for sires. We always keep some from castration when they're calved."

She wanted to laugh as he spoke of the inner workings of a ranch she'd never known about. "Okay," she said, not knowing what else to say. "So you've been selling cattle. Because that's the only source of income, right?"

"Right. Well, I mean, sometimes we sell our excess hay, but we really don't have much of that."

"But there are no records of any income from sold cattle in the past five years. We need to find those documents." Her mind buzzed with this new development. She'd found the problem. She *was* capable of doing this job.

"I'll come to your office tomorrow."

"Nine o'clock." She couldn't wait, and that scared her almost as much as needing to learn about the calf-cow market. She was so out of her league at Three Rivers, professionally and personally.

Squire couldn't sleep. The walls of his cabin kept his thoughts and worries so close. He wanted to call Kelly, just to hear her voice over the line. No amount of cocoa butter lotion had been able to soothe him, and with the softest hands he'd had in years, he slipped out of bed and pulled on his boots.

Once he reached the stables, he clucked his tongue for Juniper. She appeared a moment later, Hank right behind her. He wore gym shorts, so Squire carried their apples in his hands.

"Hey," he said, grateful neither horse questioned him for his midnight visit. They crunched through their treats, their swishing tails bringing him comfort in the strangest way. His mind wandered, no longer contained by walls.

He thought back to his conversation with Kelly as they'd walked to the picnic. He'd hoped if he could get her to the park, she'd come with him. But her hesitance had poured from her in waves. Squire had some intelligence, and he'd walked away with a straight back. When he finally got the courage to look behind him, he'd found only an empty street.

Hank nudged his thigh, reminding Squire of his confession that he had no one here that needed him. Intellectually, he knew that wasn't true. His parents were relying on him more than they even knew.

God must need you here. Kelly's words echoed through his head. If she was right—and Squire desperately wanted to believe her—he wished God would let him know how to be the most useful.

He stroked the horses for a few more minutes before going back to his cabin, where sleep finally claimed him in the early morning hours.

The next morning, he arrived in Kelly's office before she did. The view from her window offered a slightly different angle than his. The door to the building slammed, and Squire instinctively ducked his head, his forehead meeting the glass with a sharp thunk.

Equal parts frustration and foolishness bubbled in his system, giving the bump a pulse all its own.

Kelly'd already seen his limp, shown her horror at his war

stories. He didn't need her pity for his PTSD too. He straightened at the sound of her delicate footfalls and prayed for patience.

"Squire," she gasped, coming to a stop just inside her office. "You scared me."

He turned from the window, his heart still doing a double-time beat in his chest. "It's only eight-thirty," he said as he took in her tight jeans and sleeveless blouse. The crimson made her hair look lighter, more like wheat than honey. "Why are you here so early?"

"Finn slept late," she said as she ran her fingers through her hair. "So I didn't have any reason to hang around the house this morning."

He nodded and joined her at the wall of filing cabinets behind her desk. "What are you looking for?" He took a deep breath, trying not to let her tropical scent distract him from the work they needed to accomplish.

"Anything I can find," she said, giving him a full appraisal. Her eyes roamed his face, filled with concern. Attraction sparked inside Squire, but he extinguished it with a bucketful of memories of him hiding on the sidelines of the prom.

"You look tired," she said.

"You told me our ranch has five years of missing income documents." He ground his teeth together, the way he'd been doing for the past twelve hours. "So no. Not much sleeping happened last night."

"Did you say anything to your dad?"

Squire shook his head, his mind rattling with a thousand different ways to start that conversation. "I want to tell him when we have good news, not bad."

"What if we never have good news?" Kelly looked into his eyes, somehow right past all his emotional defenses. Right through him, like she always had. She fiddled with the collar of his shirt, fixing it flat. He resisted the urge to lean into her touch and close his eyes to capture the memory forever.

"Don't talk like that, Kel." He ran his hands through his hair, wishing he was in a position to touch her. He hadn't been a decade ago as his sister's younger brother, and he wasn't now as a broke cattle rancher who didn't even know how his ranch generated revenue. He'd never felt so inadequate, even with her decade of silence and seeming nonchalance about how she'd treated him.

"I like it when you call me Kel." She gave him a closed-mouthed smile and returned to her filing cabinet drawers.

He pulled open a drawer and peered inside. Jam packed with files, his heart pretzeled into a painful knot. "Oh, darlin'."

"I know," she said. "Pull out anything that looks like it could be related to sales, income, herd size, calving, or anything else you can think of that would be money coming *in* to the ranch."

He thumbed through a couple of folders that were labeled *Medical 2007*. "Do you think that's where the lost money is?" he asked. "We haven't had income?"

"No." Kelly turned back to her desk, where several thick files lay. "These are the tax files for the past five years." She flipped open the top folder. "Look. Hector reported an income of almost two hundred thousand dollars last year. I don't know where he got that number."

She rustled the papers, making an angry sound with her fingers. "There's no attached documentation. It's a miracle you haven't been audited."

Sharp fear pinched his stomach. "A miracle," he murmured, feeling untethered to the ground, like gravity had stopped pulling on him. He sent up a silent prayer of gratitude for the lack of an audit.

"We have to find the missing income statements," she said. "We have to keep accurate taxes for seven years in case of an audit." She went back to her filing drawer, her jaw set and her eyes determined.

That strange sensation—forgiveness—stretched his mind, moving him away from the past and anchoring him in the here-and-now. Focusing him on the Kelly in front of him, blurring the one who'd injured him.

Squire liked that she'd been an employee of the ranch for three days and yet spoke like she was part of the "we" that was in trouble. He admired her determination and the way her sharp eyes searched with exactness.

He turned his attention to the files. He didn't know what to do. Helplessness poured through him as he wondered how long it would take to go through these drawers. Weeks, maybe. He took a deep breath, considering what he could control. He had nothing but time. The extended tax deadline wasn't until October.

He'd once played a football game with a separated shoulder. He'd driven a tank through the deserts of Kandahar. He'd once carried his best friend, Pete, on his back after they'd taken an indirect hit in Afghanistan.

He could find a few missing files, especially if he could keep Kelly by his side during the operation. "Let's do this," he said.

By lunch, his shoulders ached, a sharp pain shot through his lower back on the right side, and his hands looked like they'd been dipped in dust-coated cobwebs. His slacks had gray streaks on them from where he kept trying to remove the grime.

Kelly hadn't fared much better, but somehow the dirt made her more beautiful, the soreness in her shoulders made her arch her back in a pose Squire darted his gaze away from.

"Let's go eat," he said, trying one last time to wipe his fingers clean as he stood. He reached a still-disgusting hand to her and pulled her to her feet.

"We've found nothing," she said, vocalizing the despair and frustration rising through him.

"We will," he assured her, giving his voice more power and hope than he possessed. He followed her down the hall, and Benson trotted to his side as soon as he descended the stairs. Squire automatically leaned down to scratch him behind his ears. The animal's comfort infused him, allowing him to erase the outward worry that his mom would be able to spot through a pair of binoculars. Which he wouldn't put past her using.

"What's his name?" Kelly asked, indicating the dog.

"You don't remember Benson?" Squire squinted at her. "I think that hurts his feelings."

On cue, Benson whined before licking Kelly's hand.

She jerked her fingers back, and Squire barely stopped himself from laughing as she wiped her hands on her pants. With her ranch-approved footwear, Squire didn't have a problem keeping pace with her. She took the path that led into the backyard and toward the patio.

"You look scared," he said as they neared the steps.

"I am scared," she said. "I don't know how to pretend that everything is okay. Especially when it's not."

He stopped walking, and she did too. "Haven't you ever had to keep a secret?"

"Yeah, sure."

He stepped into her personal bubble, wanting to be closer to her and using this hushed conversation as a way to do it. "Like what?"

She tilted her head back to keep her eyes locked with his. "You know, Santa Claus, birthday presents." She looked petrified, like Santa carried a chainsaw. Squire wondered what she was afraid of.

He shook his head. "No, like a major secret that you don't want anyone else to know. Like, in high school when you had a crush on someone and you didn't want them—or anyone—to know. Or like—"

"When your husband has another woman in another city?"

He flinched like she'd punched him. "Oh, darlin', I'm so sorry." He hooked his pinky in hers, gave a quick squeeze, and let go.

She blinked a few times as her eyes shone with sudden liquid and stared toward his cabin. "It's fine. I mean, I'm over it."

Squire cupped her elbow in his palm. "Are you? Because it doesn't sound like you are." If the rumors his mother brought home from the salon were to be believed, she'd only found out about her husband a few months ago.

She blew out her breath. "It's like Scott said a couple of weeks ago. God requires us to forgive."

Squire cocked an eyebrow and shifted his weight to his left leg.

She couldn't seem to meet his gaze. "I'm still working on it," she finally admitted.

"Which part?" he asked. "Forgiving him? Or forgiving yourself?"

Her eyes flew to his, and now they held. Time stretched as they looked openly at each other. He wasn't sure what was running through her head, but he knew she hadn't found peace on either point.

"Can I ask you a question?" she asked, her expression taut.

"Of course."

"Do you think God forgives us, even when we make the same mistakes over and over again?"

She looked so frail, the pleading note in her question hanging between them. Squire wanted to clamp both of his hands on her shoulders and impart strength to her.

"I think God is very forgiving. Sometimes it's us mortals who have to let go of the past and focus on becoming what God wants us to become."

He still didn't know why God called some men home, while others had to stay behind with puckered skin, shattered bones, or broken minds. But he absolutely knew that God was forgiving.

She turned away from him and swiped quickly at her face.

"Thank you. I'm working on that too."

"We all are," Squire said, wishing forgiving someone was as easily done as he'd just vocalized. Truth was, he was still working on forgiving *her*. This conversation urged him a little closer to that goal.

Kelly faced him and drew a deep breath through her nose. "So I have to pretend like everything is okay, like I'm just sifting through papers in my office, not looking for ranch-saving files."

"Exactly." He flashed a smile in her direction. "Because I'm sure you haven't told Finn the whole truth about his dad."

"No." Her eyes widened. "I would never—it would kill him."

"And this could kill my father," Squire said, looping his arm through hers and starting up the stairs. "So we put on our happy faces, and we pretend everything's fine."

His mom didn't make lunch every day, and today was one where the kitchen sat clean and empty. Kelly stalled in the doorway. "I brought a sandwich. I don't need to eat your food."

Squire continued to the fridge and pulled out a container of last night's sour cream noodle casserole. "But you can. Ma made that noodley stuff you and Chelsea used to inhale."

Kelly put one hand on her hip. "I did not *inhale* anything."

"Uh...." He stuck the container in the microwave. "Yes, you did."

"I've seen you eat a milkshake in thirty seconds flat."

He pointed a fork at her, glad the tension between them had evaporated. "*That* was a dare." He chuckled. "I can't believe you remember that." The woman obviously had an iron memory—at least on some points. Why couldn't she remember he'd asked her to prom?

Why did it still feel like a branding iron against his lungs? He gulped for air, reached for the courage to ask her if she'd gotten the balloons.

"What was that guy's name?" Kelly asked, obliterating his questions. "The one Chelsea was so enamored with?"

"Todd," Squire answered through a too-tight throat. Chelsea had managed to get Todd to go get ice cream with them after a basketball game, claiming a bunch of friends were going. It was just her and him, and Squire and Kelly. For that one night, he'd felt like the other half of a couple.

"That's right." Kelly snapped her fingers. "Todd Hurley. What ever happened to him?"

"You've been out of the rumor mill for too long," he said as the microwave beeped. He pulled out the food and stirred it before dividing it onto two plates. Nudging one toward an empty spot on the bar, he gave her a meaningful look. "Sit. Eat."

She slid into the seat and he sat next to her. "I have," she said. "I get most of my information from Glenda at the salon."

He appraised her. "You don't look like Glenda does your hair." He fingered it, simply because he could and it wouldn't seem weird. Silky and soft, and absolutely beautiful with a hint of red he hadn't noticed before.

She laughed, tipping her head back. "No, but she knows everyone and everything that happens in town. If I need to know something, I ask my mother, who knows or can find out at

Glenda's."

He wondered what everyone was saying about him, about Three Rivers. "I'm sure the grocer is a hotbed for gossip too."

"Definitely." She took a bite of her noodle casserole. "Mm, I remember this now. You're right. I totally inhaled this." She forked another bite into her mouth.

He ate a little more slowly than Kelly, finally working up the nerve to ask, "What have you learned about me?"

She leaned back, her plate empty. "Let's see. Your dad is going to retire soon, and you're going to take over Three Rivers. Oh." She grinned at him. "You're incredibly handsome, and Glenda wishes her daughter still lived here so she could set you up. Apparently Glenda likes a man in uniform." She waggled her eyebrows at him.

Always with the uniform. Squire tired of it, especially now that he couldn't wear his uniform for anything but show. "Believe it or not, I've heard that before."

"Oh, yeah?" She punched him lightly in the arm. "That you're incredibly handsome? Or that women swoon at the sight of a uniform?"

He crossed his arms, pride parading across his vocal chords as he said, "Both, actually. Why do you think I joined the Army?"

"Because you needed money for school."

"I never should've told you that." He picked up his plate, gathered hers, and walked around the counter to the sink. With his back to her, he asked, "So what about you?"

"What about me?"

"Do you think I'm handsome? Do you swoon at the mere sight of a uniform?" He rinsed the plates and loaded them in the dishwasher, very aware that he was playing with matches very near the open flame of his heart. The pause created by the clacking dishes lengthened even after he finished.

He turned around and leaned against the counter, his eyebrows raised. His pulse sat heavy in his throat, and heat streaked his neck. But it was about time they had a real conversation. He'd seen her fear, her confusion, and he wanted answers.

She studied the counter, braiding her fingers together again and again. "I'd have to see you in your uniform to decide if it's swoon-worthy," she said. "But you're definitely handsome. You know, for girls who like the tall, rugged, cowboy type. Like maybe Susie Randall."

He groaned. "Susie Randall is barking up the wrong tree."

Kelly folded her arms and peered up at him. "Are you calling that gorgeous, blonde woman a dog?"

"If the boot fits," he said, shrugging.

"Squire Ackerman." She stood and put both hands on her hips, a prerequisite to her lecturing him. She'd done it countless times as a teenager, and once last week in his old bedroom.

He wasn't sixteen anymore and he wouldn't back down. "I'm just not interested."

"In dating?" Kelly's eyebrows rose.

Squire pinned her with a look that made her squirm. "Who wants to know? You? Or the ladies at the salon?"

"Not me," she said, though her voice went up in pitch. "I mean, if you want to date, you should. But if you don't, then that's your right too, you know? I mean, are you interested in women?"

"I don't owe you an explanation." His words sounded like rockets inside his own ears. So much for trying to tame his commanding tone.

Kelly flinched. "You're right." She paced away from him. "I shouldn't lecture you. Especially about dating." She spun and met his gaze. He watched her gear up, watched her mouth open.

"I'm so sorry about the prom. I didn't know who'd invited me." Her fingers fumbled, fumbled, fumbled as his heart tumbled, tumbled, tumbled. Her bottom lip would be hamburger by the time she stopped chewing it.

"It was you, wasn't it?"

Shocked into muteness, Squire nodded.

"I popped all those balloons and couldn't find a name on any of the confetti. I hoped whoever had brought them would try again or call me or come to the prom and ask me to dance or...." Her words rushed, crashed, broke over Squire like white-capped rapids.

"I would've said yes," she said. "I'm sorry, Squire."

He twisted in the river of words and emotions and revelations and feelings, trying to right himself.

She hadn't ignored him. Hadn't rejected him. She simply hadn't known.

And he'd been too angry and too afraid to approach her.

Squire broke the surface of the waves her apology had caused. "I want to try again."

Their eyes locked, and everything he'd just admitted was blown wide open. The good news was Kelly had some of her own feelings she'd been hiding. He identified hope, happiness, and helplessness before she buried her emotions deep, deep.

He pushed away from the counter before he could blurt another embarrassing comment. "Well, those files won't go through themselves." He headed for the patio door, the backlash of her apology still uncoiling in his ears.

"Files?" his dad asked, coming into the kitchen. "You two still going through all the paperwork?"

Squire froze, meeting Kelly's panicked gaze. "Yes."

"Find anything yet?" He shuffled to the fridge.

"No, sir," Kelly said, her voice on the verge of a tremor. "Nothing we need, at least."

She'd spoken true, and Squire gave her thumbs up while his father's back was turned.

"Let me know when you do," his dad said, and Squire confirmed that he wanted to know too. He gestured for Kelly to go in front of him, which she did.

"Slow. Steady," he whispered as she passed him. She looked like she was scampering away, not just going to back to her office for a long afternoon of work.

Her steps slowed, and Squire made to follow her.

"Son?" his dad asked.

"Yeah?" He turned back to the kitchen as Kelly left.

He waved his spoon toward the window. "How's she doin'?"

"Better than I thought, actually."

"You keepin' an eye on her?"

"Two," he said, sure his dad wouldn't read the double meaning in his statement the way his mom would. He glanced out the window and found Kelly waiting for him at the bottom of the steps. "I'll keep you updated." He waved good-bye to his father, determined not to make a fool of himself in front of Kelly again. But she had a way of making him comfortable. Maybe she hadn't been looking *through* him all those years ago. Maybe she could see past the surface to what seethed beneath.

Benson yipped when Squire stepped onto the deck. "I know, boy," he murmured, his pulse teetering on the edge of needing to bark. "Gotta take a step back." Too bad he wanted to sprint now that he knew Kelly would've said yes.

Chapter Seven

Kelly walked a half step behind him on the way back to her office. If she stepped right next to him, maybe their fingers would brush. Maybe he would hold on, or maybe she would.

She'd liked holding his hand, and that meant it absolutely could never happen again. If Frank hadn't interrupted Kelly felt certain she'd have continued spouting her feelings. Yes, she thought Squire was beyond handsome. Yes, she'd very much like to see him in his uniform, but that his everyday clothes stirred her as well. Yes, his scruffy three-day-old beard made her think about kissing him just to see what it would feel like against her cheek.

No, she would not be repeating the mistake of getting involved with her boss.

Kelly nodded hello to Clark, who watched her with narrowed eyes. She ignored him and regained her professionalism as she strode ahead of Squire down the aisle.

Ethan leapt from his chair and sauntered toward her. Kelly could barely refrain from rolling her eyes as he stepped into her path.

"Hey, sugar," he drawled, his Texan accent too false for her liking.

"Hey, yourself," she deadpanned, her own accent drawing out the words. She felt more than saw Squire's clenched fists and jaw.

"So I'm free this weekend," Ethan said, and in any other circumstance, Kelly might have thought he was attractive. Or maybe next to Squire, Ethan didn't hold a candle.

"You wanna go to the rodeo with me?"

"There's a rodeo this weekend?" Kelly wrinkled her nose, though she loved a good rodeo as much as the next Texas girl.

"In Amarillo." Ethan grinned.

The thought of riding in a truck with him for over an hour made Kelly slightly queasy.

"And there's the Fourth of July celebration coming up," he said. "I'm sure you'll be somethin' special wearing patriotic colors." He scanned her from head to toe and met her eye with a smile.

Kelly squirmed just thinking about what he might be visualizing. "Listen, Ethan, I'm sure you're a nice guy—"

"He's not," Squire growled, moving so close his body heat brushed her skin.

"But," Kelly said. "I'm coming off a divorce I haven't finished paying for yet. I'm not really ready to start dating again." She tried to sound as sympathetic as possible. Firm, but friendly. "I'm sure you understand."

Ethan stepped back, a flush crawling up his neck. "Yeah, sure I do." He turned and shuffled back to the table, much less swagger now.

Ultra-aware of how close Squire stood, Kelly released her breath and headed for her office. "I don't need your help," she said over her shoulder.

Squire's uneven footsteps quickened. "We still have heaps of files."

"With Ethan." She stopped outsider her door and folded her arms. "I can take care of myself."

Doubt clouded his expression; his mouth flattened into an angry line. But he held up his hands in surrender. "I'm sure you can."

He moved past her and picked up a folder, his eyes hidden by that blasted cowboy hat.

"The Red Barn Cattle Company," she read from a yellowed piece of paper. "Could that be where you sold some cattle?"

She scanned the paper, and it certainly seemed like a receipt. "Three hundred seventy-four cow-calves, second year, thirty-seven thousand, seven hundred seventy-four dollars. There's a copy of a check attached."

Squire bent over her shoulder, his breath cool on her neck. "It's made out to the ranch," he said. "It's from two thousand eight. That was a record year for beef."

"The market is at it's highest right now, too," Kelly said. "I did some research over the weekend."

"Of course you did," he said, those eyes twinkling with a tease.

"Last year was a boom, what with the falling feed prices. Everyone is predicting the prices will stay stable, or get better, throughout this year too." She pulled the entire folder out of the cabinet. "A ranch like Three Rivers should be pulling in major profits."

Squire removed the thick file behind the one she'd just taken. He moved to her desk, rolling his shoulders as he went. She couldn't blame him. Her muscles ached like she'd been hit by a truck and then backed over.

"I don't get it," Squire said, leafing through the pages in his folder. "We have a computer program for this. Every receipt, every purchase, every sale. It just goes into the computer."

Kelly glanced up, a zing of worry sliding through her. "I don't have that program on my computer."

Squire frowned, pulled out his phone, and typed something into it. "I'll ask Clark about it."

"Maybe Hector was too old-school." Kelly didn't want to speak ill of the dead, but if Three Rivers had invested in financial software, it should be on the *accountant's* computer.

"Maybe Hector was a thief," Squire said bitterly.

Kelly's heart hurt for him. "We'll find the money, Squire." She smiled at him when he looked at her, and she put her hand on his, squeezing his fingers for only a moment before pulling back.

Awkwardness settled on them as Kelly cursed herself for touching him—again. She needed to stop doing that, especially after their joint confession in the kitchen. She couldn't encourage his crush on her. That was all he had. A soda pop, boss-like crush.

She opened a spreadsheet and began entering the receipts of purchase she'd found. The Red Barn Cattle Company bought a lot of cow-calves from Three Rivers. But nothing else. No heifers; no bulls.

"Jackpot," she said near the end of the file. Holding up a piece of paper, she said, "Two thousand eleven. Stuffed way at the back of this file that begins with a two thousand eight receipt and goes backward to nineteen ninety-four. Then suddenly." She waved the paper. "Two thousand eleven."

Squire took the page, his face grim, and examined it. "I was in Afghanistan for most of two thousand eleven. I don't know how things on the ranch were going."

"Seems no one did," Kelly reminded him. "We're going to figure this out. I promise." She created a new sheet in her computer file and entered the profits from The Red Barn Cattle Company.

Next she found the tax return for 2011. "We're still ninety thousand dollars short, according to what Hector reported as income for this calendar year."

Neither of them found anything over the course of the next hour. Kelly finally finished her second folder, closed it, and stacked it against the wall where they'd decided to put the looked-at files.

"Do you think he hid the records on purpose?" Squire asked, setting his own file against the wall.

Kelly stretched her back, moaning with the cascading ache in her spine. "I hate to say it, but yes. Otherwise, they'd be in the tax returns. And they'd be in the right place in the files. They're not."

His piercing eyes pinned her to the spot. "Thank you," he said. "I'm sure this isn't what you imagined your job to be when you were hired."

She hadn't imagined anything, because she hadn't had a real

accounting job before. "It's a job I desperately need," she said. "So I should be thanking you."

Squire drew her into a soft embrace, and she went willingly though her mind was screaming at her to put distance between them. She pressed her cheek to his chest, enjoying the softness of his shirt and the scent of fresh cotton—along with his manly, spicy smell.

His strong arms held her close, and she felt his muscles relax though the hug remained tight.

Kelly's heart rippled like a flag in a stiff Texas wind, and she disentangled herself. She'd told him she could take care of herself—but against him she had little defense.

"I'm going in for feed tonight," he said, his eyes like lasers, focused and intense on hers. "Want to meet for dinner?"

There was no mistaking the invitation this time, despite his casual shrug and feigned nonchalance.

"Like I told Ethan, I'm not ready to date, and—"

"It's not a date," he said quickly. "I just want to thank you. You're doing so much for us."

"Us?" she repeated, tilting her head to the side to study him. Why couldn't she read him? Did they teach Majors in the Army to be complete enigmas?

He gazed steadily back, one hand tucked in his pants pocket like he hadn't a care in the world.

"Yes, us," he said. "If you find this money, my parents will be able to retire. You'll be our savior."

She heard the sincerity behind his words, but something else lingered there too. She'd wanted him to say she was helping *him*, but he hadn't.

"You're paying me a salary," she said. "It's my job."

"Consider it a bonus."

Her heart stalled and her throat went dry. Taylor had often called her "his little bonus" at work.

She shook her head, her resolve hardening with the memory. She would not be Squire's *bonus*. "Sorry, I can't tonight." She stepped away, opened the drawer where she'd stowed her purse, and headed for the door.

"Kel, wait." Squire didn't move to block her, but the pleading tone of his voice was enough to make her pause. "It's just dinner. It's not prom."

"Squire, I just can't," she said without turning around. She wanted to use Finn as an excuse—he would be the easiest way out—but she couldn't. She found her inner well of strength, the place she'd dug down to when she'd discovered the truth about Taylor. It was pretty dry after her outburst in the kitchen, but she still had some guts.

Turning back to Squire, she steadied her nerves with a deep breath. "You're my boss." Her words, simple as they were, seemed to stutter the motion of the earth. "And I've made that mistake before."

He started nodding, his jaw tight and his eyes gathering clouds. Kelly was grateful he'd understood what she meant without her having to spell it out.

"Another time, then." His words clipped from his teeth. He'd become a statue. A statue that didn't move when she took a step nearer to him.

"Definitely another time." She ducked her head, her pulse bouncing, bouncing, bouncing through her veins. "But as things stand right now, I simply can't. I hope you understand." Kelly didn't wait for him to respond. She held her head high and walked out.

Squire didn't go home after Kelly left. Mentally kicking himself—had he seriously invited her to dinner mere hours after she'd told Ethan she wasn't ready to date?—he got in his truck and just drove. Benson sat on the front seat, his tongue lolling out of his mouth. If only things in Squire's life could be so carefree.

After a half hour of silence, he slammed his palm against the steering wheel. Benson barked as Squire yanked the truck to the side of the road and dialed Chelsea.

"Hey, little bro," his sister answered. "What's up?"

Squire leaned his head against his window as Benson laid his head in Squire's lap. "How's the job?" He stroked the dog to get his fists to uncurl.

"I'm surviving," she said. "It's our busy season, so I'm actually still here."

"Oh, do you need to go?"

"No, I've got time. You don't call everyday." Chelsea's way of saying, *What's going on? Is Dad okay? What about Mom? What is important enough for Squire to call?*

He heard all the questions, and he sighed. "Mom and Dad are great. Three Rivers will survive."

He paused, not quite sure how to ask Chelsea about Kelly without giving specifics. She didn't know about his high school crush, and he wanted to keep it that way. Though if he'd told her he'd asked Kelly to prom, maybe the date he still longed for would've actually happened.

"So this is a Squire problem," Chelsea said.

"Yes." The word hissed out of his mouth. "A girl problem, actually."

"Oooh." She squealed, and Squire held the phone away from his ear lest he go deaf. "You haven't called me about a girl since Tabby."

"Come on, Chels," he said. "She was no good for me."

"I know that," she said. "But since you don't trust anyone, you needed to give her a chance. And when you did, you found out who she really was."

"Hey," he protested. "I trust people." Even as he spoke, he knew he only gave a select few his trust and only with certain information.

She scoffed, but he continued undeterred. "This is a past girl problem." His mouth turned dry, the affliction coating his throat and seizing his chest.

"A past girl problem?" Chelsea asked. "Did Tabby come back into town?"

"No. Ah...." He swallowed his nerves. He trusted his sister. "Do you ever remember Kelly Armstrong getting asked to her senior prom?"

He could practically hear Chelsea turning back time in the few seconds of silence.

"Yeah," she said. "She got a ton of balloons, but we never found a name. Her parents didn't know who brought them as they'd both been at work." Chelsea gave a light laugh. "Kelly really wanted to go, too. Made me buy a dress and go stag."

The confirmation Squire needed surged over his walls of distrust for Kelly. The bricks around his heart crumbled, releasing years of seeing Kelly through the colored film of his bruised ego.

"Why are you asking about prom?" Chelsea asked.

"Kelly's back at the ranch."

Chelsea heard the unsaid sentiment. "And you like her," she singsonged.

"I was the one who asked her to prom."

The lighthearted atmosphere over the line dissipated.

"No...why didn't you tell me?"

He released the pent-up air in his lungs. "I was embarrassed. Humiliated. I thought she didn't want to go with a sophomore."

"I sense a but...."

"But yes. I'm interested in getting to know her better. The—the old feelings are still there."

"So it's a new girl problem." Chelsea wore a smile in her words.

"She's hardly the same girl." Squire thought of the picture of her son. "And technically, I'm her boss, and I can't act on how I feel. Right?"

"I don't know, Squire.... Lots of people meet and fall in love at work. But at Three Rivers? I'm not sure it would work."

"Ollie married Ivy," he said.

"He took care of calves, and she cleaned the admin building in the evenings. It's not the same." Chelsea sighed. "You *own* the ranch, Squire."

"But I don't want it," he said, the truth exploding out of him. With those words, Squire felt like he'd taken the antidote to a powerful poison. He rolled them around in his head. *I don't want the ranch.*

"I sort of asked her out," he said. "It was a disaster."

"I hate to say this, little brother, but there's your answer."

He pressed his eyes closed, knowing she was right. "So how's Danny?" he asked, changing the subject.

Chelsea went with it, the way she always did. He vowed as he listened to her talk about her boyfriend that he wouldn't be returning to the subject of a relationship with Kelly.

Because Chelsea was right. Kelly had given her answer, and it didn't fall into a gray area. He'd seen her face when he'd said dinner with him could be considered a bonus. She'd looked like she'd witnessed something horrific. The wide eyes, the rapid pulse. That was clearly the wrong thing to say, and he wanted to know why. He wanted to know everything about Kelly. The good, the bad, the ugly.

After hanging up with Chelsea, he ran his hand through his hair, turned the truck around, and returned to the ranch that was his destiny.

"Smithfield Cattle Auctions," Squire said upon opening another folder. He couldn't read fast enough, or find the date. "This has to be another place we sold cattle."

Kelly hustled to his side, leaning over his arm to get a better look at the purchase receipt. "Yes," she whispered. She plucked the paper from his fingers without getting too close to touching him. "Nice work, Major Detective."

He didn't like it when she called him Major, but he didn't let his frustration show. "It's from two thousand five. But if we did business with them once, we probably did again."

That was what they'd discovered over the past few days of digging through the files. They now had four stacks against the walls. Kelly had created a folder for each year of missing income, each now held a few slips of paper. It seemed that Three Rivers sold cattle in many and various auctions, to slaughter houses, and even to private merchants.

Since his dad had done all the selling, Squire hadn't been able to ask him to list all the different places they'd sold cattle. He didn't want his dad to know about the missing paperwork, or that even when they found the documents, the numbers didn't align with the income reported in the tax returns.

Kelly wiped the back of her hand across her forehead. "Another auction house." She clicked a few times on her computer. "They're out of Lubbock, which isn't unreasonable."

For the past two days, she'd been entering everything from the files into the program she'd found and installed, while Squire continued to look for cattle sales documents.

He thought they made a great team, and she'd even said those exact words. He said very little. Kept his distance. Hardly smiled. His aloof behavior had become the only way he could think of to survive.

Kelly leaned away from the computer and pulled two sandwiches out of her desk drawer. She tossed him one, slid an apple across the desk, and placed a bag of potato chips between them. "Lunchtime."

"My mom has plenty of food at the house." He picked up the sandwich. "Peanut butter and jelly? What are we? Ten?"

She smiled, revealing her perfect teeth and ratcheting up his heartbeat. "Sometimes I wish we could be." She took a bite of her sandwich and closed her eyes. "I used to love coming to the ranch. My house was so lonely."

"Used to?"

Her eyes popped open. She met his eyes and then ducked her head. "Yes, I still love coming out here."

He picked up his sandwich and opened it. "Why?"

"Chelsea was my best friend, and there was always something going on here." She gave him an innocent shrug. "I used to have a huge crush on one of your cowhands."

Squire coughed around his bite of peanut butter and jelly. "You're kidding. Who was it?"

"I couldn't keep them straight. I was a sucker for a man in a cowboy hat." She peered up at him through her lashes. "Still am."

Her smile felt infectious, and Squire found that he couldn't straighten his lips. "So that's why you're so nice to Clark."

"Clark's helpful."

So am I, he thought. Clark wasn't the one who'd spent the last four days in her office, going through endless files. Not that Squire was complaining. If he wasn't doing this, he'd have to invent a reason to spend time with Kelly.

"So," she said, averting her eyes. "Are you going to go back to school and get your veterinarian degree?"

Startled, he glanced up. She crunched her way through half her apple before she met his gaze. "Well? Look who's doing the weird *read-my-mind-while-I-stare-at-you* thing now." Her mouth turned up into a smirk.

"I don't know." His voice came out raspy. "Do you think I have that option?"

Her light green eyes took on a new hue. One with more power, more intensity. "Of course you do, Squire. Why wouldn't you be able to finish college? Don't veterans get educational assistance? After you graduate, you could work at Three Rivers, tending to the animals here. You have enough of them."

He'd forgotten about the GI Bill that would allow him to return to school. He had not forgotten the way she lectured him, though at this moment, only appreciation tainted his tone when he said, "It's not that simple. Dad wants to retire now. I've already taken over here as foreman. Veterinarians have to go to four years of medical school. Do internships." He finished his sandwich, the unspoken words hovering between them.

It's impossible. Won't happen.

"The GI Bill probably doesn't pay for advanced degrees," he added.

"But you don't want Three Rivers," Kelly said like she was trying to coax her son into eating his Brussels sprouts. "Have you thought about telling your dad that?"

"What would be the point?" Squire mashed the plastic bag in his fist, unused to arguing with her. As a teen, he'd taken everything she's said as truth. "To hurt him? To abandon him when he needs me most?"

Kelly leaned forward. "Chelsea did."

"Chelsea isn't her father's only son."

"You deserve to be happy, too. That's all I'm saying."

"So do you," he shot back, unsure of what he meant. Maybe that she could be happy with him, even if his ranch hadn't made a penny in five years. Maybe that she should forgive herself and take a chance on dating him.

His blood pressure rose as his annoyance soared. Why couldn't he accept reality? He barely knew Kelly; she'd been back in his life for only a little over a week. She'd made it clear she wasn't interested in dating. Not just Ethan. Everyone.

Reality.

He needed to accept it.

"I *am* happy," she said.

"So am I."

She stood, taking her trash with her. "Excuse me."

He let her go, just like he had a thousand times before. He

couldn't say exactly what he wanted, because that got him into as much trouble as when he kept his thoughts to himself. Or when he spoke in riddles.

Doesn't matter, he told himself as he followed her out. The inadequacy flooding through him provided him with the invisibility he'd always possessed.

As he stomp-limped out of the admin trailer, he imagined himself as transparent as a ghost, able to move through walls. For that was all he had to offer Kelly: a broken heart, a shattered leg, and a bankrupt ranch. A ghost of a real life.

And she knew it. Had seen it.

Didn't want it. Didn't want him.

Chapter Eight

When Kelly finally returned to her office, Squire was gone. She'd walked through the calving stalls, watching the boys bottle-feed the calves. She'd helped them throw feed to the chickens; she'd visited with Heidi as she instructed Frank on how to plow their garden for planting.

She loved the ranch, everything about it. She loved the silence of the country being broken by the barking of dogs, the chatter of chickens, the whistling of the wind. She loved the wide-open sky. She'd loved coming here, because she felt like she belonged.

She hated that she'd pushed Squire further away. She could tell he was hurting, probably over several things. Kelly didn't know everything, and she wanted to.

She pulled out her phone and texted him an apology, but he never answered. She went home for the weekend with his silence, and somehow that hurt more than turning him down for dinner.

Saturday dawned early as summer had officially arrived in Texas. Kelly planned another lunch at the park, this time making sandwiches for her and Finn. She slid in a couple of extras in case Squire showed up.

She hoped he would. She hadn't told him they ate lunch at the park every weekend, because they didn't. Until now.

She claimed the bench he'd been on last week, fed Finn, and watched him play on the slide. The lampposts had patriotic banners attached to them, and Kelly remembered the huge Fourth of July celebration coming up. Children laughed; dogs barked; mothers scolded. Squire stayed away.

Her mother came and picked up Finn, and Kelly went to work with knotted organs. Her shift at Vince's was spent obsessing over Squire, not merely thinking about him.

I should call Chelsea, she thought. She and Squire were close, and maybe she'd provide some details on how to win him over without taking things past the point of professional.

Stay out of his personal life , Kelly thought. She shouldn't have asked him about going back to college, or said anything about him talking to his dad about the ranch. She'd crossed the line and not even realized it.

"Hello, dear."

Kelly looked up to find Heidi standing in her line, two carts of food behind her.

"Oh, Heidi. Hi."

They chatted about the weather, the ranch, and Chelsea while Kelly rang up scads of groceries. "Making your monthly trip?"

Heidi glanced at the full belt of food. "This is only for a week. We have a lot of boys coming out for planting."

"Oh. Where's Squire this weekend?" Kelly slipped him into the conversation casually, but surely Heidi hadn't mistaken the interest in her voice.

"He's at the base this weekend." Heidi handed her a fistful of coupons.

"I thought he'd been discharged."

"He has. They're still doing some rehab on his leg." She watched the screen as Kelly scanned each coupon. "It gives him trouble sometimes."

"Yes, he said as much." Kelly nodded, satisfied at why he hadn't answered her text yesterday afternoon. It still stung. What? They didn't have service on the base? He couldn't spare ten seconds for a text? Squire seemed to have a knack for disappearing when he didn't want to talk about something.

She finished with Heidi's groceries and handed her the receipt. "See you Monday."

Heidi looked at her a moment longer than necessary. "You don't work here every weekend, do you?"

"It's my last day," Kelly said. "I had to give two weeks notice after I got the job at the ranch. Didn't want to leave Vince high and dry."

Heidi patted her hand. "You're a sweet girl, Miss Kelly." Her eyes sharpened and her grip tightened. "My Squire deserves someone like you."

She pushed one cart of groceries toward the exit as a bagger pushed the other, leaving Kelly's ears burning. What was she saying? A passing statement that she thought Squire deserved a sweet girl? Or was she giving Kelly permission to be with Squire, despite the fact that he was her boss?

She definitely needed to call Chelsea.

"Kelly!" Chelsea's scream nearly blasted Kelly's ear off. Due to her new schedule, she'd risen early on Sunday morning despite the opportunity to sleep in.

"Hey, Chelsea. It's not too early, is it?"

"Not for you," she said. "Actually, not for anyone. We're on deadline for a new product, and I've been working seven days for a couple of weeks now."

"Wow," Kelly said. "Do you have a few minutes?"

"Definitely. I hear you're back in Three Rivers. I wish I was there with you."

Kelly wished that too. Chelsea had always been a voice of reason for Kelly, even though she was also her biggest conspirator and perpetrator of silliness.

"So…I need some advice."

"I'm getting that a lot lately. I should start charging." She laughed. "Tell me everything."

Kelly wondered who else was asking for advice, but Chelsea lived a whole new life now. Surely it wasn't someone she knew.

"So my job is out at Three Rivers," she started. "Your mom said something yesterday that made me think."

"She's always doing that." Kelly thought she detected some bitterness behind Chelsea's words.

She fiddled with a string on her shorts, unsure how to talk about Chelsea's brother without broadcasting her interest in him.

"What did she say?" Chelsea asked.

Kelly pushed the words out of her throat. "She said Squire deserves someone like me. And we've been working together to...solve some problems at the ranch, and—"

"Okay, stop," Chelsea said, accompanied by a girly shriek. "Are you saying you like him? That you want to be the one Squire deserves?"

"No," Kelly said. "Yes? Maybe. No. I just don't know what your mom meant by that."

Chelsea started laughing, but a sticky coating formed in Kelly's throat. She gazed beyond the row of trees at the edge of the backyard. She envied them. They didn't care what grew nearby and how close it was. They didn't think about their neighbor day and night. They didn't wonder what it would be like to have a second chance at something they desperately wanted.

Kelly didn't need a new love every spring like the trees blossomed and leaved. She wasn't even sure she could take such a leap of faith a second time.

Chelsea's giggles finally subsided.

"What's so funny?" Kelly asked.

"Squire called me last week. He told me he asked you to prom." She squealed.

"What else did he say?" Kelly thought her words sounded strange coming from such a curved mouth.

"He wanted to know if a relationship between him and one of

his employees would work. I—uh—I told him it probably wasn't a good idea."

Ice chased away her blurred vision, the upturned lips. "I turned him down, because he's my boss." *And I'm not ready to date again.* She'd spoken true on that point. Squire's questions about forgiveness niggled at her. She definitely hadn't forgiven herself. She didn't even know how someone went about doing that.

"But then your mom said he deserves someone like me, and I thought...I don't know...maybe...."

"Three Rivers isn't an office, with a policy," Chelsea said. "So, why not?"

Kelly's inner well was nearly dry. "Taylor, my ex-husband, was my boss when I started dating him." She took a deep breath, but it did nothing to settle her this time. "I'm scared, Chelsea."

"Oh, honey—"

"I mean, what if I cross that professional line again? What if he turns out to be like Taylor?" The questions spurted out of her, her throat bearing the heat as if lava had escaped the earth. "What if I lose my job? What will I do then? Finn and I need financial security."

Chelsea waited a few seconds, and when Kelly didn't continue, she spoke. "What if it's amazing? What if you fall in love with him? What if you and Finn move out to the ranch and the three of you become a family? What if the two of you could run Three Rivers together?"

Kelly imagined herself as Squire's wife, living on the ranch full-time. She could still be the accountant. "I don't know," she said.

"I'm not ready for another man in my life anyway. I don't know if I can do that to Finn."

Chelsea's long silence made Kelly's insides wobble like they'd been jelled. "Sometimes, Kelly, we have to let go of what we don't know, and just go with the flow."

"You sound like my cousin. She said to take the first step, and God would direct my feet."

"You have smart friends."

"But, I don't go with the flow. I need to know what's going to happen before I step."

"You must have gone with Taylor. At least a little bit."

Chelsea's words stung, because she was right. Kelly had been swept up by Taylor, by everything about him. His wealth, his good looks. She squeezed her eyes closed against the memories, against the way she'd abandoned what she knew to be right because he was charming, handsome, and rich.

Come to think of it, Squire possessed two of those qualities. And if she found the money for the ranch, he'd be rich too. The thought terrified her. She could *not* repeat the mistakes she'd made. She wouldn't. She'd worked too hard to feel comfortable at church again, spent too many nights working up the courage to send a prayer to heaven.

Help me now, Lord, Kelly prayed silently. *What's the next step?*

She had no idea, and God seemed to be silent on the subject as well.

"I don't want to make the same mistakes twice." Kelly barely recognized her voice, childlike and tinny as it came out.

"You're not going back to Taylor, are you?" Chelsea asked. "This is *Squire* we're talking about. I didn't know Taylor, but I'm willing to bet he's nothing like my brother."

"He *is* tall, dark, and handsome."

"I can't believe you and Squire...." Chelsea drew in a sharp breath. "I bet my mom can see it too. That's why she said he deserves someone like you. What have you done to make her think that?"

Kelly thought through the seven working days she'd been out at the ranch. "I don't know. We've mostly been digging through files. Your mom never comes out to the administration building."

"Neither does Squire." A heavy dose of suggestion rode in Chelsea's voice.

"Of course he does," Kelly argued. "He has an office now that he's the foreman."

"But he doesn't need to be out there," Chelsea said. "He needs to be where my dad is, learning how the ranch operates. And I guarantee that doesn't happen in an office."

Kelly hadn't seen Frank in the administration trailer once since her interview. Her heart pittered and pattered, tumbled and tripped, at the thought of Squire spending so much time in the trailer just to be with her.

The topic moved to Danny, Chelsea's boyfriend, and by the time Kelly hung up, she still didn't know what to do.

Three Rivers embodied everything she wanted: Safety, security, someone to love.

She just wasn't sure she could take the risk. It wasn't just her heart this time. It was her *life*. Her son's life. Their future.

Squire doesn't want the ranch anyway, she thought, her hopes falling. She wanted to belong somewhere, with someone, but she wasn't sure she could rely on a man to support her again—especially one with no prospects beyond a near-bankrupt ranch.

She buried her face in her hands. She couldn't reconcile the two halves of her thoughts, and she ended up going downstairs twice as confused as before.

Squire took his time returning from Sheppard Air Force Base on Monday. Anxious as he was to find the missing documents and, yes, to see Kelly again, he felt the need to delay the reunion. She'd texted on Friday afternoon, another welcome apology.

He'd ignored her.

He wasn't sure why. Maybe because he was simply hurt. Maybe he wanted her to feel what it was like to be overlooked, forgotten, ignored. She'd spoken true about his desire to be the ranch's veterinarian, not its owner. But during his physical therapy and doctor's appointments, another idea had hatched in his mind.

Maybe he could be both. Maybe everything wasn't quite so black and white.

With a new prospect bouncing around in his brain, he drove slowly, knowing that the first stop he'd make when he returned to the ranch would be Kelly's office.

By the time he'd made the four-hour drive, it was an hour past lunch. His mother had the boys working in her garden, so Squire knew the administration building would be quiet.

Against his will, his nerves stood at attention. His pulse quickened, and he suddenly needed to turn up the air conditioning in his old truck. Trying to ease his jitters, he looked at himself in the rear-view mirror.

"She already likes you," he muttered to his reflection. He let the door to the building slam closed, even though it sent a full-body shiver racing through him. Pressing the memories back, he approached her office with loud footsteps so she'd know he was coming.

She sat at her desk, leaning forward as she peered at something on her computer screen. His tension fled at the sight of her. Her hair wisped from its low ponytail, like she'd been outside in the Texas wind. She wore a black and white polka dot sheer top with a black tank top underneath. He stared for too long, but he couldn't make himself look away.

"Afternoon, darlin'," he said.

She startled but didn't look at him. "Is it really afternoon?" She glanced at her watch. "I haven't eaten yet."

"Perfect timing, then." He gestured to the chair he normally occupied. She'd placed a large stack of folders on it. "Mind if I come in?"

In answer, she hurried around her desk, doing everything she could not to make eye contact with him, and removed the files.

Squire sat down, suppressing a sigh of relief. "Sorry I didn't respond to your message, darlin'." Regret laced his words. He knew better than anyone how deep a wound like that could go.

"It's fine," she said. "Your mom said you go to the base for physical therapy. I figured you didn't have service."

"I had great service," he said, finally drawing her full attention. "Ah, there you are. I was afraid you were going to ignore me the whole afternoon." He gave her a quick smile, but she simply blinked at him.

"You got my message, and just, what? Ignored it?" A fire entered her eyes, spurring Squire to apologize again.

"I've been thinking a lot about what you said," he continued. "And I wasn't sure how to respond, and I'm sorry."

She nodded her acceptance. "What did I say that you were thinking about?"

"The part where you suggested I finish veterinarian school."

She'd completely abandoned her work and pulled out a paper sack. She broke her sandwich in half and offered it to him. He waved her away, a grin on his face. His mother made a feast during planting week. Kelly's PB&J wasn't worth eating compared to the beef ribs and potato salad he hoped would be waiting for him at the house.

"And?" she prompted.

"And nothing. I've just been thinking about what you said."

"No conclusions?"

"Not yet." A fib, but she still looked like she might run screaming from the room if he said the wrong thing.

She scanned him, the edges around her eyes softening. "You're still in uniform." Her gaze met his, and she swallowed hard, like the peanut butter had stuck in her throat. "And you've shaved."

"Thanks for noticing." A string of attraction threaded through him when she blushed. He stood, flinging his arms wide as he spun in a slow circle. "So now you've seen me in my uniform. Swoon-worthy?"

He chuckled as he sat down. "Don't answer that, okay? I don't think I can take another rejection from you." From the redness in her cheeks, he wasn't sure he'd get one.

"Squire, I—" She pressed her eyes closed for two heartbeats before opening them again. "I've been thinking a lot this weekend too. I'm really sorry about pushing you about the ranch. It's honestly none of my business. I crossed a professional line, because, I don't know, I knew you growing up?" She huffed out her breath. "I don't know. But it wasn't my place to say anything, and it won't happen again."

He studied her as she took a bite of her apple, her eyes dancing away from his again. "We're friends, right?" he asked.

"Sure." She nodded, and relief shot through him. He had very few people he counted as true friends, people he could trust no matter what. He wanted Kelly to be one of them.

He leaned forward and placed his elbows on her desk. "Then it's okay for you to talk to me about personal things. That's what friends do." He pinched off a bite of her sandwich. "I'd like the lectures to be toned down. I don't need another mother."

Her face blanched before a slow smile spread her lips. "Fair enough. But then you better start being level with me about what you thought about this weekend." She pointed her finger at him. "I can tell you're not saying everything."

"Lecturing." He chuckled, and it felt right to be sitting here with her, talking, with the knowledge that he couldn't get much past her.

"I had a thought, and it's kind of crazy, but I wonder what you think." He tried to quiet his nerves by crossing his arms tightly, like he could keep the storm inside that way. "What if I could finish school *and* run the ranch? I mean, obviously not at the same time. But I could hire a foreman while I finish medical school. Then I could come back and run the ranch, with my primary job as taking care of the animals." He watched her for any sign of emotion, approval, something. She gave nothing away.

"It's only four years. Dad could still retire. He and Mom could still move into town. The foreman could live in our basement, take care of the house, the ranch, everything. Then, when I'm done, I come back and take over from there." He pressed his arms tighter, the thunderclouds grew bigger, waiting for her reaction.

Her face lit up, making her more beautiful than ever. "That sounds like an ingenious plan. And you could still have a clinic in Three Rivers. Something you operate on an emergency basis, or a couple of days a week."

"Working with the animals on the ranch will definitely keep me busy enough. But it's something to think about."

She tapped a pen against her desktop, finished her lunch, and finally looked at him again. "So, will you say something to your dad?"

"Yes, I'm going to talk to my parents today." He stood, feeling lighter and freer than he had in months—since Hector had died. "I'll see you tomorrow, okay? We'll get back to all these files."

"Squire." She stood too. "Where would you go to school?"

"The only program for a doctorate in veterinary medicine is at Texas A&M."

Eight hours away, he thought, but didn't say. She heard the distance that would be between them, though neither one of them acknowledged it. By the turmoil in her eyes, *she* didn't even know how she felt.

He wanted to comfort her. But he didn't know if things would work out, with them, with the ranch, with anything. So he simply left her office, rehearsing the speech for his parents.

Squire strolled from the administration building to the house, words tripping around in his head.

Help me find the right thing to say, he prayed as he approached the homestead. *Bless my father with an open mind.*

He found his mother in the garden. Unfortunately, at least a dozen cowhands worked nearby, all within earshot.

"Hey, Ma." Squire stepped next to her and put his arm around her shoulders.

"You're back." She peered up at him, a smile on her face. "What did the doctors say?"

"Still healing." His pulse suddenly went into overdrive. He had so many words, and they were all suddenly fighting to come out. "Where's Dad?"

His mom didn't look away from him. "What's on your mind, son?"

"I don't want the ranch," he blurted. He took a deep breath. "Right now," he said. "I want to finish my veterinarian degree, and then come back and work with the animals."

Somehow, his dad knew he'd just said something important, because he appeared next to his mom. "What's going on?"

Squire half-hoped his mom would convey the message to his dad. But he knew she wouldn't. She raised her eyebrows and gestured to his dad.

"Dad, I don't want to run the ranch right now. I want to finish my veterinarian degree. Then I'll come back as the official veterinarian on-staff." He shoved his hands in his pockets and focused on the dirt at his feet. "I still have time to apply for this fall's program. It's four years. In College Station." He reminded himself to breathe, to speak slower. "I'll hire a foreman before I go. I know you want to retire."

His father stood there, staring at Squire. He blinked once, twice. Stared some more. Squire knew he was processing. He never reacted immediately, instead absorbing and trying to understand. It was something about his dad that Squire loved the most. He'd learned to behave the same way, though he hadn't had as much practice.

His dad glanced at his mom. She nodded, somehow completing a conversation they'd either had previously or didn't need to have.

"Okay," his father said.

The rubber band around Squire's chest snapped, the release sweet and freeing. "We should see if Clark wants to give up his desk job in favor of taking on the ranch."

"Clark?" his dad asked.

"He would be ready to retire in four years," his mom said. "He's a great choice, Frank."

Squire hadn't considered what the foreman would do once he returned, but Clark *would* be ready to retire in four years. Everything seemed to be falling into place to allow him to return to school.

Squire wanted to shout, to laugh, to dance like no one was watching. This level of happiness hadn't been present in his life since the attack on his tank.

He glimpsed a version of himself he'd been then. Hopeful for the future. A man with dreams that could come true. Someone who could feel joy.

As he headed to his cabin for a shower, his steps landed lighter, the air entered his lungs easier, the sun illuminated his life.

A life free from an old hurt. A life without resentment.

A life he wanted.

Chapter Nine

The next morning, Kelly woke to Finn's crying. He gagged, and she flew from her bed right when he threw up. She helped him, shivering, into the tub, then went upstairs to retrieve cleaning supplies.

Half an hour later, her alarm went off. She called Frank, and by his groggy tone, she'd woken him. She explained about Finn, and he said, "Don't worry about it. Hope he feels better soon. See you tomorrow."

She hated calling in sick on her ninth day, but also appreciated that she worked for a family that understood.

After cleaning everything up, including Finn, she helped him get dressed in a clean pair of pajamas and they snuggled together on the couch.

At precisely nine o'clock, she got a text from Squire. *You're sick?*

Finn is, she messaged back. She grinned as she imagined Squire standing in her office, waiting for her. *You're welcome to go through things in my office. Make a stack for anything interesting you find.*

Her mom brought a bottle of soda downstairs, stroked Finn's hair, and gave Kelly a kiss on the forehead before going back upstairs. Half an hour later, she called down that she and Kelly's dad were going into Amarillo for the day.

Kelly woke to the peal of the doorbell sometime after lunch. Finn continued to sleep, so she slid away from him and hurried upstairs. She whipped the door open, absolutely no idea who would be standing on the other side. She certainly didn't expect to see Squire standing there, holding a couple of grocery sacks.

"My mother sent soup." He lifted the bags and stepped past her, Benson bounding behind him. "Oh, can he come in the house?"

"Yes, yes." She frantically tried to flatten her hair as she followed Squire and his dog into the kitchen. She wished she wore a cowboy hat every waking moment the way he did. She grabbed a sweatshirt off the back of the couch and pulled it on to hide the fact that she wasn't completely dressed.

When she arrived in the kitchen, he'd placed a pan on the stove and was removing the lid from a container of chicken soup. Benson sat at attention in front of the aquarium, his paw flinching toward the glass every time a fish swam near.

"You know my mother." Squire poured the soup into the pan and began opening drawers. "She's got twice as many cowboys out at the ranch this week, getting her garden in. She makes enough food to feed an army."

An army of anxious ants marched along Kelly's skin at having him in her parents' house. At his large presence filling the tiny kitchen. At the way her fingers itched to hold his.

"Spoon, spoon," Squire muttered, and Kelly stepped next to him to the drawer where all the big cooking utensils were. She handed it to him, and he grinned. "Thanks."

He hummed as he stirred the soup, and she had a flash of what a life with him could be like. Then she reminded herself that if Squire went back to school, he wouldn't be home in the middle of the day. He wouldn't be able to zip over with chicken soup when she or Finn was sick. He wouldn't even be within a reasonable driving distance to see him on the weekends.

She put her hands in the pockets of the hoodie. "Did you talk to your mom and dad about college?" She couldn't help asking. Friends asked each other questions about their lives.

"Yes."

She heard the warning in his voice, and he kept his back to her, a clear indication that he didn't want her mothering him.

"And?" she asked anyway.

"You're so nosy." He turned and she found a sparkle in his eyes.

"Interested," she corrected. *Very interested*, she added mentally.

He took a micro-step closer to her, but in the small kitchen, it felt like a leap. "They agreed that I should finish. Dad's talking to Clark about being the foreman while I'm gone." His eyes bored right to the center of her being. "Thank you for pushing me to talk to my parents."

A flash of pride stole through her. "I didn't do anything."

"You did." His entire body blazed with energy. It practically leapt from his body to hers. "I wouldn't have said anything if you hadn't insisted that I could do both."

"So you're calling me pushy and insistent?" She hugged herself. "Thought you didn't want me to lecture you."

He laughed, a much happier sound than she'd heard from him before. "If the boot fits."

The sound of coughing floated up the stairs, and Kelly took the opportunity to leave the kitchen. It was getting hot, hot, hot in there.

"Hey, baby." She cupped Finn's face in her hands and searched his eyes. "How are you feeling?"

"I'm hungry."

He didn't feel feverish. He didn't seem flushed. "You think you can eat?" She smoothed his hair back. "Maybe something like toast?"

"Maybe something like soup?" Squire's voice sounded behind her, and she turned to find him on the bottom step.

"You're the guy from the park." Finn spotted Benson, who came with Squire like his shadow. "Is that your dog?"

Squire joined them near the couch and knelt down. "Do you like chicken noodle?"

Kelly noted the kindness in his voice, and how he'd gotten on Finn's level. Benson licked Finn's hand, and he giggled. He stroked the dog's head, and if dogs could purr, Kelly felt sure Benson would have.

"Can I eat soup, Mom?" Finn's stomach roared.

"I guess so," she said. He stood up slowly, a speed her son didn't usually operate on, and headed upstairs. "If he throws up again, you're cleaning it up," Kelly said to Squire before she went to help Finn get some homemade chicken noodle soup.

She ladled herself a bowl too, unable to resist the tantalizing scent of chicken broth and pasta. Behind her, Finn and Squire sat at the bar, and she served up another bowl so the three of them could eat.

When she turned, she found a freshly baked loaf of bread on the counter too. "Your mom is a saint," she said, almost ready to cry that she didn't have to cook today.

"Hey, I'm the one that brought it." Squire smirked, but Kelly looked away. She wasn't sure what emotion rode in her eyes, but she didn't want Squire to see it.

Finn made a full recovery after that, soon wanting to go outside and play with Benson. "I'll take him out," Squire said. "Benson loves a Frisbee."

"Yes!" Finn jumped up and down. "Please, Mom, can I?"

She appraised her son, as if she could tell the status of his health just by looking. "You sure you're feeling okay?"

"Yes."

Squire put his hand on her shoulder. "He's fine. Benson's practically a nurse. He'll let me know if something's wrong."

"All right," she said. Finn whooped and ran around the corner and through the mudroom. Squire started to follow when Kelly said, "Maybe I'll jump in the shower."

Squire nodded and proceeded out to the backyard. Kelly moved to the window in the kitchen where she could watch them. Benson ran around, barking, while Finn found a football and tossed it to Squire.

He launched it back. Finn jumped for the ball and caught it. He came down with a smile on his face, and Squire scooped him up with a triumphant yell. Her heart melted into her stomach, which churned with a strange mix of joy and trepidation. She'd never seen Taylor play with Finn before. The most he'd done was bring his computer to the beach so he could work from a camp chair while Finn splashed in the ocean.

Watching Squire play with her son, she again glimpsed what life could be like with a family. With Squire.

If only he was available to settle down, to run the ranch, now. Four years seemed impossibly long, and College Station impossibly far away.

Frustration solidified her heart and her resolve. Finn alone was her family, and a handsome, kind man with a dog didn't change anything. She fed herself these lies as she headed downstairs to shower.

"He can't stay," Kelly said for the third time. "He's been here all day."

Her parents had returned from Amarillo with Chinese takeout. Enough to feed half the county, in Kelly's estimation. They'd invited Squire, who was still at the house, to stay for dinner.

"He *can* stay," her mother said, bustling around the kitchen and getting out plates. Five plates.

Squire looked at Kelly, his eyebrows raised. He moved into the living room, and she followed.

"I can stay, darlin'," he said. "Really. I'm twenty-six years old." He half-smirked, half-smiled. "It's not like I need to check with my parents first."

"You don't need to waste any more time here," she said, unsure as to why she was pushing him away. The hug in her office had something to do with it. The way he'd played with Finn had something to do with it. The battering her ribs were taking from her pulse definitely had something to do with it.

"It's not a waste of time," he said, his eyes flashing with dangerous fire. "I've been invited. I'm going to stay." He removed his cowboy hat and ran his hands through his hair. Somehow, it fell into place, despite being under a hat for hours. He stepped past her and re-entered the kitchen.

Kelly heard his low voice mix with her father's. She felt off-balance with Squire here. Not because he didn't belong, didn't fit. But because he did.

She pressed her hand over her heart and willed it to beat slower before she rejoined her family—and Squire—in the dining room. Chinese food containers littered the center of the table, and her dad was helping Finn get the sweet and sour chicken he loved.

Her world righted itself, with Squire in it. She saw with clarity how easily he could fit in with her family, her son, her life. Her fingertips tingled and her eyes misted and her stomach squeezed squeezed squeezed.

"Come on, Mom." At the sound of Finn's voice, Kelly stuffed everything behind a wall in her mind to deal with later and took her place with the people she loved most. It surprised her to think of Squire like that, but while she might not *love* him, she certainly felt comfortable around him.

She filled her plate with her favorites, removed from the conversation as her father asked Squire about his military service. She had nothing to contribute, but she listened as he gave details about his deployments.

"How's your family?" her mother asked next.

"They're fine, ma'am." He leaned away from his plate, apparently satisfied. "My mother had the boys put in her garden these past few days."

Kelly's mom smiled. "If only we all had cowhands to get our gardens in."

"I could send them out," Squire offered, which made Kelly's eyebrows rise. When his mom had offered the services of the boys to help her move, Squire had vetoed it in two seconds flat.

"Don't be ridiculous," Kelly said. "Mom hasn't gardened in well, ever."

"Hey," her mom said. "Daddy always puts in some peas and corn."

"It takes them half of a Saturday," Kelly told Squire.

"Have you done it yet?" he asked her father.

"No." He leaned over and picked up the fork Finn had just dropped.

"Well, I can come help you get it done this weekend, then," Squire said.

Kelly wanted to object, but both her mother and father accepted so quickly, she couldn't. She watched them exchange a glance and she suspected that their impromptu trip to Amarillo had actually been planned.

She narrowed her eyes at her mother, who suddenly had somewhere else to look. Suspicion, confirmed. Heidi must have called to say she was sending over chicken noodle soup with a side of male goodness. Kelly abandoned her food too, finding it hard to swallow.

Finn finished eating before everyone else, as usual. Kelly started to stand to help him clean up and get ready for bed.

"I'll do it," her mother said. "Will, come help me run a bath for him."

Like it took two people to turn on the tub. Kelly watched them go, feeling very much like she was on a date in her parents' kitchen. Ridiculous!

"It's been a great day," she said to Squire. "Thanks for bringing the soup and playing with Finn." Her voice caught on her son's name. "It means a lot to him."

Squire's eyes sparkled like sapphires when he looked at her. "It was a great day, wasn't it?" He reached for his hat and put it on.

"Better than digging through cobwebbed files," Kelly said.

"I don't know," he said. "It might be a tie."

With him, everything would be like twirling through a meadow. "Well, I'll be back tomorrow, and as you massage the aches from your shoulders, I'm sure you'll change your mind." She stood and began clearing the dishes. Squire joined her, rinsing the plates and putting them in the dishwasher.

He returned to the dining room and brought in the leftovers. She pulled out plastic containers and they started putting everything in the fridge. With the kitchen clean, and Finn in the tub, Kelly didn't know what to do next. Her parents hadn't made a reappearance, which only increased the buzzing beneath her skin.

Squire went into the living room, Benson following on his heels. "Well, it's been a fine evening, ma'am. But I best be goin'."

His fake cowboy accent sent a shiver over her shoulders, and she tucked her hands in her pockets to stop herself from reaching for him. "Tell your mother thanks for the soup. And the bread." She bent down to stroke Benson. "Thanks for playing with Finn, buddy."

She straightened. The heaviness of Squire's gaze weighing against her resolve. She stepped toward him and embraced him in a two-second hug that felt every inch as awkward as Kelly did. "Thank you for coming."

"Sure thing, darlin'." Squire's whisper made Kelly want to hold onto him a big longer, but one false step could lead her down the wrong path, just as it had before.

Her heart hurt in two separate parts. One, because she knew she wasn't ready to take their friendship to the next level. And two, because she feared that if she didn't figure things out before he left, she'd lose him forever.

Squire drove away from Kelly's knowing that he'd just experienced one of the best days of his life. For a few hours, he felt like he had a family he'd like to come home to after a long day on the ranch. Or a long day of studying veterinary medicine.

As he left the lights of town behind, a cloud of loneliness

descended again. He reached over and ruffled Benson's mane. At least he had his dog.

And a future, he thought. *One I actually want.*

The next morning found him in Kelly's office with a cup of black coffee and a single slice of toast. He didn't want her to know he hadn't slept well for thinking about her, though he was sure his face bore the weight of his exhaustion.

When she arrived, she looked as fresh and lovely as ever. She'd paired black jeans with a long, flowery top that make her eyes look more like the color of grass than the color of sea glass. A silver bracelet dangled from her wrist, complimenting the hoops in her ears. He half-expected to see heels on her feet, but she'd opted for a smart pair of running shoes.

"Earth to Squire."

He startled as he realized she stood right in front of him, waving her hand. "Sorry," he said. "I don't know what happened there."

She turned on her computer, and he opened a file. A dance he was growing accustomed to, but one that wouldn't yield him the results he wanted.

When he couldn't stand looking at another piece of paper, he sighed and stood. "I'm going to go see what my mom made for lunch."

She glanced up, her eyes glazed. "Lunch?"

A flash of affection stole through him. Her beauty continued to amaze him at the most random times, and her hardworking spirit only added to her allure.

"Yeah," he said. "It's almost one." He extended his hand to her.

"Come on. I don't care if you brought something. Ma is making lunch every day this week for the boys. It'll be better than whatever you brought."

She stood, but didn't take his hand. Not that he expected her to. "I doubt it. I brought her soup."

The front desk where Clark usually sat was empty, and Squire wondered if his father had talked to him about being the foreman yet.

Benson perked up from his spot in the shade under the stairs when the door opened. Squire whistled, and the dog came to his side. "Let's go eat, boy."

Benson licked his hand, the roughness of his tongue sending a vein of happiness up Squire's arm. He chuckled as he swatted the dog away.

"Finn loved him," Kelly said. "I should get him a dog, but it's like another child to take care of."

"He can come play with Benson any time. The poor guy needs someone to run around with." He glanced down at his dog, who had gained a bit of weight since he'd started sitting in the shade. "I don't get much time to run him the way he needs to be run."

"Don't the boys take him out on the ranch?"

"They used to," he said. "But ol' Benson is getting up in years. He can't keep up with them anymore."

"Well, he was gentle with Finn. It's all he talked about last night after you left. 'Did he take that dog? When can he come back?'" She spoke in a high-pitched voice, imitating her son.

Squire couldn't help the satisfaction settling over him. He'd wanted to help Kelly with Finn, and he was glad he had. Spending the day with her hadn't been bad either. More like perfect. He followed Kelly up the steps to the patio and through the sliding glass doors.

The smell of bacon hit him as soon as she opened the door. His stomach growled and his mouth watered simultaneously.

"Ma," he called, but he didn't have to look far to find the food. "BLT's." He took two halves and put them on a paper plate. He opened the fridge and found macaroni salad and peach punch. He pulled them out and put them on the counter.

"Oh, you found the food," his mother said, entering the kitchen. "Hello, Kelly. How's Finn feeling?"

Kelly hastily put down the sandwich she'd been about to bite into. "He's much better, Heidi. Thank you so much for the soup."

"Squire insisted," she said. "He even helped chop the vegetables."

Squire steadfastly refused to look up from his plate, though he felt Kelly's gaze land on him. He couldn't believe his mom was selling him out. *Maybe* he had pushed his mom to make the soup. *Maybe* he had been a little enthusiastic about taking it to Kelly.

"I've learned there's nothing he can't do," Kelly said, and Squire's head snapped up.

"That's not true," he said at the same his mom said, "That's the truth."

"Has Dad talked to Clark yet?" he asked, shifting the conversation away from his apparent perfection. He knew he wasn't perfect. All Kelly had to do was ask his last girlfriend—

Tabby would tell her all about his trust issues, the way he put his work before his relationships. Heck, he'd had to double-check Kelly's story about prom before he truly believed her.

"Yes," his mom said. "He said he'd be honored to be the foreman. He needs to be replaced as general controller, so he and your father are working on that. As soon as those people are in place, you'll be free to work with the animals until you figure out what you're doing with college."

Sourness socked him in the mouth. "I haven't even been accepted yet."

"You will be," Kelly murmured. A drape of silence settled in the kitchen, but he didn't know how to lighten the mood.

Saturday morning, Squire loaded up his truck with fertilizer and seeds, put Benson in the cab, and headed to Kelly's. She hadn't said anything more about helping her parents plant their garden. They hadn't either, but they'd agreed to have him come this morning. And he was going.

Nerves assaulted him as he drove, but he continued on. After he pulled into the driveway and got out, he heard laughter from the backyard. At least someone was home. He grabbed a shovel and a rake before heading around the house.

Benson bounded ahead of him, barking when he rounded the corner. Squire heard Finn's delighted squeal, and a smile sprang to his face. The sight in the backyard brought a pang of longing to his heart.

Finn rolled around on the grass with Benson, a baseball bat abandoned nearby; Kelly stood near her mother as they both hung clothes on the outside line. And her dad watched everything from the deck.

Squire felt like perhaps he'd just run to the store to get more clothespins or bring back lunch. Like he could integrate himself into this family with a quick kiss to Kelly's cheek and a ruffle in Finn's hair.

As quickly as his comfort and happiness had come, it bled away. He wasn't part of this family, and his time in the Texas panhandle was rapidly ending. He'd sent in his application on Wednesday, and though he couldn't have been accepted yet, he checked the status online every day.

"Hey," he said to Kelly and her mom. "Do you guys still want help putting in your garden?" He balanced the tools he'd brought next to him.

Ivory blinked a couple of times, a gesture he now realized that Kelly had gotten from her mother.

He hooked his thumb back toward the driveway. "I brought seeds and everything. Whatever you want."

"What have you got?" Will sauntered over.

Squire shook his hand. "Corn and peas, I think you said you liked."

He glanced at his wife before heading toward the front. "Let's do it."

Squire didn't have any grand illusions about having Kelly work by his side. So he was surprised when she wielded a rake as he returned to the backyard with a load of seeds.

"Got 'er tilled last night," Will said. "I was just gettin' up the gumption to go to the hardware store."

"Now you don't have to." Squire set the stake for the first row of peas. Kelly walked the length of the garden and secured the other end of the string with her stake. He dragged the end of his hoe along the string, making a shallow trench for the seeds.

Will helped Finn get a handful of seeds and taught him how to space them. Then he took his rake and covered them. "Then we'll water," he told his grandson.

"What are they?" he asked.

"Those're peas."

"Grandpa likes to eat those right out of the garden," Kelly said, taking Finn's hand as they walked back to the shed to get another set of stakes for the next row. "You'll be lucky if you get any." She threw her dad a playful smile, and he shrugged.

"She's right," he said to Squire.

With all of them working, the small garden space was finished in less than an hour. Squire didn't want to leave yet, but he had no reason to stay.

He loaded his tools in the truck and shuffled back to get Benson. "Well, I guess I'll be off. My mother needs a couple of things from the grocer."

"Oh, so do I," Ivory said. She turned to Kelly. "Maybe you could go with him. Get what's on the list on the fridge so we don't have to go out on the Sabbath."

Kelly raised her right eyebrow, but her mom said, "I'll go get the list, and then I'll need to help your dad dig through the shed to find the sprinklers."

"Mom—" Kelly started, but the woman could move fast for someone getting up there in years. Squire watched her go, feeling like he was somehow being set up.

"I can get it all," he said. "Bring back what she needs."

"I want to go," she said without moving her lips. "They're driving me crazy, asking all kinds of questions." She took the hand rakes and buckets Finn had been playing with into the shed.

Squire watched Finn chase Benson, never quite able to catch him. Will came out of the shed and thanked him, and Squire shook his hand again. The gesture felt formal, but also casual.

"Questions?" he asked when Kelly reappeared. "What kind of questions?"

"About my job, about the ranch, about where I'm going to live. On and on."

"Your mother is from the same generation as mine," he said.

"The nosy one?"

He put his hand on her elbow to guide her out of the way of an oncoming Benson. She stiffened at his touch, and he dropped his hand. "Maybe just *interested*."

Kelly shoved him away from her, danger in the set of her mouth, but playfulness riding in her eyes.

Ivory came bustling out of the kitchen, a paper flapping from her fingers. "Here you go," she said, handing the list to Kelly. "Thank you, Squire."

"Ma'am." He tipped his hat to her and waved for Kelly to go

first. She shot him an apprehensive look as she stepped past, but he kept his smile hitched in place. He sensed her nerves—he had the same lightning bolting through him. But he wasn't backing down from this, from her, from his second chance.

Chapter Ten

Kelly kept adjusting her jeans, then her shoes. She hated the jittery feeling coursing through her veins, along her skin, tightening her muscles. At the same time, it kept her hyper-aware of everything in the cab of Squire's truck. He whistled along with the radio, seemingly without a care in the world.

"Heard anything from Texas A&M?" she asked just to get him to stop.

"I only applied three days ago."

"You'll get in," she said.

"We'll see. Where are you planning to live?" He pulled into Vince's, and Kelly felt the burden of dozens of eyes. Watching. Staring. Judging.

"I don't know," she said. "I haven't had any time to look for anything yet." When he asked, she didn't feel the same level of annoyance as when her mom had. No pressure, no defense needed to be played. He asked because he was curious or wanted to help, not because he wanted to tell all his friends at the salon.

They walked into Vince's, and he chose a basket he could carry while she got a cart. "Gonna show me up with your muscles, huh?"

she teased.

In response, he flexed for her, and she laughed. They meandered through the aisles, getting what their mothers wanted. Kelly noticed every glance that came their way, but she found she didn't care. *Let them talk*, she thought. Heaven knew they already were.

"Ice cream?" the checker asked as she finished ringing up Squire's groceries.

"Yes," he said. "Two." He handed over his money before Kelly could protest. She rang out next, and they stopped by the customer service counter to get their soft serves.

"I haven't had one of these in ages," she said after she'd gotten her chocolate and vanilla twist.

"You worked here. I would've gotten one at the end of every shift." He'd gotten plain chocolate, and Kelly couldn't help watching him carefully lick around his ice cream. She wondered what his mouth would feel like against hers.

She numbed her lips with a huge bite of ice cream, her synapses firing. Was she ready to start dating again? So soon? It would only take a single step, and she'd be on that path.

"My favorite kind of ice cream is Rocky Road, but they don't serve that from a machine." He stowed his groceries in the back of his truck and nodded toward the park. "You game for a walk?"

"Sure." With her bags in the truck too, they headed across the street.

The conversation lulled, but the silence didn't need to be stuffed with words. Just being with Squire felt natural, like she'd known him her whole life. Which, of course, she *had* known him her whole life. She'd been comfortable with him in high school too. But her feelings hadn't been mixed up; her eyes hadn't wandered his way; her mind hadn't fantasized. As she walked next to him, she wondered if that would've changed if they'd gone to prom together. If she would've started dating him. If she would've stayed in town instead of leaving for college.

They bypassed the playground and the field where a few people were throwing Frisbees. As they moved into a more secluded area, her insides puddled like her ice cream. He glanced down the path, which turned from sidewalk to dirt path. "There's a well back there—or there used to be. Me and my friends used to toss all kinds of stuff into it."

"A well?" She looked into the trees. "I've never seen a well back there."

He swallowed the last of his ice cream cone and turned a Cheshire cat face toward her. "Well, today is your lucky day."

Kelly fell into step beside him, the mischief from his grin infecting her. "What? You threw quarters in and made wishes?"

He slid her a sideways glance that screamed dreamy. "Sometimes. But mostly we threw in our old jerseys and shoes after football season. Sort of a rite of passage from one season to the next."

They rounded a bend, effectively shielding them from the rest of the world. Squire stepped closer and captured her hand in his.

Her first instinct was to pull away. It happened as a flinch, a reaction she couldn't control. He held on tighter. "I'm not your boss anymore." The words seemed swallowed up in the leafy trees, or maybe his voice was just low and husky.

Her fingers relaxed, and she reveled in the warmth of his skin against hers. The sky shone a deeper blue. The trees whispered romantic advice. The birds quieted, as if they too sensed holding hands with Squire Ackerman was life changing.

As she finished her cone, Squire tugged her toward a side trail, barely wide enough for one person. "It's down here."

"No wonder I've never seen it." She had to let go of his hand to navigate the steep terrain, stepping over fallen branches and tree roots.

He made it down first, and turned back to help her with the last few feet, which was a straight drop-off. She put both hands on his shoulders, and he put both his on her waist, lifting her down.

Once on her feet, with his hands gone, she experienced a sense of loss she didn't understand. Along with the rush in her stomach and the swooping of birds in her chest, she simply felt…whole when he touched her.

Tucked against the incline they'd just come down, sat a well. Old, with the stones crumbling, it possessed a charm that gave Squire a run for his money. He held out a quarter, and she strolled over to the well, allowing the swell of magic that came from wishing to encompass her. She closed her eyes and tossed in her coin.

Seconds later, Squire threw in his quarter as well. She met his eyes, and for the first time in a long time she felt as alive as he looked.

He closed the distance between them, effortlessly taking her in his arms. "Kelly," he murmured, almost a question but not quite.

She wrapped her arms around his strong back. She was safe; secure; home. "Hmm?"

His answer came as he brushed his lips against her temple. The birds in her chest rioted, pushing her pulse into the rapid beating of wings.

"Can I kiss you, darlin'?"

"I wished you would."

"We wished for the same thing, then." He leaned down, his eyes sparking with the hope of a second chance. The first touch of his lips to hers made her world stutter, stop, spin spin spin. She lost herself in the kiss, in Squire's touch, in the easiness of being with him.

And Chelsea was right.

Squire was nothing like Taylor. Everything he did was vastly superior, and Kelly knew she'd be ruined for life. Every kiss would be compared to this one, and none would ever be this spectacular.

"You know, I didn't want to come back to Three Rivers," she told him as they picked their way back to the park.

Still on the dirt path, his hand still in hers, he lifted his eyebrows. "Oh?"

"No, I didn't think it was the best place to get a job. I mean, everything is owner-operated. Who was going to hire an accountant?" She glanced at him, hoping for a reaction. Major Ackerman stared straight ahead.

"A bigger city would've been a wiser choice. But my mom insisted. She said we could live here for a few months just to catch our breath. And then the job at the ranch came up." She wasn't sure why she was telling him this.

He squeezed her fingers. "Well, I'm glad you came back."

Her heart slipped through the cracks between her ribs and landed in her shoes. She realized she was hinting that she could come to A&M with him. She'd have a good chance at finding a job in a city the size of College Station. Then she wouldn't have to live five hundred miles away while he completed his medical degree.

She said nothing, though. The magic of the kiss by the wishing well faded as they stepped from dirt to cement, as Kelly realized that Squire would be leaving town soon. Had he felt his pulse in every appendage when she'd left? How had he managed to put his organs back where they belonged? Kelly felt scrambled up inside, a tangled mess she couldn't unravel.

"Kel?" he asked.

"Yeah?"

He lifted their joined hands a fraction of an inch. "This okay in public?" His bright blue eyes danced with hope.

Kelly warred with herself. She wanted to announce their relationship to the world. But she preferred to do it from another city—like College Station—so she didn't have to endure the questions, the sideways glances, the gossip in the diner, the grocery store, and the salon.

He let go of her hand, the light in his eyes dimming even though his lips twitched upward. "Okay. Later." He moved, much quicker now, down the sidewalk.

She hurried to catch him but didn't reach for his hand. "Squire," she said. "What are we doing?"

"Walking in the park." He pushed his cowboy hat lower to cover his eyes.

"No." She pulled on his elbow to get him to stop. "I mean, us." She gestured back in the general direction of the well. "That." She breathed like she'd been underwater for too long. "I mean, I liked that." She studied her running shoes next to his boots. "I like *you*. But I have my son to take care of. And you're leaving...."

"Ah, okay." He lifted her chin gently with two fingers, searching her eyes. She didn't know what answers he found, and she couldn't ask because his phone broke into their lives with a loud buzz.

"We'll work it out." He pulled his cell from his pocket, frowning as he read the incoming message. "I need to get back to the ranch." He kissed her again, quick and without the same careful passion as at the well, barely a meeting of mouths. She clutched the disappointment at such a short union, and then released it.

"I'm sorry. I have to go."

She wasn't sure if he just meant for the day, or if he meant forever. She didn't know what the text said. But she did know that it felt like he was running away. Even though he'd said they'd work things out, all she saw was his retreating back.

Squire explained about the mare giving birth at the ranch as he drove Kelly home. "I'm the new animal care," he said. "At least for a little while." He frowned as he looked out the window, wishing he hadn't vocalized the end-date to his veterinarian duties.

After all, that was obviously a point of concern for Kelly. *As well it should be*, he thought. She did have a job in the panhandle, and she did need to take care of Finn—and herself. He toyed with the idea of asking her to come with him to College Station, but she barely seemed ready to be alone with him.

He couldn't go too fast. Which was why he needed an airtight game plan about College Station before he said anything.

"I gotta get Bense," he said after he helped her bring in her groceries. He moved toward the backyard to find his dog. Kelly followed him, and Squire caught her wrist as she reached for the door. Her skin felt like silk, and he took a deep breath of her creamy scent, catching a hint of earth from gardening and a blast of chocolate from her lips. Just thinking about her mouth sent him into a tailspin.

"Squire," she whispered. "My mother is right there."

"Can I sit by you at church tomorrow?" He touched his lips to her forehead. "I'll behave myself."

She pushed against his chest but only succeeded in putting an inch between them. "Like you are now?"

It may have been his imagination, but she sounded beyond breathless. Surprised he could influence her to forget to breathe, he stepped back. "Better than now," he promised. "Like choir boy good. I swear."

She cocked her head to the side and studied him. When she smiled, he smelled victory.

"Okay," she said. "But nothing funny."

"Oh, I'm serious about you, darlin'." He pushed open the door and left her standing in the house. "Hey, Mrs. Armstrong." He scanned the backyard, which was devoid of dogs and little boys. "I'm lookin' for Benson. I have to get back to the ranch."

"Oh, Will took him and Finn down to the creek," Ivory said. "I'm sorry. We didn't know you'd need to go so quickly."

"It's fine," Squire said. "Kelly can bring him to work on Monday." He turned as she joined them on the deck. "That okay, Kel? Bringing Benson out to the ranch on Monday?"

"Or you could come over after church tomorrow. Have lunch with us?" She raised her eyebrows at her mom, who nodded.

"Lunch sounds great." Her beauty made him ache, but his attraction to her had always gone deeper than that. Watching her care for Finn only reminded him of how sensitive she was, how selfless to take care of others before herself.

Clark texted again, and Squire cursed the timing of the universe. "I really have to go," he said. "I'll talk to you later."

He left, frustrated even though he'd gotten his wish. But five hundred miles was a long way, and four years a very long time. Especially for a beautiful woman like Kelly. He could see and feel her walls going back up. She wasn't ready for more yet, but his time in Three Rivers was running out.

"What happened in town?" his mom asked later that evening.

"Nothing." Squire looked up from his silent phone, trying to eradicate the hope that Kelly would text.

"Well, something did," his mom said. "You've been acting moody since you got back."

Not surprised that she'd noticed, but definitely worried that he had been acting different, he shrugged. "Nothing. Planted a garden, got your groceries."

Kissed Kelly.

She set aside her sewing, which ignited Squire's nerves. His mother's undivided attention meant a conversation he wouldn't enjoy.

"Please. Give me some credit. I know you like that woman."

"What woman?" he asked innocently, silently begging his mother to drop this. Especially before his father came in from the stable. Squire had successfully helped the mare through birth, and Raven was resting quietly with her foal. Clark and his father had stayed in the barn to discuss what they should do with the new horse. Ranch business. Stuff Squire didn't care about, and now didn't have to pretend he did.

His mother clucked her tongue. "You can't keep everything bottled up," she said, picking up her sewing again. "It's not healthy."

He rolled his eyes. "I'm not Chelsea, Ma. I don't need to talk everything to death."

"It would be nice if you said *some*thing. Women like it when men talk about things."

He considered her advice. He wasn't great at expressing himself. It was one of the things that served him well in the Army, but not in his past relationships. If he'd said something to Kelly, to Chelsea, to anyone, ten years ago, everything might have turned out differently.

"I'm going back to veterinary school," he finally said. "That's what's the matter."

Her needle went flying through the fabric. Up and down. "I thought you wanted to go back to school."

"I do," he said. "Kelly doesn't." Rather, he didn't know how she felt. He had no idea if she'd uproot her son and move with him to College Station. Neither of them knew if she could get a job. Squire didn't even know if his GI Bill would pay for school, or how he'd have enough money to live. He'd probably have to get a job too.

Before his mom could answer, his dad came in, wiping his hands on his jeans. His mother abandoned her sewing and crossed the room to ask him about the new foal. Squire had thought he wanted company tonight. As his parents discussed the newest addition to the ranch, he slipped out the patio door in favor of his empty cabin—where he didn't have to talk about how he felt, his future, or his failures.

As Squire neared his cabin, his Army warning radar blared. Louder and louder. He paused near the edge of the garden, the row of cabins in plain view. They looked like any other Saturday night. Dark and empty, as the boys usually trucked into town on the weekends.

The parking lot, where he might have seen a visitor's car, was blocked by the equipment shed and the calving stalls. His stomach flipped as a noise—a small clink—sounded to his left. He spun just as a man came out of his cabin.

Squire squinted into the rapidly darkening sky. His pulse pounded for several beats until the man laughed.

"Major Ackerman," he said, striding forward.

Recognition washed over Squire. "Pete?" he asked, but there as no doubt it was Squire's First Lieutenant, Peter Marshall.

Squire didn't have to look to know Pete's entire left arm was covered in bright pink scar tissue. The burn extended onto his torso and kissed his neck. Pete had undergone a number of skin grafts, his texts about the surgeries and recoveries always the same: *At least my face is still as pretty as ever.*

"What are you doing here?" Squire asked.

Pete clapped Squire on the back in a man-hug, still chuckling. "I just got discharged." He glanced around, examining the sky. "You're right. This place is magical. Just as much sky as Kandahar, but not nearly as hot."

"Wait a few weeks," Squire said, smiling. "It turns sweltering."

"I'm planning to stay a while," he said. "Your dad offered me a job."

Squire hadn't realized how checked out he'd been while buried in dusty files and entrenched in figuring how to make things work with Kelly. "When did you talk to my father?"

"Couple of days ago. Called that number you gave me. Your controller said you were busy, but gave me to your dad. I got here this morning, but I guess you were off planting someone's garden."

Pete shoved his hands in his pockets and rocked back on his heels, a knowing smile on his face.

Though Squire outranked Pete, a flush still warmed his neck. He employed his military training to keep from clearing his throat. "So you thought you'd invade my cabin?"

"Your dad said I could bunk with you since all the other cabins are already doubly occupied."

"Sure, yeah," Squire said. "You get settled in?"

"Yes," Pete said, cuffing him on the shoulder. "So let's go out. I talked to a couple of guys who said there's a great place for wings in town. I haven't had anything good to eat in ages. Hospital food is disgusting."

"Well, you came to the right place."

"I know, I know." Pete rolled his eyes. "You've been bragging about your mother's cooking since the day I met you." He nudged him toward the parking lot. "But I want wings tonight, Major. *Wings.*"

He strode away, and Squire didn't hesitate before following his friend. With Pete, he knew exactly where he stood. It was easy to laugh with him, reminisce about the desert they'd experienced together, and help him flirt with the waitress Pete thought was pretty.

Squire supposed the tall woman with dark hair could be considered pretty. "You know I know all about Tammy," he said, stirring his bleu cheese dressing with a celery stick.

Pete tore his gaze from her retreating figure. "Oh, yeah?"

"Yeah." Squire related what he knew—the most embarrassing

things. Who she dated in high school, that she'd once worn a bathing suit to school just to see what old Principal Henderson would do. She'd been sent home to change and never came back.

Squire chuckled just thinking about it. "Tammy's never a dull moment."

"Just what I need, brother." Pete's gaze wandered back to Tammy, his appetite for the wings obviously satisfied. "What about you? You see anyone here you like?"

Squire almost choked on his water. "You must not remember me," he said. "I don't look for women in a sports bar."

Pete laughed, the sound boisterous and infectious. "Oh, that's right. You're in love with that girl from high school."

"No," Squire said, coughing to cover his embarrassment. He couldn't remember telling Pete about Kelly, ever. He'd never felt the need to relive the humiliation.

"So." Pete's eyes glinted with humor. Squire knew that look, and he didn't like it. "Pick one." Pete swept his arm out, indicating the whole bar. He wore a compression sleeve over his arm, and on the drive to town Squire had learned that the hospital in West Virginia where Pete had been all these months had finally done all they could for him.

Now, Pete practically wore a laugh on his face. "Just pick one, Major. You don't have to marry her."

Squire narrowed his eyes, wondering why it mattered if he kept Kelly a secret from Pete now. "Fine," he said. "I pick the girl I knew in high school." He lifted his soda to his lips. "But I didn't tell you about her." He raised his eyebrows, clearly asking how Pete knew.

"Your mom said you'd gone into town to plant someone's garden," Pete started. "I asked questions until she said you'd gone to help your girlfriend's parents." He threw back another chicken wing. "After that, she had *a lot* of stories to tell."

"Kelly is not my girlfriend," Squire practically growled. His mom had no right to be saying such things. With a start, Squire realized that words like *girlfriend* could get back to Kelly in a matter of minutes. He glanced around to see who was sitting close enough to overhear.

A trio of women twittered nearby. None of them looked at him, and he focused back on Pete. "Please don't say anything. I'm just— we're just—she works at the ranch."

"So I'll get to meet her on Monday." Pete leaned back and crossed his arms. The king on his throne.

"Tomorrow, if you want to go to church," Squire said.

Pete's jovial mood finally deflated a notch. "Church, Major?" He took a swig of his club soda. "Not really a church goer."

"Really?" Squire asked. "But we talked about religion all the time."

"I believe in God. I just don't go to church."

"You should come with me," Squire said. "Our pastor says good things."

"Maybe." Pete sat up straighter as Tammy approached.

"Just a couple more minutes on those fries, boys," she said, sashaying away as fast as she'd come.

Bright lights in red, blue, and green lit up the front window, following immediately by the sharp snap and pop of shooting. Squire ducked his head, sliding off his chair and getting as low as he could.

Four seconds passed before he realized he wasn't in the Abrams, wasn't driving through the desert, wasn't being attacked by the enemy. By five seconds, he realized the sounds and lights had been fireworks.

By six seconds, he met Pete's gaze without having to look up, because the lieutenant had slid under the table too.

At seven seconds, he and Pete straightened. Embarrassment crawled up Squire's neck as he took his seat, the tension in the air as thick as black smoke.

"Dropped my napkin," Pete announced to the ladies at the next table over, all of whom had turned toward them.

They went back to their business, leaving Pete and Squire to look at each other. Squire broke the tension by chugging his soda. "Glad it's not just me that's jumpy."

"And you've been home longer than me," Pete said. "The hospital is no Texas paradise."

"No shooting, though."

"Unless you count the drugs they kept pumping into me with those sharp needles." Pete glanced away, his somberness disappearing as Tammy approached with his cheese fries. "Help me get her to go out with me," he hissed to Squire. "He-ey," he said louder as she set the plate in front of him. He seemed to have nothing else to say, because he kicked Squire under the table.

"Hey, Tammy," he said, throwing Pete a glare. Luckily, he knew exactly how to get Pete back. "You goin' to church tomorrow?"

Pete's look could've murdered Squire. He chuckled as Tammy said, "Sure am. Will you boys be there?"

Chapter Eleven

Kelly fiddled relentlessly with Finn's tie after they'd sat in the fifth pew, where they usually did. Her stomach had become a hangar for airplanes, their propellers roaring at full speed. Why had she agreed to sit by Squire at church? *Everyone* would see them.

"Hey." Squire's voice interrupted the unrest slicing through Kelly. He sat next to her, but not too close. Close enough to stretch his long arm across her shoulders, sure. A shiver wound down her spine at the thought of cuddling into him during the sermon. She set her jaw. She wouldn't. She'd set personal boundaries for him, and she intended to keep them.

"Hey." She noticed another man sliding onto the bench next to Squire. Tammy Olson seated herself next to him. Kelly leaned forward to see the man better. He wore a gray suit that didn't seem to fit quite right around his bulging muscles. Still, he had a good air about him, and when he turned toward her, she got a full view of his dazzling smile and bright green eyes.

"You must be Kelly," he said, extending his hand across Squire for her to shake.

"Kel, this is my First Lieutenant, Pete Marshall. He just got back from overseas, and he's starting out at the ranch tomorrow."

Surprise shot through Kelly, though at least Pete's physique could be explained. "Nice to meet you." The hand she shook was puckered and pink, clearly the victim of a fierce fire.

She sat back, very aware of Squire subtly shifting closer to her. He leaned down. "I should've called you, but I didn't have time. I can't come to lunch now that Pete's here."

Kelly's spirits fell. She'd helped her mother bake their famous cheddar biscuits that morning in anticipation of hosting Squire for lunch. "Oh, that's okay," she said, making her voice carefree. "Another time."

The organist began playing, meaning it was almost time to start the service. Kelly focused her attention on the pulpit, determined to remember that sitting by a man at church meant nothing. Absolutely nothing.

You know where liars go, she thought, her shoulders sinking as she admitted defeat. Already she could hear the whispers on her right, where Glenda sat with her other widowed friends. Kelly might as well snuggle up to Squire while she could. They would assume she was anyway.

"Maybe you can come out to the ranch," Squire whispered, slipping even closer to her. If he thought this was behaving himself, he was sorely mistaken.

"Bring Finn," he said. "He can see the new foal."

"Maybe," Kelly said, keeping her face forward. "I'll talk to my parents." As soon as she said the words, she wanted to take them back. One glance to her right, where her mother sat, only irritated her further. Glenda had actually come over and was whispering to her mom.

She groaned, not bothering to keep her voice down. Crystal turned around, and Kelly nodded toward the gossip circle. In church! Didn't they even have the decency to wait until the picnic?

Crystal reached back and patted her knee. As soon as her cousin's hand vacated the spot, Squire's took its place. Kelly sucked back a gasp, working hard to keep her composure.

"You're twenty-eight years old, darlin'," Squire teased, his breath falling softly against her earlobe. She couldn't move even if she wanted to. "You don't have to ask their permission."

She angled her head toward his, and he removed his hand from her knee. Another few inches, and she could kiss him. Her heart rate sped, sending adrenaline all the way to her pinky toes.

Glenda might die of a heart attack if Kelly kissed Squire in church. But apparently, gossip was the Lord's work.

"They're expecting you for lunch," she said, trying to ignore his sugary smirk and so-delicious-she-could-eat-them dimples. "I have to talk to them first."

He leaned in and smelled her hair. "Please come," he whispered just as Scott started his sermon.

True to his word, Squire didn't try to hold her hand, or put his arm around her, or touch her at all. Kelly had a hard time focusing on Scott's voice, though she got the general gist of his message: Trust God's will.

With Squire so close and smelling like pine and fresh air, even Finn's restlessness couldn't distract her. Finally, the lecture ended.

Finn hadn't fallen asleep, and Kelly leaned over. "Mom, Squire can't come for lunch. A friend of his came into town."

Her mom's face fell, but she recovered quickly. "That's fine, dear. We can take our biscuits to the picnic."

"He invited Finn and I out to the ranch." Kelly glanced at her son. "He said you could see their new horse. You want to do that?"

"Yeah!" Finn jumped to his feet and stumbled around Kelly's legs to Squire. "How many horses you got?"

"A lot," Squire assured him. "You can ride whichever one you want." He ruffled Finn's hair. "But you have to bring Benson back. He's the only dog who knows how to make the horses behave."

Finn turned back to Kelly. "Can we go, Mom?"

She cast a quick glance at her mom, who nodded. "Sure, buddy. We have to go home and get changed, though. Can't ride a horse in loafers." She looked at Squire when she spoke. "Trust me, boots are required gear for a ranch."

He laughed, and she wished they were alone so she could kiss him again. The depth of her feelings startled her, and she got to her feet to put distance between her and Squire. She examined the stained glass window, wondering how she could even be considering pursuing this relationship. She hadn't even finished paying for her divorce.

Take the first step, she thought, echoing something the pastor had said. *And let God guide you.*

She stepped into Squire's right side as he stood, causing him to slide his arm around her waist if he didn't want to fall back. Their eyes locked, and though she couldn't stretch up and kiss him right here in front of everyone, she felt confident he'd gotten the message: She wanted to.

"I thought you said Kelly wasn't into you," Pete said as soon as he'd climbed in the passenger seat of Squire's truck.

"She's…." Squire didn't quite know how to articulate how Kelly felt about him. He'd seen her fight her attraction to him. He'd felt the passion in her kiss at the well. And just now? He could've sworn she'd have gone to the moon with him. But College Station would do just fine.

"Into you," Pete finished. "I'm obviously better at reading women than you are, Major." He puffed out his chest. "It's okay to admit it."

"So how does Tammy read?" Squire asked to get the spotlight off himself.

"She's interested," Pete said. "I mean, I might only be here for a few months, until I figure out what I'm going to do next. But she seems interested for now."

They drove out of town in silence, Squire occupied with thoughts of Kelly and Finn out on the ranch. He wanted to see her again, smell her perfume, maybe hold her hand. After he and Pete returned to the ranch and changed out of their church clothes, Pete went up to the house for lunch. Squire puttered around the tack room, knowing he needed a few minutes before he faced his mother and her relentless questions.

When the soft hum of an engine met his ears, he sauntered over to the doorway. He blinked a couple of times to ensure he wasn't hallucinating. But when Benson practically knocked him to the ground and licked his face, Squire laughed.

"Did we make it in time for lunch?" Kelly wore jean shorts and a tank top; clothes he hadn't seen her wear since high school. He swallowed hard, scanning down to her feet. Knee-high boots. Black. With a heel.

He muscled Benson out of the way so he could step closer to Kelly. Finn hovered near her, shyly looking past Squire and into the barn.

"You're never too late for lunch, darlin'," Squire said, brushing his fingers against hers on the side where her son couldn't see. "You want to see the new foal?" he asked Finn.

"What's a foal?"

"A baby horse." Squire moved down the aisle that split the horse barn in half. "Come see. He's a beauty." He led the boy to the stall where the foal was romping around. Raven poked her nose from the doorway in the back that connected the two spaces.

"What's his name?" Finn said, hanging back.

"Doesn't have one yet." Squire leaned against the bars. "You can come right up here. He won't bite."

Finn joined him, pushing his face between two bars. Kelly crouched next to him, and they tried to get the foal to come over. He was skittish, and moved back into the private room with his mother.

"Can we feed him?" Finn asked.

Squire smiled down at him, smitten by the wonder in the boy's bright eyes. "Sorry, bud. He only drinks milk right now." He glanced at Kelly. "Let's go get something for us to eat."

He wanted to take her hand in his, but he wasn't sure how she'd react, what with Finn there. Pete had probably already informed his Eagle Eye mother of Kelly's imminent arrival, so Squire stuffed his hands in his pockets. Sure enough, inside the kitchen, his mother had a basket out and was tossing silverware into it. Pete sat on the couch in the living room, watching football with Squire's father.

"Hello, Kelly." Squire's mother paused when she saw Finn. "And this handsome boy must be Finn."

He looked at Kelly, and she said, "Mind your manners now."

Squire loved the Texas accent in her voice. He shifted closer to her just because he could.

Finn stepped forward. "Nice to meet you, ma'am."

Squire laughed with his mother, while Kelly beamed at Finn.

"He's quite the charmer," his mom said, tossing in a roll of paper towels. "Here's your lunch. When I saw you pull up, I grabbed whatever I had in the fridge. I hope it's okay."

Squire stepped forward and kissed his mother on the cheek. "Thanks, Ma."

"I'm sure it will be fantastic," Kelly said. "I've never eaten anything you made that I didn't like."

He carried the basket outside and down the patio steps. "You guys want to ride horses out on the ranch? Or go in the ATV?"

"I promised Finn a horse ride, so—Oh!"

Squire turned to find her lilting on her toes, trying to get away from a big, red hen. He wasn't sure who was squawking more,

Kelly or the chicken.

"Shoo!" He kicked toward the chicken, and she puffed out her chest feathers, taking one more nip toward Kelly's leg before strutting away.

He couldn't help laughing, and not a gentle guffaw or a carefree chuckle. The kind of laughter that rattled his insides and filled the wide sky with sound.

Kelly shot him a glare while she tried to catch her breath.

"Watch out," he said. "There're dangerous animals around here." He sobered as Finn fell into step beside him, linking his little fingers between Squire's.

A swell of what felt dangerously like love started small in his center. It grew, morphed, expanded until it burst from him in the form of a smile.

They reached the stables, and Squire set down the picnic basket so he could saddle up the horses. "Maybe you can ride with him?"

"I haven't ridden a horse in, well, ever." She glanced around like they kept man-eating dinosaurs in the barn's storage.

"Yes, you have." He threw a blanket over their mildest horse. Baywatch only grazed these days, having put in many good years on the ranch as a working horse. "Remember you and Chelsea rode out to the bull pasture once? When the boys were moving them." He watched as her cheeks turned pink. "Oh, I get it. You were tryin' to show off for one of the cowhands. Betcha can't even remember which one."

She shrugged one shoulder as she fiddled with a string on her shirt. Squire focused all his attention on saddling Baywatch lest he allow her to distract him. "Well, this here horse is the gentlest one on the block." He spoke in a fake cowhand accent. "A pretty little lady like you won't have no trouble with 'im.'"

"Stop it." She pushed him away from the saddled horse. "Also, I can't believe you can remember the *one time* I've ridden a horse."

Squire covered his rising embarrassment by lifting Finn onto Baywatch's back. "Hold these," he said, handing the reins to Kelly. "I'll help you up as soon as I have Juniper saddled."

He had his horse ready in record time and he put a stepping stool next to Baywatch. "Okay, step here, and then throw your leg over his back."

"I'm so going to regret this," Kelly said, placing one heeled boot on the stool. "You already saw me freak out over a chicken. What if I fall off this horse?"

"Then you're fired," he joked. "Every ranch needs their *accountant* to be horse-worthy."

"Ha." She put her hand in his for balance.

"Hold onto the horn there," he said. She leaned over Finn and pushed off. Squire held all her weight for a moment, and then she landed in the saddle.

Baywatch startled, which for him, meant he took a step forward when he should've kept still. He gave Squire a cynical look, the horse equivalent to a human eye roll. Squire patted his flank in assurance as he went to mount Juniper. She pranced over to Baywatch, where Squire tied the reins to his saddle horn.

"Ready?" he asked.

Finn cheered, and Kelly managed to nod. Both reactions

burrowed into Squire's memory, and he vowed never to forget them.

Kelly wasn't sure how Squire balanced on his horse, what with the large picnic basket riding tandem on his lap. She doubted he could even see where he was going, and a wisp of unease tickled her mind. Yet somehow, after about twenty minutes, they ended up in the shade of a large oak tree. It stood a solitary watch over the prairie, the keeper of Three Rivers Ranch. She waited until Squire dismounted and put the food down, then she practically fell off the horse and into his arms.

She didn't miss the grunt as all her weight collapsed on him. A rush of heat flared in her cheeks as she stepped away and adjusted her clothes. Squire helped Finn down, who immediately galloped off toward a fence line with Benson.

"Stay where I can see you!" she yelled after them, with absolutely no idea if her son had heard her.

Squire let the horses go to graze, first removing their saddles and spreading out a blanket from the bottom of the picnic basket. He knelt right in the center of it, pulling out bottled water and various containers of food. No matter where she chose to sit, she'd be next to him.

She sat on his left and picked up what turned out to be a container of macaroni salad. "I love this stuff."

"Try this," he said, taking away the salad and handing her another dish. She sniffed it and got a noseful of raspberries and cream cheese.

"With pretzels?" she asked.

"It'll blow your mind." Squire handed her a spoon, and she scooped out a bite. One taste of the tangy raspberry, the silky cream cheese, and the salty pretzel, and she was sold.

"Mind, blown." She loaded up her spoon again.

"So if you're in a good mood," he started, his voice low and soothing, like she was an animal he didn't want to spook. "You wanna talk about me going to College Station?"

Kelly groaned, took one more bite of the delicious raspberry salad, and nodded.

"So I don't have all the details worked out, and there are so many things we can't control." He cleared his throat. "Number one, I haven't even gotten in yet."

"You have experience with animals. You just birthed a horse, for heaven's sake."

He took a bite of a sandwich and chewed slowly. "True."

"What's number two?"

"I can't afford medical school. Not unless we find that missing money."

"We'll find it," she said. "We're getting close." She plucked a sandwich out of the basket for Finn and glanced around for him. She couldn't see him anywhere.

"How do you know we're getting close?" he asked, shifting a bit closer to her. How close she wanted him, she didn't dare admit—even to herself.

"I just have a good feeling about it." She met his gaze. The same magnetic pull that had been drawing her to him for weeks yanked. She relived the last few seconds at church, when his hand on her lower back had been firm, but gentle.

Just like his lips, she thought, focusing on his mouth now.

"Okay, number three." He ducked his head so she couldn't see his face under his cowboy hat. "I don't really want to leave you here."

She didn't miss the emotion in his voice. Joy that he wanted to be with her rotated with a heavy rope of fear. Was she really ready to start another relationship? She had Finn to worry about.

Finn.

Her rational mind seized onto Finn. Panic joined the party as she scanned the horizon without seeing Finn.

"Hold that thought." She stood, brushing sandwich crumbs from her shorts. She shielded her eyes with her hand, her throat closing more and more the longer she looked. "Did you see which way Finn went?"

He stood and joined her. "He ran off toward the hay fields."

Five minutes. They'd been sitting on the blanket for five minutes. She had a *child;* she couldn't afford to let herself get distracted by a handsome man. Not even for five minutes.

"Squire—"

He put his fingers in his mouth and whistled. The horses startled, and far away in the distance, a thread of dust rose from the earth. "There."

"That's moving too fast to be Finn."

"Its Benson," Squire said, striding forward to meet his dog.

Kelly's emotions teetered on the edge of a cliff, ready to jump off if it meant she'd find Finn at the bottom.

Benson barked like mad and raced in circles around Squire. He tried to stroke him, to calm him, but the dog wouldn't settle down. He streaked back the way he'd come, and Squire swung onto his horse, bareback style.

"Something's wrong," he said, reaching for her hand. He pulled her onto the animal in front of him and kicked the horse into a gallop.

After what felt like hours but was only seconds, Squire pulled the mount to a stop. "Stay here." He leapt down and hurried toward where Benson was circling something.

Like she was going to stay there. She slid off the horse, not anticipating quite how far it was to the ground. Her ankle twisted as she hit the dry earth, and she cried out. But she kept going. Her heart hammered; the sun burned so bright; she couldn't see much past the tears in her eyes.

She stumbled, almost going down. Then Squire was walking toward her, Benson barking excitedly on his heels, carrying someone.

Finn!

"Is he okay?" she asked, rushing toward him as quickly as she could.

"He fell, and he's scraped up," Squire said, eying her from head to injured toe. "Just like you. Let's get back to the house."

He put all three of them on his horse and told her, "Home." He didn't steer, didn't correct her course. Half an hour later, she delivered them safe and sound to the homestead. He took Kelly and Finn inside and set his mother to work on them.

"What about the other horse?" Kelly asked. "The picnic." Her ankle throbbed, and she kept the ice pack Heidi had given her on it.

"I'll go out in a bit," Squire said. "Did you hurt anything else when you fell off the horse?"

"She fell off a horse?" Heidi shook her head as she pressed a cloth to Finn's knee. "What are you doing to the poor girl?" She put a bandage on Finn, who seemed to be absolutely fine. Benson whined before he licked Finn's fingers.

"I told her to stay." He frowned at his mom. "She didn't listen."

"I'm *not* a horse, and I didn't *fall* off a horse," Kelly said. "I slid down, and it was farther than I thought."

Squire looked away, but not before she caught a smile on his face. A moment later, he started laughing. "I'm sorry," he said between chuckles. "I can't help it."

She punched him playfully on the arm. "Stop it."

"Not too fond of cowboys now, are you?" he asked, smirking.

She lifted her chin, not willing to tell him she now held him in even higher regard. He was more than just a good-looking cowboy. He was her hero. Who rode horses bareback, tamed wild bulls, and had absolutely roped her heart.

Chapter Twelve

The next morning, Kelly arrived at Three Rivers, without Finn, without a limp, and without her pride. She was sure the story of her falling off that blasted horse would be all over the ranch, and she held her head high as she entered the administration building.

The cowhand who'd delivered her to her interview sat at the desk. He had a calm air about him, a welcome change from Clark's narrowed eyes and gruff voice.

"Good morning."

"Ma'am." He tipped his hat, giving her a glimpse of brown hair and gray eyes. "Squire's in your office already."

Her heart somersaulted at the same time her defenses went up. "Thank you...."

"Tom," he supplied.

She smiled at him before she hurried through the trailer. Squire stood at her small window, his hands in his pockets. "Morning," she said, entering her office and putting her lunch and purse in her bottom desk drawer.

He slid his hands around her waist, and she turned into him. "Oh, okay. So it *is* a good morning."

"No lasting damage from yesterday?"

"I think we'll both heal."

"You think he'll ever come out to the ranch again?" Worry skimmed through his eyes, like he really thought a scraped knee was something new for Finn.

"Are you kidding? All he's talked about since we left is the baby horse, the fences he got to climb, and that dog." She looked toward her door. "I really need to get that kid a dog."

"Mm." Squire lowered his face into her hair and took a deep breath. He tipped her back a few inches so he could kiss her.

The hair on her arms and neck rose, though that could've been from Squire's fingers along her jaw. Still, she couldn't relax into his embrace, fully enjoy the taste of sugar on his breath.

He pulled away, concern in his tone when he asked, "What?"

"I just...." Her super-hearing continued as she heard Clark call the cowboys to order. "I'm just not used to this being okay in my office."

"I didn't get to do that yesterday." He released her and stepped back. "But I get it. I'll keep looking for any records, and you keep putting everything into the computer."

She glanced around, feeling sluggish at the thought of diving back into the thousands of sheets of paper in her office. "We can probably finish this soon."

He stood there, watching her, a look of absolute adoration on his face. She felt like she was viewing him through glass. She saw past his Army-trained mask and into his soul. He was kind and heroic—exactly the kind of man both she and Finn needed.

She'd seen her son clasp Squire's hand yesterday. She'd felt a blanket of love then, just as she did now.

The trailer vibrated, shaking Kelly from her thoughts. "Squire?"

"Hm? What?" He shook himself as if he hadn't realized he'd gone into staring mode.

"I said, we can probably finish soon." She stepped around her desk to turn on her computer. "That is, if you don't stand around, staring at me all day." She didn't let on that she'd done the same and enjoyed the redness that colored his neck.

Though she didn't catch him staring at her while she worked, something had shifted between them. Something good. Something hopeful. The soft leafing of pages punctured the silence in her office. The words on her papers started to blur as the minutes passed. Her mind wandered to what Squire had said under the oak tree. *I don't want to leave you here.*

She didn't want to stay here without him. But her life wasn't all about what *she* wanted anymore. If she didn't have this job, she couldn't provide for Finn. She and Squire needed to talk through a lot more before she could actually follow him to College Station.

Please guide me, she prayed.

Squire triumphantly lifted a page. "Houser Cattle Auctions."

Kelly blinked and took the paper from him. "From two thousand twelve." She located the correct folder on the edge of her desk and placed the paper inside. "Nice work."

He focused on his task again, and Kelly admired him again. His broad shoulders, his mouth set in a determined line.

"Here's another one." He turned the page. "And another one.

These are in order." He flipped until he had several pages, all from the years they needed.

"And it looks like we sold at Houser's more than once each year." He handed the papers over so she could examine them.

"What else have you got?" she asked as she sorted the financial documents into their correct years.

"Nothing," Squire said. "The rest of this folder is from ages ago." He put it in the stacks against the wall and retrieved another pile to search.

She barely had time to pick up the first receipt he'd found before he said, "Oceanview Cattle Company." He flipped pages nearly as fast as he could look at them. "All in the same place."

She felt like laughing; she felt like crying; she felt like dancing around and yelling. Their progress over the past week had been slow, tedious. But finding so much at once felt like progress. Like an answer to a prayer. Kelly closed her eyes and gave a brief word of thanks.

Crystal pulled her car to a stop in front of a red brick house that Kelly eyed like it had done her a personal wrong. "I don't know, Crys...."

"If you say that one more time, I'm going to call Squire and tell him you love him."

Kelly swung her attention from the house to her cousin. "You wouldn't dare."

By the playful look on Crystal 's face, Kelly knew she wouldn't.

"No, I wouldn't. But you've said 'I don't know' about everything. I don't see how you can't know if you like Squire. Or how things are going with him."

"Fine, I like Squire."

"And how are things going with him?" Crystal nestled into the driver's seat, as if she was getting ready for a juicy movie.

Kelly thought about the kiss in her office, the adoration she'd seen on Squire's face. "He said he didn't want to leave me here in Three Rivers while he finished his medical degree, and I freaked out because I hadn't seen Finn in five minutes."

Crystal 's brow furrowed. "So you never answered him? Told him you'd gladly accept his diamond and move out of your parents' basement? You want to go with him, right?"

Kelly covered her face with her hands. "I don't know?"

"No!" Crystal pulled Kelly's hands down. "You know. Listen to your heart. Or your gut. Better yet, listen to God. But you know."

Kelly turned away, staring at the house she'd come to see. "I'd go with him," she whispered to the glass. She twisted back to her cousin. "And how stupid is that? It sounds even worse saying it out loud." She barked out a laugh. "I mean, I only met him two weeks ago!"

Her cousin covered Kelly's hand with her own. "You've known him your whole life, baby. That's a lot longer than two weeks."

An insane amount of hope flooded Kelly. She took a deep breath to steady herself before her imagination bled into her reality. "Let's go look at this house."

She wandered through the rooms, imagining her table and chairs in the dining room, Finn's racecar bed in the second bedroom. But it didn't feel like home. The only place that had felt like that lately was the ranch.

Or maybe it felt like that because of Squire. Maybe no matter where he was, she needed to be there too, because *he* was beginning to feel like home.

The email came on Wednesday morning.

Dear Major Ackerman,

We're pleased to inform you that you have been accepted to the Doctorate of Veterinarian Medicine (DVM) program on the campus of Texas A&M in College Station, Texas.

The words blurred, black on white. Gray. Gray like a Texas thunderstorm.

Gray, like the area between right and wrong.

Gray, like the distance between Kelly and College Station.

He focused, almost hoping the words had changed. Denied him entrance. It would make some things easier and others harder.

Easy. Hard. Gray.

He leaned away from his laptop, trying to come up with a plan. He didn't want to approach his parents—or Kelly—without a solution to the problems they shared.

For his parents, he needed to find the money. And then ask them to pay for his doctorate degree.

His stomach threatened to release the coffee he'd consumed. His parents wouldn't need all of the missing money; they could afford to pay Squire's tuition. With his GI Bill, he might not even have to work to pay for rent and utilities.

Kelly presented a whole new issue Squire still hadn't been able to solve. He felt himself falling deeper and deeper in love with her. He closed his eyes, surprised that he'd admitted to himself that he loved her.

He'd always had a soft spot for her. She'd been his first crush. The first to destroy him and resuscitate him. The first woman he'd forgiven. The one he'd forgive over and over to keep her in his life, even if she did lecture him sometimes.

Over the past two weeks, he *had* fallen in love with the Kelly Armstrong of now. How could he leave her here?

Helplessness welled in his chest, pressed against his flopping heart. Could he ask her to come with him? *Should* he? They didn't have to get married right away. She could get a job, find an apartment. They could date until she was ready. Squire was willing to wait as long as she needed.

"You got in to your DMV program." Pete's voice behind Squire reminded him that he no longer lived in his cabin alone.

His first instinct was to slam his laptop shut and tell Pete to mind his own business. But Chelsea's accusation about him not trusting anyone echoed in Squire's mind. He'd trusted Pete with his life. He could trust him with this too.

"Yeah," Squire said, scrubbing the back of his neck. "You can't tell anyone."

Pete retreated to the kitchen nook and picked up a leftover muffin. "Why not? Major, this is good news."

He heard Chelsea's voice in his head, telling him to trust Kelly. To tell her, and to work out all the details together. But just like he hadn't told his dad about the missing money, he couldn't tell Kelly about the admittance. He didn't want to hurt either one of them.

"I just don't want anyone to know yet," Squire said. "I have some things I need to work out first."

"Lady friend things?"

"Yes."

"And you don't want your parents to know, because...?"

"They'll tell Kelly." Squire's gut squirmed with the lie. He didn't lie to his men. They counted on him to be one hundred percent truthful with them. "I just need to figure some things out," he said again. "Don't tell anyone. That's an order, Lieutenant."

Pete saluted. "Yes, sir. I'm just glad I'm not the only one who has no idea what to do with their life."

A pang of guilt stole through Squire. "Any headway on that front?"

"No," Pete said. "But I'm happy here, just like you said I would be. I'll figure it out."

Squire nodded before ducking into the bathroom to brush his teeth. He paused in front of his mirror. He didn't look like a man keeping a secret. But he knew when confronted with his mother, she'd know something was up, the same way the horses always did.

So he bypassed breakfast at the homestead in favor of the administration building. He'd have to face his mother eventually, but not with the acceptance so fresh.

When we find the money, he promised himself. *I'll tell everyone everything when we find the money.*

Squire seemed unnaturally moody when he arrived in Kelly's office. He reminded her of the initial Squire she'd met upon arriving at Three Rivers. She didn't know what had happened, so instead of engaging him, she put her head down and got to work. Together, they found more documents, ate lunch, and seemed to get along just fine. But he didn't kiss her, didn't even glance her way when he stood and stretched his back near four o'clock.

"You're still coming with me to the animal shelter, right?" she asked.

His gaze found hers for the first time that day, and she found a troubled expression in his eyes. "Is that tonight?"

"It was," she said. "Finn's birthday is on Friday." She stood too. "You said you could house the puppy here and then bring him in on Friday for the party." She took a step toward him and put her hand on his arm.

He looked at her fingers, watched them as she slid them up to his shoulder. "Squire, what's wrong?" She expected him to relax, maybe lean down and kiss her.

Instead, he watched a spot over her shoulder. "I just…need to get out to the stables. I can't handle being inside all the time."

Kelly heard the strength in his voice, layered behind the tension. "Okay, well, go now. When I'm done here in an hour, we can drive to the shelter. Okay?"

He nodded, wrapping her in a hug with his strong arms and

dropping his face into the crook of her neck. He breathed deeply. "Okay." Squire flashed her a smile that vanished before she'd truly seen it and left her office.

An hour later, she found Squire in the stable, his hand stroking the muzzle of his tall, black horse. As she approached, another horse—this one taller, with a beautiful black mane against a reddish body—ambled over. He huffed at Kelly as she stepped to Squire's side.

"Hey," she said softly so as to not disturb the horses.

Squire glanced at her, and the calmness in his eyes told her she'd found the man who made her heart wilt and regrow into something stronger, better, more beautiful. "You remember Juniper," he said, lifting both hands to stroke the horse's cheeks. "She decided she was mine when I got home."

"Hmm, she did, did she?"

Squire chuckled. "If I didn't know better, I'd say you're jealous of a horse."

"Maybe you're not as smart as you think." Kelly bumped her shoulder into his bicep.

He let his hand fall to hers, slipping his fingers between hers. "That's Hank." He whistled and the stallion nudged Squire's shoulder, dropped his head to Squire's pocket, and then nickered against his knee.

"He knew I was hurt the first time he met me," Squire said, his voice little more than a murmur. "Juniper too. They…comfort me. Calm me down when I get stressed."

Kelly squeezed his hand in silent support. "They're beautiful."

Juniper dropped her head to Squire's pocket too. "They're gone, guys," he told them. "You ate all the sugar cubes."

Kelly marveled at his gentle tone, how he spoke to his horses like they were people. Not just people, his friends. Friends he brought treats for and petted like cats.

"She didn't bring you any apples," Squire said as Hank swung his body around Juniper's and sniffed Kelly's pocket. "She didn't know." He tossed a flirtatious grin toward Kelly. "I'm sure she'll bring you something next time."

He pushed the horse's head away from Kelly's waist. "Go on, now."

Reluctantly, Hank moved back.

"Sorry," Kelly told the horses, though a vein of ridiculousness wormed through her. Talking to horses like they understood her was new for her. Squire didn't seem to notice her nerves, but Juniper startled and stepped away.

Squire did too. "Should we go?"

"Yes," Kelly said, turning away from the horses. "Let's go."

"I don't know," Kelly said an hour later. "I like that chocolate Lab...." She glanced over her shoulder to the three-month old puppy, still watching her through the bars of his enclosure.

"Border collies love to run," Squire said from where he crouched, scratching a pup's ears. "But I can see you won't be persuaded." He stood. "Maybe I'll take this one. I kinda like him."

"And I'll take the chocolate Lab," Kelly said. Labrador retrievers were supposed to be good dogs for kids, and she'd fallen in love with the energetic fur ball the moment she'd laid eyes on him.

"I'll go get the paperwork started," the attendant said, turning and walking back down the row.

"So you'll take him until Friday," Kelly said. "Finn's party starts at six."

"I'll box him up and bring him in." Squire offered his hand to Kelly, and she appreciated that he didn't just grab on like he owned her. She slipped her hand into his, wondering if Squire would amaze her forever.

"So I heard there was a rodeo next weekend," she said. She'd heard it from Ethan, when he'd asked her out—again. "Fireworks afterward, the whole nine yards."

"Are you askin' me out, Miss Kelly?" Squire tugged her closer, released her hand and put his arm around her shoulders.

She leaned into his strong side. "Yes, sir."

He laughed, the sound bouncing against the cement. "I want to," he said, sobering. "I do. But can we go somewhere else?"

"Sure," Kelly said, surprised that a man who never took off his cowboy hat wasn't interested in the rodeo. "Can I ask why?"

Apprehension filled his eyes and his jaw clenched. "I—well, I don't do so well with explosions." He took a deep breath and continued, "Last week, Pete and I went out for wings, and some fireworks went off. We both hit the floor, heads down. It was embarrassing."

Kelly's brain raced with something comforting to say. "I'm sorry," she said, the lamest words on the planet, at least in this situation. She clasped her other hand around his. "What would you like to do?"

He cocked his eyebrows at her. "What do I want to do?" He stopped in front of the chocolate Lab's pen and slid his arms around her. "This." He leaned down and touched his lips to hers.

She drank him in, wishing she could infuse him with good memories to wipe away the bad ones. Kelly kissed him until she was one taste away from the highest sugar rush she'd ever experienced. Then she pulled back. "Well, we can't do that all night."

"Let's go to the rodeo. Finn will love it. But we have to leave before the fireworks. Maybe we can go back to your place and make ice cream sundaes. Finn would like that too."

Kelly fell down another rung on the ladder of love. The way Squire assumed Finn would come with them on their date, and how he wanted to plan something her son would enjoy, made her want to take a big jump and leave the ladder behind completely. But with this water new and possibly cold, one step at a time was smarter.

She told herself a single rung at a time wasn't too fast to fall in love. She wasn't sure if she was lying to herself or not.

Kelly put in long hours looking at files and computer screens during the day, and longer hours at home planning for Finn's birthday party. She felt the weight of being both his father and his mother on his first birthday away from Taylor. Her ex-husband had texted earlier in the week to find out if he could send Finn something, and Kelly had given him her parent's address. When she left for work on Friday morning, nothing had arrived.

She spent the half-hour drive to the ranch fuming over Taylor's nonchalance. He'd said he'd pay half of everything, but at the first event of Finn's life, he hadn't sent the gift on time. She finally rolled down the window to air out her anger.

Please let the package arrive today, she prayed. She did not want Finn to be disappointed. Her mother texted just after two o'clock.

Taylor's package just arrived.

Kelly grinned from ear to ear just as Squire looked up. "What did you find?" He stood and came around the computer, his face holding so much hope.

"Nothing," she said quickly, flipping her phone over. "My mom just sent me a text."

His expression tightened again, and Kelly really wanted to help this troubled, tense Squire become the warm, kind, funny man she'd started to fall for.

He paced to the window, his limp pronounced when he didn't try to hide it. "I've got to take a break." He glanced at her as he headed for the door. "I'll see you tonight at the party, okay?"

"Six o'clock," she reminded him. "Dad's grilling."

He waved and she watched him go, wishing she had the therapeutic powers of Juniper and Hank. But she didn't. The only thing she could do to ease Squire's worries was find the money. She knew he carried that weight alone, and that it was one-point-six million pounds of heavy.

Chapter Thirteen

Kelly tried to set aside her worry as Finn's birthday party began and Squire still hadn't arrived. Crystal, Scott, and their three boys brought laughter and love to the house, as well as a gift for Finn. Kelly couldn't believe she wouldn't have a present for her own son.

Her insides felt shredded by nails. She checked her phone again, like maybe it had died in the last twenty seconds.

"Kel, you want a hamburger or a hot dog?" her dad asked, his tongs poised above the grill.

"Hamburger," she answered, sending another message to Squire. She'd sent two already and certainly didn't need to fire off a third. But she couldn't help it. If she didn't have that puppy for Finn, she'd be worse than Taylor.

The spikes raked over her lungs and she gasped for breath as she fixed her burger with lettuce, tomatoes, and one of her dad's perfectly cooked over-easy eggs. Crystal had taken care of Finn's hot dog without Kelly even knowing.

She stuffed her phone in her back pocket and loaded her plate with potato chips. "Happy birthday, Finny." She smiled at him and picked up her burger, though the idea of eating it had her stomach leading a revolt.

"When are we going to open presents?" he asked.

She choked on her first bite. "In a little bit," she said. "We're going to eat first, and you have to show your cousins how you can throw the football."

Thankfully, that got Scott into the conversation, as well as Crystal 's two older boys. Kelly nearly choked for the second time that night when her phone buzzed against the bench. She whipped it out of her pocket, praying with every fiber of her soul that it was Squire.

It was. *Sorry I'm late. Crisis with Pete. Tell you about it later. Be there in twenty.*

True to his word, Squire texted only nineteen minutes later. *Out front. Should I come through the house with the puppy?*

Kelly jumped up from the bench where she'd been talking with Crystal . "Squire's here. Be right back."

"Can't wait," Crystal said in a purr. Kelly sprinted up the steps to the deck and into the mudroom. At the front door, she gestured to Squire to bring in the chocolate Lab.

"Hey," he said, wielding a large cardboard box. "I'm so sorry I'm late." He set down the box and drew her into a hug. "It's so good to see you."

He sounded exhausted, and Kelly wondered what crisis had happened and if it had anything to do with his service overseas. She was beginning to realize that Squire had more wounds than just the one in his leg.

"Pete could've come," she said.

"That wasn't the problem," Squire said, pulling back. "Though he does want to come to the rodeo next weekend with Tammy. Is that all right?"

"Sure," Kelly said. "He's always welcome."

Squire gazed at her with adoration evident on his face. "You're amazing, you know that?"

"Not really." She fiddled with the top button on his shirt. "You're the amazing one, bringing my son a dog." She hooked her thumb over her shoulder. "Come on. Everyone's in the backyard."

He retrieved the box and followed her to the picnic table. "You bought the dog, darlin'."

She directed him to put the box on the table bearing the other gifts. With it in place, a sense of calm soothed the scratches inside.

"Hey, let's open presents," she called. The boys came running over, and Kelly's parents followed. Crystal and Scott wrangled their kids into submission long enough for Finn to open the gift they'd brought.

He enthusiastically ripped off the paper, yelling with delight at the Lego set his cousins had brought for him.

"What do you say?" Kelly prompted.

"Thank you," Finn dutifully replied, hugging Crystal and then Scott.

"Mine next," Kelly said, nudging the box closer to him. He lifted the first flap and the puppy poked his head out.

"A dog!" Finn shouted, dancing away from the table and then back. "Is he mine, Mom? All mine?"

She laughed at his exuberance. "Yes, baby. He's yours." She

lifted the Lab out of the box and set him on the grass in front of Finn. He crouched down and scratched the puppy behind his ears.

The dog licked his face, causing Finn to laugh.

"What are you gonna name 'im?" Squire asked as he bent down to pet the puppy too.

"What's a good name?" Finn looked to Squire for advice, his face open and unassuming.

Kelly's heart warmed as she watched them. If this could be her reality, every day, she'd be the luckiest woman in the world. Crystal gave her nudge with her elbow, her expression knowing.

"I don't know," Squire said. "What's something you like?"

Finn's eyebrows creased as he thought. "How about Buster?"

"Sure," Squire said.

"Do you like Buster, Mom?" Finn looked at her with eyes wide with innocence.

"Sure, baby." She drew him into a hug. "Happy birthday."

Kelly could never love anything or anyone as much as she loved Finn in that moment. As Squire stepped to her side, she thought it might be natural for him to put one arm around her shoulders and the other around Finn. Her chest narrowed, telling her Squire had just claimed a piece of her heart—permanently.

Squire stood in Kelly's backyard, watching Finn and the other boys chase Buster. The chocolate Lab had a cheery disposition, and he didn't mind when five-year-old hands grabbed onto him.

Kelly, Crystal, and her mom cleaned up the dinner dishes and brought out a cake. As flames lit Kelly's eyes, a twinge of guilt stole through him. He needed to tell her about his acceptance into the veterinarian program. Soon.

But not tonight. Tonight was about Finn, and Squire could see he wouldn't be getting any time alone with Kelly. Certainly not long enough to have a serious conversation about their future.

So he sang Happy Birthday, and cheered, and ate cake and ice cream. He presented Finn with his gift—a Frisbee—and taught him how to throw it so Buster would learn to catch it. By the time dusk settled, Crystal and her husband started rounding up their kids.

After they left, Kelly's dad took Buster and Finn and went inside. Her mom had gone in when Crystal left, and Squire wondered if maybe now *was* a good time to talk with Kelly.

But he didn't want to. He didn't want to ruin this perfect night with uncertainty and serious conversations.

"How's Pete?" Kelly sighed as she sat down at the picnic table next to Squire.

A crease troubled Squire's brow. "He's all right." Though he wasn't sure if Pete really was okay. "Some of the boys were practicing their calf roping. Someone had a whip, and when it cracked, Pete freaked out."

Squire had too, but not nearly to the same degree. There was just something about that sound that instantly brought a bright, white light to Squire's mind. He had no idea what Pete saw or smelled, but he knew it transported him right back to the bombing.

Kelly's hand landed on his knee, breaking him from the cage

inside his mind. "You okay?"

The heat from her hand soaked through his jeans. "Yeah."

"You disappeared." Concern rode in her eyes. Those beautiful eyes Squire wanted to look into every day of his life. "I asked you twice without a response."

"Sorry." He didn't know what else to add. "Anyway, Pete should be okay. I got him out of the arena and into the house. My dad was talking to him when I left." Squire took off his hat and ran his fingers through his hair. "Then I forgot the blasted puppy." He chuckled at his own stupidity. "Had to go back for 'im."

Kelly moved her hand from his leg to curl it around his elbow. She leaned into him, and he felt like she was claiming him as hers. "Thanks for bringing him, and thanks for coming."

"Nowhere I'd rather be." He pressed a kiss to her forehead. They sat watching the stars appear in the midnight blue sky, and Squire couldn't work up the courage to mention his acceptance.

Not tonight, he told himself. *But soon.*

By the following Wednesday, Squire's eyes blurred at the thought of looking at another piece of paper. He dutifully went to Kelly's office, but at lunchtime, he escaped to the stables. He found Pete standing at Raven's stall, feeding her foal sugar cubes from his palm. "Hey," Squire called. "You want to go riding with me?"

"Yeah, sure. Haven't been on a horse in a while though."

"Today's a great day to get back to it." Squire pulled down a blanket and his saddle. The smell of leather and horse settled the raging river inside. They hadn't found the money. He was beginning to seriously doubt they ever would. A hot poker jabbed his chest. It felt very much like abandoning hope.

"My gramps used to take me out bareback," Pete said as he watched Squire saddle Juniper.

"How long's it been?" Squire asked, retrieving more equipment for Pete. He selected Peony, a sweet Quarter Horse who had sprinted her last race over a decade ago. The color of eggshells, Squire had taken it upon himself as a teenager to make sure she was always clean.

"Too long," Pete said. "Gramps died a few years ago, during my first deployment. I was able to visit his grave before I made my way here."

Squire didn't know what horrors haunted Pete's mind, but by the way he stared out the open door of the stables, Squire knew it wasn't good. "You guys had a horse ranch in Tennessee, right?" he asked, hoping to draw Pete back to the present.

"Not really a ranch," Pete said. "It was a boarding stable. I got to work the horses a lot, but they weren't ours."

Squire finished saddling Peony. "Well, these ones are. Let's hit the range." He needed the freedom of the wide, open space. The quietness of the wind slinking through the grass. How clean the air smelled.

He mounted Juniper and together, he and Pete set out. The steady clomping of the horses hooves almost lulled Squire to sleep.

"How long are you going to be off getting your veterinarian degree?" Pete asked, breaking the peaceful silence.

"At least four years," Squire said, the weight of being gone from Three Rivers for so long descending on him.

"By that frown, you don't seem happy about it."

"I am," Squire said. "It's just a long time to be away from the ranch. But I know it's the right thing to do." He just didn't know what to do about Kelly and Finn, both of whom had carved a place inside his heart. How could he leave them behind?

"A long time away from the ranch?" Pete repeated. "Or a long time away from Kelly?"

"Both," Squire said. "But she's...not ready to be uprooted again."

"You mean she's not ready to get married again."

"That too." Squire shot his Army pal a sideways glance. "What about you?"

Pete refused to look at him. "What about me?"

"You're shoveling stalls for my dad. That's what you want your life to be?"

Pete exhaled heavily. "I have no idea what I want my life to be." He met Squire's eyes. "How pathetic is that?" He raised his burnt arm. "I'd always thought I'd be career Army. I don't know what to do now that I can't do that."

"Maybe you need to take the first step," Squire said carefully. "Like what Pastor Scott was saying last week about forming our will to God's." They'd been to church a couple of times now. While he knew Pete might not have gone without the extra encouragement, he was attending and he didn't put up a fight about it.

Pete harrumphed, but didn't contradict Squire. "If I knew which step to take, Major, I'd take it."

"Maybe God can help you with that too."

"Maybe," Pete said, his eyes roaming the skies like they'd have the answers. Squire watched them too, enjoying the time away from the business of the ranch, from his cell phone, from everything. He felt the most content out here, just him and his horse. He felt closer to God here than he did anywhere else.

He knew going to College Station and getting his medical degree was the right thing to do. Maybe he needed to take his own advice and find out what to do about Kelly.

He closed his eyes and prayed. *Lord, help me see clearly. Help me to know what to say or do with Kelly Armstrong and her son, Finn, even if that means walking away from them.*

His heart constricted painfully at the thought, but he had to trust that God would lead him where he needed to be. After all, He'd led Kelly home. He'd allowed Squire a glimpse at how freeing forgiveness could be.

Help me—

The answer came as plain and strong as wind or lightning or daylight.

Trust Kelly.

With no progress on finding the missing money, Squire bid goodbye to Kelly on Friday afternoon, with the promise that he and Pete would be at her house the following evening for the rodeo.

He trusted Kelly, but every time he considered telling her about his acceptance, his tongue swelled like a bloated fish. He couldn't say anything, and the hours slipped away like dust through his fingers.

He spent Saturday morning helping his mother weed the garden, and most of the afternoon with Pete in the stables. The horses calmed them both, and an idea formed in Squire's mind.

"Why don't you do something with horses?" he asked Pete. "You seem to like them, and they like you. Does your family still have the boarding house?"

"No," he said. "When Gramps died, my uncle sold it. With my dad already gone, there wasn't anyone to run it."

"Except you." Squire's eyebrows pinched together.

"I was half a world away, with no promise of ever coming back."

"But maybe now, you could. Get a new place. Something."

"Something," Pete echoed, looking longingly at Peony and Raven, the two mares who'd attached themselves to him. "Come on, let's go get ready for this rodeo."

When he arrived at Kelly's house, he smoothed down his blue flannel shirt before ringing her doorbell. Finn answered, wearing his own button-down flannel, jeans, and a brand new pair of cowboy boots.

"We're goin' to the rodeo!" he announced, as if Squire didn't know.

Squire knelt down to be eye-level with the boy. "Is Buster a good pup?"

"He's the bestest," Finn said. "My grampa is keepin' him for me tonight. Buster likes my grampa."

"That's great," Squire said. "Where's your mom?" He looked over Finn's shoulder, but there was no one in the living room. He could see into the kitchen, but she wasn't there either.

"She's downstairs," Finn said, fitting his small hand into Squire's. "Can I sit by you at the rodeo?"

"Sure thing, buddy." Squire loved this kid, and a sharp pin pressed into his chest. He couldn't leave Finn here for four years. He'd never felt so strongly about something in his life.

Kelly and Finn had to come with him to College Station. But how?

Trust Kelly.

She came up the steps, and Squire followed every move she made. She wore tight jeans paired with a sparkly navy top. She'd curled her hair and artfully painted her face. Her lips, pink as roses, glistened.

"Evenin' ma'am," he said, tipping his hat when he really wanted to tilt her back and kiss her.

"Evenin', yourself," she drawled. "I just need shoes...."

"Hurry up, Mom," Finn said. "I don't want to miss the ropes."

Squire grinned at him as Kelly moved into the mudroom for her shoes. "The calf roping? I can show you how to do that, you know."

"You can?" Finn looked at Squire like he'd just told him he could make it be Christmas every day.

"Sure," Squire said. "You'll have to come back out to the ranch, though. Think you can talk your mom into that?"

"Sure!" Finn said. "She goes there everyday. She'll bring me."

"Bring you where?" Kelly asked, returning to the living room wearing cowboy boots made for a rodeo.

"To the ranch!" Finn yelled. "Squire's gonna show me how to rope."

"Is he?" Kelly's amused eyes met his. "I didn't know Major Ackerman could rope."

Squire laughed. "Major Ackerman has a lot of skills you don't know about." He offered her his elbow, and she slipped her hand into his arm.

"I can't wait to see them all," she said as they headed for the front door. Squire had never felt so complete, with Finn hanging on to his left hand and the woman of his dreams clinging to his right. He needed these two in his life all the time. Now he just had to figure out how to make that happen.

As Kelly settled girlfriend-style next to Squire in his truck, her hopes were high. She wanted this man beside her through everything, the hard times and the good. The way Finn looked at him made her insides a quivering mess.

Just as quickly, though, reality came roaring back. Her divorce had only been final for three months now. She'd been back in Three Rivers for two, and the day she found out about Taylor was only four months old.

Was she ready to risk her heart again? So soon? And what about Finn?

The way he babbled on about roping and calves and horses, she thought he'd be just fine with Squire in their lives permanently.

"You okay?" Squire asked as he pulled into the parking lot. Kelly realized that the conversation around her had been easy, casual. And that she hadn't participated once.

She gave him a quick nod, determined not to spend this date inside the worried recesses of her mind. Pete helped Finn out of the truck, then reached for Tammy. Kelly slid out after Squire on his side, pleased when his hands found her waist and squeezed.

"You don't seem okay," he said.

"I am," she insisted. "A little distracted, but not anymore." She smiled at him, feeling some of her cares fly away. "Come on, I don't want to miss the ropes either."

Finn came bounding around the front of the truck, and Squire released her to pick him up. They both laughed before Squire settled Finn on his shoulders and reached for Kelly's hand. She gave it to him willingly and stepped with him.

Peace filled her as they joined the crowd entering the arena. She'd taken the first step. She was with Squire—and everyone in Three Rivers could see it.

"Hey, have you heard anything from A&M?" she asked as they moved through the turnstile and into the bleachers.

Squire stiffened, but didn't look at her. She followed his gaze to see Susie Randall blocking their way, her arms folded tightly across her chest. "Evenin', Squire," she said, her voice poisoned. She cast a withering glance at Kelly. "Miss Kelly."

"Hey, Susie," Kelly said, inching up the ramp so Pete and Tammy could join them. "Have you met Squire's Army buddy, Pete? And you know Tammy, of course."

"Of course," Susie said, turning her attention back to Squire. "You said you were too busy to come to rodeos."

Kelly couldn't see his face, but tension poured from his boxy shoulders.

"Things have really settled down," Pete said, a huge smile on his face. "The Major here was in real trouble until I showed up on the ranch." He clapped one big hand on Squire's forearm before brushing past Susie. "Nice to have met you, Miss Susie." He tipped his cowboy hat at her, but the genuine warmth he normally possessed was nowhere to be found.

Squire followed him, his fingers tightening around Kelly's as he pulled her past the other woman. Kelly felt every second of Susie's glare, and the weight of the townspeople as they took in the sight of her hand in Squire's and the way he carried her son on his shoulders.

She didn't take a full breath until they'd settled in their seats and the barrel racing began. Then she realized Squire had never answered her question.

Squire's fingers fisted against the steering wheel half a second after the first firework went off. Sitting right next to him, Kelly got blasted by wave after wave of tension. When she dared to look at him, she found his jaw ground tight, his eyes straight ahead.

"Hey, Finn," she said. "Why don't you tell Squire about how you trained Buster to speak?"

Her son started to babble, but it did nothing to ease the palpable, pungent odor of fear coming from the man next to her, as well as the man in the backseat.

"Hey, Major. Can you make this truck go any faster?" Pete's voice sounded rusty and unused.

Squire pressed on the accelerator, but it didn't do much. Still, with every passing moment, he took them further and further from the sound of popping and bombing and exploding.

The night seemed so dark to Kelly. She couldn't even begin to imagine what Squire was seeing right now. Remembering.

She placed her hand on his knee, curling her fingers along the inside of his leg. She didn't want to coddle such a strong, capable man, but her touch worked its magic.

He released his breath and his fingers unwound and the sky seemed to lighten with his mood.

He skidded to a stop in her driveway, his chest heaving. He spilled from the cab, Pete not far behind him. Together, they limped into the blackness that seemed so absolute outside the halo of the headlights.

"Is he okay?" Tammy asked.

"Which one?" Kelly helped Finn out of the truck. "Go get your pajamas on, baby." He raced off toward the front door while Kelly searched the yard for Squire and Pete.

"Pete looked like he was going to be sick." Tammy pulled her hair out of its ponytail.

"They served together overseas," Kelly said by way of explanation. Low voices met her ears, and she followed them to the cluster of trees in the corner of the front yard.

Squire stood a couple of inches taller than Pete, making him easy to identify. Kelly moved right into his personal space and linked her fingers with his. They radiated a chill she hadn't expected for such a hot summer night.

"You okay?"

He gripped her hand and put his other arm around her, drawing her close. They swayed to music only Squire could hear, his inhalations and exhalations steadying.

"Sorry."

"Don't you ever be sorry," she said. She felt like she was navigating uncharted territory, as she had no experience with helping post-traumatic stress disorder victims. Just being nearby seemed to soothe him.

"Mom!" Finn called. "Where you at? Gramma says its time for ice cream." The screen door slammed. Squire jumped and Kelly wrapped him in a tight embrace.

"You don't have to stay." With her cheek pressed to his pulse, she discovered he wasn't as calm on the inside as he appeared on the outside.

"I'm not leaving."

"I bought Rocky Road for you."

His lips skimmed her cheek, her jaw, her lips. "Thank you."

She knew those words were for more than just ice cream, and a hint of joy tugged through her as they strolled toward the steps.

The next morning at church, Squire slid onto the bench next to Kelly, his hand finding hers easily. He managed to squeeze once before Finn climbed into his lap, talking fast about Buster and how he'd fetched a stick that morning.

Squire hadn't gotten out of bed until nearly nine, which was three hours later than usual. He hadn't been able to sleep last night, the sound of those fireworks still echoing in his head, his heart, his soul. A shudder rolled through his shoulders, vibrating the little boy and drawing Kelly's attention.

At that moment, with her examining him, he felt stretched too thin. Too thin like healing skin over a wound. Too thin like plastic wrap about to break. Once that happened, the truth would spill out and stain everything.

She patted his knee just as the organ began. Thankful he couldn't blurt out that he'd gotten into his DMV program, he focused his attention on the pulpit. He trusted Kelly. He just didn't see a point in causing waves until they found the money. Without it, he couldn't pay for school anyway.

"Interesting sermon today," Kelly said an hour later as she scooped a sleepy Finn from Squire's arms.

He'd perfected the art of dozing with his eyes open—another perk of serving in the Army—and hadn't actually heard a word the pastor had said. "Yeah," he said anyway, hoping she'd just talk and talk and talk, using her pretty voice to paint beautiful pictures of mercy and love and forgiveness.

"You want to go home, or to the picnic?" she asked Finn.

"Picnic!" He charged down the aisle after his cousins, leaving Squire alone with Kelly. He seized the opportunity to hold her hand as they left the church. And all the way to the park. And while they waited in line for potato salad and rolls and brisket.

If he could've eaten with her hand in his, he would've. She fit into his life like she was made to be there. A trickle of apprehension prickled down his spine, but he ignored it. They were together for now.

"I want to show you something." He stood, gathered their plates, and made sure Finn was with Crystal before leading Kelly away from the crowd.

"Another well?"

"Not quite." He ducked behind a large cypress tree, the trunk thick enough to conceal him from the dozens of eyes sitting at the tables. He tucked her against him, his hands heavy at the end of his arms as he placed them on her waist.

He couldn't breathe without her this close all the time. Gazing at her, the smoky haze he'd been operating in since last night finally cleared. He smelled her cocoa butter lotion. The lines of concern around her eyes were crisp. He memorized the feel of her body next to his.

"Squire—"

He slanted his mouth over hers and kissed her and kissed her and kissed her until she couldn't seem to stand on her own. Until he heard Finn call for them. Until the ache in his soul sealed shut.

Chapter Fourteen

Kelly arrived at work on Monday morning, a giddy mess. Her weekend with Squire had been picture perfect. The stolen kisses they'd enjoyed at the picnic, behind the thickest tree trunk, still made her muscles soggy. The warmth of his strong hands against her face sent shivers through her, though the summer sun was brutal this morning.

By the end of the day, Kelly thought she might scream. "If we don't find something soon...." She sent a glance Squire's way. He'd shown up just after lunch, but his mood had been subdued, taking hers with it. She didn't know how to finish the sentence, because the fact was, they hadn't found anything worthwhile in days.

"Maybe this is all there is." Squire indicated the towering piles on her desk.

"It can't be," she said, her voice rising in pitch as desperation overwhelmed her. "It just can't be."

"Kel," Squire said. "It's going to be okay."

She nodded as he gathered her into the safety of his arms. He held her for a few moments before she straightened her spine and strengthened her determination. "Okay." She took a deep breath.

"Let's keep going."

That evening, after dinner, her mom put her hand on Kelly's. "You look distracted, baby."

Kelly couldn't deny it. For some reason, the drive to find the missing money at Three Rivers was eating at her. "I'm okay," she said. She'd told herself that every ten minutes, but she wasn't quite feeling it yet.

"I'm going down to Glenda's to get my hair done," her mom said. "Might be a good distraction. Do you want to come?"

Thinking it would be good to be around other people, Kelly agreed to go with her mother. She double-checked her phone to make sure it was still on before they left. Why, she didn't know. In case Squire called and said he'd miraculously found every missing document? They'd looked through nearly all the folders, and he always left her office when she did.

Her foot tapped as Glenda set her mother's hair. Their idle chatter barely permeated her eardrums—until she heard one of them say, "Squire Ackerman."

She jerked her attention toward them, hoping she wasn't being too obvious. Her mother wasn't facing her, so she couldn't see her expression, but Glenda was the one who'd spoken.

"I heard he got into that veterinary program at Texas A&M." Glenda set another roller. "He's leaving the ranch in August. Won't be back for years." She clucked her tongue. "Such a shame. A handsome man like that needs to find a wife and have babies."

"He's leaving the ranch?" her mom said, her voice louder than usual. Her words landed like bombs in Kelly's head.

"That's what I heard."

"For good?"

"I think he'll be back after he finishes school. And then what will he do? Live out at Three Rivers by himself?"

Kelly couldn't stand to hear another word. She leapt from her chair and practically ran from the salon. She had Squire's number dialed before she could think. As it rang, she came to her senses and hung up.

She couldn't believe she'd heard about his college acceptance through the salon gossip circle.

Maybe it wasn't true. The very definition of rumor indicated it might not be. But the way sounds blurred into sights told her everything she needed to know.

She hadn't wanted to believe her ex had another woman in Santa Monica. But she'd seen the brunette. Seen the gold band on her finger. Seen her husband kiss that other woman.

Smell, sight, sound—they had all melded into one sickening sensation. She felt that again as she limped down Main Street.

Her insides twisted, and she swallowed like she might throw up. The first tear fell before she could call it back.

"I'm goin' out on the range tomorrow," Squire told Pete at breakfast on Tuesday. "Saturday night was too close to the fireworks." If Kelly hadn't been there, Squire felt certain he'd have ended up on the lawn in a protective position.

"I'm with you, Major."

"You want to come, then?" Squire slid the fried egg out of the pan and onto a plate. "We'll saddle up, ride out until we're good and lost in the middle of nowhere, and then camp for a few days."

"Good and lost?" Pete glanced up from his breakfast of cold cereal.

"Figuratively speaking," Squire said. "I don't think Juniper can actually get lost."

Pete nodded as he pulled on his work boots and left the cabin. Squire stayed home for a few more minutes, then followed Pete out the door and into the stables. He should be in Kelly's office, looking for the missing files, but the same desperation he'd seen in her face yesterday clogged his throat today.

Maybe this is all there is, he'd said yesterday. He didn't want that to be true, because then his parents couldn't retire, and he couldn't finish his medical degree. Worse, Three Rivers was bankrupt without that money, and he had no way to provide a good life for Kelly and Finn.

Without those documents, he had nothing.

Maybe this is all there is, he thought again, looking around the stables as cowhands mucked out stalls and fed horses.

I refuse to believe that, he thought. There had to be more to his life than a failing ranch and unrealized dreams of a life with Kelly. Otherwise, he didn't need to be saved in that attack when so many others had died.

Kelly's office was dark when Squire arrived. He frowned as he checked his watch. Lunchtime. Could she have gone to the house?

He pulled out his phone and called her. She didn't answer, and something cold settled in Squire's chest. He couldn't explain how or why, but he knew something had happened.

He called her mother, who answered on the third ring.

"Hello, Mrs. Armstrong. It's Squire Ackerman. Is Kelly at home?"

"Oh...." Mrs. Armstrong let her voice fade to silence, further solidifying Squire's suspicions.

"Mrs. Armstrong?" he prompted.

"Kelly doesn't want to talk to you right now," she said. "She came and got some files from her office this morning, and she's working on them here at home."

Squire turned and examined her desk. Sure enough, the five folders for each year of missing income were gone, as was the stack he'd been steadily working through over the past few weeks.

"So she's there," he said.

Scuffling came through the phone. "Squire," Kelly said, her voice sharp and even. "Please do not come here. I don't want to talk to you, or see you, right now."

His heart leapt at the sound of her voice, then fell when it comprehended the words she'd spoken. "Why not?"

"Did you get into your DMV program?"

Thick ice threaded through him, pushing aside bones and slicing muscles with sharp, cold edges. She knew about the acceptance letter. "Kel—"

"Don't," she bit out. "It's a simple yes or no question. Did you get into your DMV program?"

Squire could barely unclench his teeth long enough to say, "Yes."

This silence didn't speak of comfort like that he'd experienced in the park with Kelly.

This silence didn't soothe his mental aches like that he'd felt at church with Kelly.

This silence cut, jabbed, stabbed, sliced at his heart.

"Why didn't you tell me you'd gotten into the veterinarian program?" Her voice broke. "Never mind. Don't answer that. I know why. It's fine. I get it. I'll find your money and then you can be on your way."

"If we don't find the money, the acceptance doesn't matter. That's—"

"No, you don't get to explain," she practically yelled over him. "Do you know how much I hate the salon gossip circle? But that's how I had to hear about your acceptance. *You* should've told me."

She sounded broken, and Squire didn't know how to fix her. He cursed himself for inflicting more pain to her still-healing heart. She hadn't been ready for a new relationship, and while he'd convinced himself he'd given her enough time, he knew he hadn't. He was on a deadline, and he wanted his second chance so badly, he'd pushed too hard, too fast.

"Without the money, I can't go anyway," he tried again, but

she'd already hung up.

Squire stared at his phone, his heart hollowing, chipping off in places and drifting like ashes to the ground.

Her bitterness and anger were so raw. His shoulders sagged as he dropped his head. He couldn't believe she'd ended everything just because he hadn't told her about the acceptance letter.

He wondered about the real story behind her divorce. She'd indicated that Taylor had been the one at fault, but he'd had enough relationships to know the street went both ways. Had she refused to talk to him too? Refused to work things out?

He shook his head to dislodge the growing distrust. He should've told her about the acceptance, plain and simple.

He dialed her number again, sure she wouldn't answer. She didn't. He once again tried to silence the thoughts running through his mind. He'd forgiven her once; he needed to learn to trust someone now, more than ever. Not just someone.

Her.

The next day, Tom informed Kelly that Squire would be out on the range all day. She'd gotten his text about going out on the range to avoid the Fourth of July fireworks. She supposed if the circumstances were different, she would've encouraged his campout.

The last thing she wanted for him was a repeat of Saturday night after the rodeo. His wounds were too fresh, still bleeding.

Kelly realized hers were too. That was why she'd driven to the ranch at six AM and confiscated the files. The steady drip, drip, drip of her broken and bleeding heart echoed through her body from top to bottom.

She worked alone in her office, missing Squire more than she thought possible. She hadn't realized how nice it was to speak whenever she wanted and have someone there to listen.

Not just someone.

Him.

At the same time she missed him, she found herself growing angry with him. He should've been man enough to tell her about the acceptance. Even without the money, they should've had that conversation. She felt like he'd robbed them of advancing emotionally together. Of helping each other stop the internal bleeding so they could each heal.

Over the next couple of days, she took over Squire's job of looking for financial documents. Only a few folders remained, and she found nothing new. She hadn't been tallying the pages as she went, so she set to that on Friday.

Midafternoon, a knock interrupted her work. Tom stood in the doorway, holding a CD. He'd always treated her kindly, with respect. He didn't let his gaze linger too long, like some of the other cowboys did.

"Hey, Miss Kelly." He entered and set the disc on her desk. "I found this in Clark's stuff. It says taxes on it."

Her throat muscles clenched, making it impossible for her to speak. Her poor heart stuttered, hardly able to take any more afflictions.

"I thought you might need it."

"Thank you," she said, adding a smile to her words. But she felt like throwing up.

He tipped his hat and left, his cowboy boots thunking the way back to the general controller's desk.

She hadn't finished entering all the income into the computer yet, but maybe she wouldn't have to. Maybe this CD contained everything she needed—including the bank account number where the missing money sat gathering loads of interest.

With shaking fingers, she slid the disc into her computer, drumming her nails as she waited for it to spin.

When she was able to access it, she scanned the five items. She fumbled for her phone and texted Squire, though she knew he likely wouldn't get the message.

911! Come to my office ASAP!

Five folders sat on the disc, each labeled with the word "taxes" and a year. The missing five years of information.

Kelly's stomach tightened, and it kept twisting and twisting. She'd always thought Clark was so nice, if a bit gruff and overly watchful. Could he be the one who'd stolen one-point-six million dollars from Three Rivers? From Frank and Heidi? From Squire?

She double-clicked on the Taxes 2010 folder, hardly daring to hope to find everything she needed inside.

But find it, she did. She clicked on the folder labeled *Income*. Inside, every piece of income was neatly organized. Digital copies of the statements they'd found in random places. Labeled meticulously, so that Kelly knew immediately why the reported income on the hard copies of the tax returns didn't match up.

One document was labeled "November, 2010, Oceanview Cattle Company (unfiled)." She clicked it open and sent it to print.

After printing everything for 2010, she compared them with what she and Squire had been able to locate. Those pages added up to the reported income in the hard copies of the tax return for 2010.

The printed documents showed that Three Rivers had actually brought in an additional four hundred ninety thousand dollars. She sat back in her chair, stunned. If blinking and breathing weren't involuntary, she wouldn't have done them.

Clark had been siphoning money from the cattle sales. Several thousand dollars here, a complete sale there. Enough to total almost five hundred thousand dollars in a single year!

She grabbed her phone and dialed Squire, praying he was riding Juniper and they happened to be in a spot where he had cell service. *Please, God.*

As she listened to his phone ring, she got up and locked her office door. She didn't want anyone walking in right now. Sourness spread through Kelly's mouth and crowded her stomach, an odd sensation she couldn't will away.

Squire didn't answer, and desperation clogged her throat as she hurried to the window and looked outside. She half-expected Squire to come riding along on Juniper, but he didn't.

She closed the blinds and set to work printing out the rest of the digital income documents, cross-checking them with the paper items, and tallying up how much money Clark had failed to report.

One million, six hundred and thirty-seven thousand dollars and eighty-four cents. The exact amount that Kelly had discovered was missing.

She needed to talk to Squire. Now.

She texted him again. *Found the missing documents. Come to my office.*

She called him. No answer.

She paced the length of her office, the lights off and the door locked. She didn't want to leave for the weekend without talking to him. She couldn't. She swallowed to ease the thickness pressing against her tongue. Squire was unreachable. She didn't know how to get to him, short of walking onto the range with a prayer in her heart.

She thought of Finn, and decided against putting herself in danger. If she got lost on the range and something happened to her....

Kelly headed out to Tom's desk. "Do you know where Squire and Pete went? Like, is there somewhere on the range they're likely to be?"

"There's a cabin in section twelve," he said. "They might go there. They might sleep on the ground. I don't rightly know, Miss Kelly." He peered at her with concern in his eyes. "Is everything okay?"

"No," she said. "I need to speak with Squire immediately. It's a matter of extreme importance."

Tom stood. "I'll get Frank, and we'll go find 'im."

Kelly checked her watch. How long could she afford to wait? She'd promised Finn she'd take him to Crystal's for dinner and a sleep over.

"I have to get home for my son," she said, noting that it was already half-past five. She should've left thirty minutes ago. "Please call me as soon as you find him."

"Will do." Tom headed out the door while Kelly hurried back to her office. She tucked the CD into the side pocket of her purse— the only one that zipped closed. She scooped up all the printed documents and stuffed them in the bottom of her bag. Standing in the doorway, she decided not to lock it down or put everything away. She never had before, and she didn't want Clark stopping by and finding something to raise his suspicions.

She dialed Squire one last time as she pulled onto the highway. "Squire," she said to his voicemail. "It's Kelly. Please call me as soon as you get this. I have so much to show you. I have it all; not at my office. I'm taking Finn to my cousin's tonight, but come by my house anytime."

The next morning, Squire still hadn't responded, called, texted, or shown up. She worried her lip while Finn ate breakfast, while she helped her mother hang the laundry.

She couldn't believe Squire had chosen now of all times to disappear, despite the Fourth of July holiday that brought such strong reactions. He seemed to have a knack for walking away without much of an explanation.

Her worry turned to anger, and then resentment. She didn't have time to waste with a man who couldn't even tell her where he was going and when he'd be back. Who couldn't respond to a phone call or a text.

And these weren't needy calls and messages. This was *business*—*his* business. Matters *he* should care about.

Her resentment faded back to concern. Maybe something had happened to him out on the range. Her stomach knotted when she thought about him out in the middle of the wilderness, coming face-to-face with Clark. The only consolation she had was that Pete had gone with him.

She oscillated between wanting to give him a piece of her mind and hugging him fiercely next time she saw him.

If she saw him again. Maybe she should quit while she was ahead, get another job, and end her communication with Squire. That piece of her heart that she'd given to him felt like a huge hole in her chest, and she realized that whether she liked it or not, he now owned her whole heart.

Squire woke on Sunday morning, his back one giant knot from sleeping on the ground for the past four nights. He stretched, trying to work out the tightness in his muscles, while Benson nosed his way into Squire's pack for something to eat.

Squire hadn't been sleeping well. He felt so guilty for not telling Kelly about his acceptance. Even under the blanket of stars, he hadn't been able to figure out how to make things right with her. All he could hear was the break in her voice when she asked why he didn't tell her.

To protect you sounded lame. And *to protect myself* sounded selfish.

He wished Pete hadn't gone back to the homestead last night. Without his phone, which he'd abandoned in his cabin, he felt truly alone. The service out this far was non-existent, but he could at least pretend he could send Kelly a text.

He wasn't sure how much time had passed when Benson barked, drawing Squire's attention. He turned toward the sound and immediately saw a trail of dust rising in the air.

"Who is it, boy?" He reached down and scrubbed behind Benson's ears. He whined, which meant it was someone friendly. A few minutes later, Squire recognized his father's horse.

Concern caused his heart to beat quicker, and he pulled on his boots, jammed his hat on his head, and rolled up his sleeping bag. By the time his dad and Tom arrived, he was ready to go.

"What's wrong?" Squire asked his father, swinging himself up onto Juniper's back. "Is Mom okay? One of the calves?"

"Everything's fine," his dad said. "Except for this." He held out Squire's phone.

He took it, a frown pulling at his jaw. "I left this behind on purpose."

"Miss Kelly's been trying to get in touch with you," Tom said. "Said it was a matter of extreme importance." He looked from Pete to Squire, his expression unreadable.

His dad fixed him with a look that meant trouble, and Squire squirmed in his saddle. He was used to getting the evil eye from his mother, but from his dad? Tom wore a dark look that said Squire should've known better than to keep secrets from his family.

"Kelly's been texting and calling for two days," his dad said. "Tom came to the house on Friday night, and we got your phone from your cabin to read the messages. Something about some missing money. Why don't I know about this? What's going on?"

Flames and ice crystals warred in Squire's head. The scorching fire would force out the truth about the money. Regret tipped the blaze, but Squire focused on what he could control. The shards of ice cut new pathways for fresh possibilities. Had Kelly found the money? He almost wept that he might be able to finally drop these burdens he'd been shouldering alone.

"Son," his dad said, swinging his horse around. "We need to get back quickly. And you better talk the whole way."

"I can't believe you didn't tell us," his mom said, her hands winding around each other. Tom had looked exhausted as he'd headed into the stables to brush down the horses. Inadequacy pooled in his fingertips at his demonstration of incompetence. His dad was too old to be sleeping on the hard ground and they didn't pay Tom enough to babysit all the cowboys, and an old man, and apparently Squire.

"Frank, how can we leave Three Rivers now?" His mother sounded near tears, and Squire wished he'd told his parents the truth months ago.

His father had done nothing but listen on the way back. Then he'd made Squire explain everything again to his mom. Squire had never seen his dad cry, but he certainly looked like he might now.

"I have voicemail messages from Kelly," Squire said. "Let me listen to them." He went down the hall to his old bedroom as he dialed his voicemail. Kelly's voice, urgent and beautiful, came through the line.

"Squire, it's Kelly." His pulse jumped at the simple sound of her voice. "I know I told you I didn't want to talk to you, but please call me as soon as you get this."

Beep.

"Squire, it's Kelly. Tom said he found a CD in Clark's desk. I don't know if it's his, but I think you should be careful around him. It has all the financial documents on it, even the ones that were unfiled. Just...be careful."

Panic struck him like a blow to the back of the head. He spun, expecting to see Clark standing in the doorway. But there was no one there.

Beep.

"Squire, it's Kelly. I have all the documents, and I'll give them you so you can show your father and figure everything out. Please, just call me as soon as you can."

Beep.

Squire tried calling Kelly. She didn't answer, and he got a taste of his own medicine. It was bitter, and frustrating. Surely she must have been frantic to get in touch with him. Just as he was to talk to her right now, to ensure her and her son's safety.

He hurried back into the family room, where his parents still sat. "Squire, what's going on?" his mom asked.

"Tom found a CD in Clark's desk and gave it to Kelly. It had all the missing documentation on it."

"Clark?" his father repeated, his eyes lined with exhaustion. "Where's the CD?"

"Kelly has it," Squire said. A wave of realizations washed over him. Kelly trusted him. She hadn't held anything back from him. She said she'd give him all the documents to show his family. She could've insisted he let her do it so she could get the recognition she deserved for a job well done.

He'd kept secrets from her, didn't tell her everything so she could make the most informed decision for her and Finn. Kicking himself for a lot of things, he pulled out his phone and fired off a text to Kelly. *Keep the CD safe.*

"Kelly said she printed everything off the CD, but I don't have it right now." He glanced at his father. "Kelly believes they took the money from our cattle sales for themselves. It's enough money for you to retire comfortably and for me to finish school before I come back and run Three Rivers."

His words faded into silence, leaving him wondering what he'd been so afraid of discussing with his parents. He realized he didn't have any excuses left. Nothing to keep him from finishing his degree. Nothing from asking Kelly to go to College Station with him.

Only his own insecurities about being good enough for her, strong enough to finish school, wise enough to be a father.

Tom burst into the house, his dark gray eyes storming. "My desk has been ransacked," he said. "My cabin too."

A sharp barb of fear punctured Squire's lungs, causing the air to leak out in a slow hiss. "Clark." He turned to his parents. "Where's Clark?"

"He left this morning," Squire's mother said. "Said he was going to Amarillo."

Squire scrubbed his hands through his hair, forcing himself to focus on one task at a time, the way the Army had taught him.

"Squire, what do we do now?" his mom asked.

"I think we need to call the police." He checked his phone again. "I'd just hate to accuse Clark if he wasn't the one at fault."

"Who else would go through their old desk?" Tom asked, his eyes glittering with the same anger cascading through Squire's body. He felt like smashing his fist through the wall. Money didn't matter if he couldn't have Kelly. Being a veterinarian would mean nothing.

Everything shattered inside Squire. He squeezed his phone, imagining his grip to be strong enough to splinter it into a thousand pieces. He hated that he'd driven Kelly away, kept secrets from her and his parents, hidden how he really felt about things. Even though his mother had warned him not to do it, he *had* bottled everything up.

No more, he thought as he glanced around his ranch. He wanted to finish his veterinarian degree, and he wanted Kelly and Finn by his side while he did it.

"I'm going to Kelly's," he said, his determination growing when his father nodded. "Tom, please stay here and make sure my parents stay safe."

"You got it, Boss."

Squire drove faster than he ever had before, calling Kelly twice without getting her to pick up. With every passing mile, his Army radar blared and then screamed. He dialed Pete.

"Where are you?" he asked when his friend answered.

"Nice to hear from you too," Pete said in a quiet voice.

"I don't have time for games, Lieutenant," Squire barked. "Kelly could be in trouble. Where are you?"

"I'm at church." Scuffling came through the line. "I'm heading outside. What do you mean, Kelly could be in trouble?"

Squire's heart leapt, but his alarm kicked up to a steady wail. "Is Kelly at church?"

"No," Pete said. "Her parents are here with her son. But she's not."

"Can you meet me at her house?"

"I think I remember how to get there," Pete said.

Squire hung up. He trusted Pete. He could count on him for anything, even in the middle of church. Why hadn't he been able to trust Kelly, even after prompted to do so?

He didn't know, and he didn't have time to psychoanalyze himself. The only thing he could do was drive faster. So he did that.

Chapter Fifteen

Kelly stared at the ceiling in her bedroom, wishing the walls around her life existed in a completely different city. The thought felt false, though, and Kelly admitted that the only walls she wanted to see in the morning were out on the ranch.

But she didn't want to be with someone she couldn't trust, who didn't trust her. Still, she hadn't been able to sleep on Saturday night, the Fourth of July fireworks notwithstanding. She'd laid in bed, reliving the kindness in Squire's eyes when he played with Finn, the adoration she'd seen when he looked at her. She remembered how he'd come to plant her father's garden, how he'd helped Finn on the range, how honest he'd been about not wanting Three Rivers.

But now she knew he wasn't honest all the time. She didn't know when he'd gotten his acceptance letter, but she guessed it had been several days ago. Glenda and all the girls already knew, and Heidi didn't come to town that often.

It doesn't matter, she told herself as she got up and padded into the bathroom. Just like she'd said on the phone to Squire. He was free to do whatever he wanted. He'd made his choice, and it wasn't to share his life with her. Taylor had made the same choice, but as Kelly thought about him, the usual bitterness and shame didn't well up in her throat.

She looked into her own eyes in the mirror. "I've forgiven him." A powerful wash of peace filled her. She felt relieved of a heavy burden she'd been carrying for months. Thinking of Taylor reminded her of something he'd taught her years ago as an intern. She locked the bedroom door and put the CD in her laptop.

She could find out who created the files on the disc. Taylor had taught her how to look at the data created when each file was. It usually included the username of the computer who created it, as well as the date and time.

She clicked on the CD icon on her desktop and opened the information pane. The username attached to the disc left little doubt in her mind.

Cowboyclark stared back at her, along with the date of creation. December 12, 2010. The last date the disc was modified was yesterday, and Kelly knew she'd done that.

She wanted to call Squire and tell him that she now knew Clark was the one to blame. But she'd turned off her phone as soon as she'd gone to bed last night. She hadn't been able to bear the thought of another night of checking it every four minutes. She'd even left it upstairs, out of reach. If and when Squire returned to civilization, he'd find her messages. She had a sudden longing to hear his voice, but she pushed it away.

She took the disc out of her computer and put it back in its case. She'd printed everything off of it, but Squire would need this. No matter what, she couldn't lose it. She held it close to her heart as she listened to the silence in the house. She took a calming breath. What had he been truly been avoiding while out on the range? How to ask her to come with him? Or how to break up with her? Or simply fireworks that sparked his trauma?

She didn't know, and she hated that. She hurried into the bathroom and opened the cabinet over the toilet. Too obvious, though the cabinet was too high for Finn, and her parents never came downstairs. But there was a decorative lip on the top of the cabinet, and she slid the slim case over the top, careful to keep it where she could touch it.

Satisfied that no one would disturb the CD until she could return it to Squire, she left the bathroom and went back to bed, praying that sleep would claim her for a good long while.

When she woke, the silence in the house loomed like a physical being. She felt like she did when she was single, like no one would know when she got up or what she did next. She hated it. As she dressed, she heard footsteps upstairs, slow and steady, like her father's. A cold chill skated down her spine, and she opened her bedroom door slowly so as to not make any noise.

She waited for Finn's rapid-fire steps to accompany her father's. Or the more clipped steps of her mother's heels as they returned from church.

Nothing stirred, and whoever had entered the house wasn't moving now. Kelly held her breath, desperately wishing she had her phone with her. She glanced at the alarm clock on her nightstand, seeing that it was just before lunchtime. Church hadn't ended yet, unless Scott had run out of things to say a little early.

Kelly moved silently through the downstairs living room to the steps, stopping and looking up before she committed to climbing them. Heart pounding and throat dry, she made a snap decision.

"Dad?" she called, forcing herself to move around the corner and start up the stairs. "Finn?" She climbed the stairs steadily, as if expecting to see her father and son. She didn't want whoever was here to be in the basement, where the CD was stowed.

She wasn't entirely surprised when Clark stepped into her path. She was completely terrified, though, of the dark look on his unshaven face.

Squire parked down the street from Kelly's house, behind the ranch truck Pete had taken to church. His Lieutenant climbed in the cab. "That truck was here when I got here, about ten minutes ago."

Clark's truck, which was parked in Kelly's driveway. Squire's heart stopped, then restarted at three times its normal rhythm. He pulled out his phone and sent a text to his dad.

Clark is at Kelly's house. Come into town, quick. He included her address and silenced his phone.

"Pete, I need you to call the police," he said slowly, not taking his eyes from the truck. "Tell them someone broke into the Armstrong house, and that he could be armed and dangerous."

"Whoa, Major. You're freaking me out. Whose truck is that?"

"Clark's," Squire said.

"The foreman?"

"Yes," Squire said. "I don't have time to explain. Call the police. I'm going in there."

"Major." Pete put his hand on Squire's arm. They looked at each other. "Be careful."

Squire nodded, reading the concern in his friend's eyes. "If I don't come out in fifteen minutes, come in after me."

"You got it, Major."

A dozen scenarios went through Squire's mind as he snuck around the side of the house and up the back stairs to the deck. He kept himself low, so no one could see him through the kitchen window. His injured leg protested, but he bit back the pain.

Squire calmed himself, employing his Army training for stealth and steadiness. He took a deep breath and held it, poking his head up to peer through the window. The kitchen sat empty, not a utensil out of place. Squire crept to the back door, his senses kicking into overdrive. He eased the door open, careful to move it inch by inch to avoid making any sound.

Kelly's parents owned an old home, and he hoped he could avoid causing any creaks or squeals as he slipped inside. He removed his boots and left them on the deck to reduce the noise his feet would make.

He listened through the open door, and he could hear a low, masculine murmur coming from the living room.

Lucky for him, Kandahar had taught him to move great

distances silently. He sat on the floor and pulled his legs through the doorway. Pressing his back against the wall, he managed to stand, even though his injured leg stuttered as he did.

Four steps and he'd be able to hide behind the wall while he assessed the situation. He took them quickly, never letting his full weight settle onto the balls of his feet.

He took a deep breath, then another, listening. The shrill ring of an old-fashioned phone had his fists curling tight and his breath hitching.

He couldn't clearly hear what the man said, but it sounded like, "You won't be answering that."

The ringtone stopped. "Who was it?" Kelly asked, and she sounded strong and safe.

"Your boyfriend's father," the man said, and Squire easily recognized Clark's voice. He wanted to bang his head against the wall as he speculated on how long he'd been here.

"He's not my boyfriend," Kelly said, and the words cut Squire. "He's my boss."

"Right," Clark said. "I hear you have a thing for bosses."

"Shut up," she said, her voice on the outer edge of fury. "Why don't you just tell me where the money is? Frank and Heidi are reasonable people."

Squire pulled out his phone and opened the video recorder, but he needed to get closer to make sure he got a quality sound. He ducked low and peered around the corner. A cutout in the wall separating the kitchen and the living room allowed him a partial view, and he watched as Clark sauntered by, his eyes cast low, like he was watching someone sitting down.

He moved out of sight, and Squire took the opportunity to scamper past the cabinets on his right to the half-wall with the cutout. He didn't stop there, but crawled past the fish tank, bypassing the kitchen, and continued into the attached dining room.

Past the table, another doorway allowed access into the living room. He paused, his right shoulder only inches from the molding. One peek around the corner, and he'd be able to see Kelly.

His chest coiled without oxygen, and his leg throbbed. Through controlled breaths, he waited, straining to hear any footsteps against the carpet. When he heard nothing, he took a chance and did a fast check around the corner.

Kelly sat on the couch facing him.

Deep breath.

Check.

Clark sat on the coffee table to her right, his back to Squire.

Breath.

Check.

He seemed hunched at the shoulders, like he was reading on his phone. Or worse, Kelly's.

Squire didn't pull back as quickly this time, and Kelly kept her attention squarely on Clark though Squire silently prayed she'd look up and see him.

Her feet and hands were tied. Her hair looked mussed, like she'd put up a fight, and her face seemed redder than usual. No blood, and definitely no tears. She was strong and confident, a lot like the first day she'd come to the ranch for her interview. But now she looked more vulnerable too. Definitely scared. Squire had also seen her kind streak. Her endless worry. Her anger and distrust.

"I know you have the CD," Clark said at last, looking up from his lap. "It says so right here."

"I wouldn't know," Kelly said dryly. "As you haven't let me see my phone."

Squire raised his hand at the same time she moved her head to shake an errant lock of hair from her face. She saw him, and her eyes widened. Just as quickly, she glanced away, playing her part perfectly.

"Squire texted, 'Keep the CD safe.'" Clark held her phone toward her. "So you obviously have it."

"I *don't* have it," she insisted. "You searched my basement and didn't find it. I don't have a CD. I don't even know what you're talking about." She glanced back to Squire. He held up his phone, hoping she'd get the hint that he was recording and she needed to get Clark to confess to everything.

He ducked back behind the wall when Clark started to turn his way. "What are you looking at?"

Sure footfalls came his way, and Squire *moved*. Past the table, the aquarium, and all the way around the wall and into the living room. He ducked behind the couch just as Kelly gasped.

"Where is he?" he whispered, his back pressed into the couch and his eyes trained on the cutout that showed a slice of the kitchen.

"Just went around the corner," she whispered back.

"I'm recording. Get him to talk."

"Don't be tryin' to trick me now," Clark said, his footsteps shuffling against the carpet on the other side of the couch as he returned to the living room.

"I'm not," Kelly said. "You're the one doing all the trickery. You stole millions of dollars from Three Rivers."

"You don't *know* that," Clark said. "You don't even know who you can trust."

"I thought I could trust *you*."

Clark chuckled darkly, the sound like sandpaper against bark. Squire wanted to burst from his hiding spot and punch him in the throat.

"Where is the money?" Kelly asked.

Clark said nothing, and Squire's heart sank. He'd had enough experience with hostiles to know when someone was going to talk. And Clark wasn't in a chatty mood.

"I really thought Squire would come," Clark said, and a shaft of light fell across the floor near Squire, like Clark had parted the curtains. "But there's no one coming."

Squire couldn't judge where Clark was, and he didn't dare take a peek. He'd been pinned down before. The best thing to do was wait for a lull and then go in, guns blazing.

It was definitely a lull. He didn't have a gun, but he leapt from behind the couch, yelling at the top of his lungs.

Clark sat on the coffee table, looking down. Squire was practically on top of him before he even raised his head. They collided; Kelly screamed; phones and cowboy hats went flying.

Squire's momentum took both men to the floor. He landed one punch to Clark's chin before he heard the sirens. He had his hands pinned when the red and blue lights came through the wispy curtains.

With Clark snarling, but unable to move because Squire had his knees locked securely around the man's waist, the police crashed through the front door.

Despite his injured leg, Kelly watched Squire pin Clark in two seconds flat, a clear testament to his Army training and impressive physical condition. While three police officers took care of the situation on the floor, another untied her feet and hands.

"Ma'am, are you okay?" He helped her stand, but Kelly could only nod. She took a shuddering breath and told herself not to break down now. But bent pins and bits of string wouldn't hold her together for long.

"My parents and my son," she managed to say.

"Are they here?" the police officer asked.

"He said they went to church." She turned on numb feet. "He has my phone somewhere."

"He stole one-point-six million dollars from my ranch," Squire said. "He tied up a woman in her own house. I want him arrested." He stared coldly at Clark, who glared back.

Two officers cuffed Clark and recited his rights as they led him outside, leaving Kelly with Squire and two additional cops. One was glancing around and jotting down notes. The other remained by Kelly's side.

"Ma'am, I'm Officer Swenson. Can you tell me what happened?"

Kelly squeezed her eyes shut like she could disappear that way. "I woke up late, and my family was gone." She suddenly needed to hear her mother's voice and Finn's laughter. "Where's my phone? I need to call my parents."

"I'll do it." Squire thumbed on his phone and stepped into the dining room.

Kelly sank back to the couch and cradled her head in her hands.

"You woke up late?" Officer Swenson prompted.

Kelly nodded just as Squire returned. "No answer." He sat next to her and wrapped his arm around her shoulders. "I'm sure they're still in church. I called Pete and asked him to go get them."

Kelly nodded as the officer said again, "So you slept late...."

Clark's dark eyes filled her vision, blocking out the sunlit living room and the weight of Squire's arm. The ropes bit into her wrists. Her own pleas—high-pitched and hysterical when she asked about Finn—painted the inside of her skull.

"Kelly."

Squire's commanding tone broke the web of fresh memories. She looked into his eyes, easily finding the love and concern swimming inside their depths.

"I heard footsteps upstairs. At first I thought it was my father, but it wasn't. It was Clark Paxton, the foreman at Three Rivers Ranch where I work."

"And that's your ranch, sir?" Officer Swenson asked, writing though he focused on Squire.

"Yes, we've been working for a few weeks to find a substantial amount of money that's been missing for years. Kelly figured out who'd taken it." He lowered his head until his lips leveled with her ear. "I'm so sorry I wasn't here."

She squeezed his hand; she didn't want to have this conversation in front of a police officer.

"So Clark Paxton entered your home without your permission?"

"Yes," Kelly said. "He tied me up and left me on the couch while he went downstairs. I live in the basement with my son." An involuntary shiver ran down her spine. If Finn had been here with her…. She couldn't complete the thought.

Squire kept one arm across her shoulders and brought their joined hands to his lap. She relished the warmth and steadiness he provided, grateful he'd come despite the harsh words she'd said to him.

"I could hear him down there going through everything. I heard crashes and stuff. I don't know what he did, but he didn't find what he was looking for."

"Which is?" Officer Swenson asked.

Kelly exchanged a glance with Squire, who nodded. "A CD that has irrefutable evidence that Clark is the one who took the money from cattle sales at Three Rivers. He has all the missing documents in digital format on the CD, and his username is in the electronic data on the files."

"Where is the CD?" Squire's eyes blazed with emotion. Anger, hope, love.

"I put it on top of the cabinet above the toilet in my bathroom. I know Clark didn't find it. He was livid when he came back upstairs. He kept asking me where it was."

"May I?" Squire asked Officer Swenson, who waved at him to go down and retrieve the CD. The radio on his hip beeped, and a voice came through the line.

"Cory to Swenson. I caught Will Armstrong just as he was leaving. Seems someone had told him about the situation at their place. They're on their way home now."

Relief slammed against Kelly like waves against cliffs. She wept with the release of fear and worry, with knowing her parents and son had been safe at church.

Officer Swenson patted her back and excused himself. When Squire returned with the CD in his hand, Kelly wiped her tears. "I kept it safe for you."

He sat on the couch next to her, his knee pressing against hers. "I don't care about the CD, darlin'."

She studied the red marks ringing her wrists. "You don't?"

He reached for her hands and rubbed the lines like he could erase them through his touch. "Are you okay?"

"I'm fine."

He gently lifted her chin to look into his eyes. "You're not fine."

Her chin shook as she tried not to cry. "I've never been tied up before."

"I have," he said. "And you looked much better than I did."

She half-laughed, half-cried, and he pulled her into an embrace. "I'm so, so sorry, Kel. I made so many mistakes. I should've told you about the acceptance letter. I should've asked you to come to College Station with me as soon as I thought of it. I should've—"

"Wait," she said, leaning away from him though in his arms was where she wanted to stay. "Go back to that last one."

He took a deep breath, his eyes round with anxiety. "I want you and Finn to come to College Station with me. I can't leave either of you here for four years."

"You can't?"

He shook his head slowly. "I let you go once before. I don't want to make the same mistake twice. I'll wait as long as I have to. I love you and want to be with you."

Her chest exploded like she'd swallowed firecrackers. He loved her.

How should she respond? Was she ready to repeat the sentiment to him?

Squire ran a hand over the scruff on his face. "I was scared to talk to you about things."

"You?" She leaned into his chest to feel the comforting thrum of his pulse against her cheek. "You just attacked a man, after sneaking through my house silently. I didn't see an ounce of fear in you."

"Adrenaline," he said. "Army training. It was nothing."

"And yet somehow I scare you?"

"Not you." He pressed a light kiss to her temple. "Being with you. Or not being with you. Or something. And with the money obstacle out of the way, all that was standing between me and you, was, well, me."

"If I'd known finding the money was going to freak you out, I wouldn't have worked so hard to do it." She twisted so he could see she was teasing.

He kissed her, the pure love in his touch erasing the pain in her wrists and the horror of the morning. She pulled back when she heard the crunch of gravel under tires. She rushed to the door, outside, and down the steps. "Finn!" she called as her father got out of the truck.

Her mom exited on the other side and paused to help Finn down. They met at the front of the truck, where Kelly hugged Finn so tight she thought she might break him.

"Kelly, what happened?" her mom asked, glancing at the patrol car still in their driveway.

She shook her head as she glanced at Finn. "A little problem in the basement," she said with a false note in her voice. "We'll need to stay upstairs." She held back the tears and took her son's hand as they moved into the house.

Squire waited by the door, his hat perched on his head. "I should go. My dad needs me down at the station."

"You can't go," Finn said, pouting. "Buster can catch the Frisbee now. You gotta see 'im."

Squire crouched in front of him. "That's great, buddy." He glanced up at Kelly. "Can I come back later?"

Finn studied him as Kelly nodded. "You'll come back, right?"

"Sure thing." Squire ruffled Finn's hair and stood. He tipped his hat to her parents and slipped out the front door.

"Squire," she said from the doorway. He paused at the bottom of the steps and peered up at her. She wanted to tell him she loved him too, but the words wouldn't form. "Come back soon."

He bounded back up the steps, his gaze intense and unwavering. "As soon as I can, darlin'."

She watched him move down the driveway and get in the patrol car with Officer Swenson before she turned away. "Finn, let's get some lunch." She nodded toward the stairs. "Dad, you might want to check out the flood downstairs."

"Are we going to have to sleep somewhere else?" Finn asked, a dose of worry in his voice.

Kelly's heart constricted. "No, baby. We'll sleep up here if we have to."

"I call Grampa's bed." Finn skipped into the kitchen, where Kelly started making his favorite meal: macaroni and cheese. With the water on to boil and Finn happy with a couple of his cars, Kelly told him to stay upstairs so he wouldn't get hurt. She joined her parents in the basement. The sight before her looked like a tornado had blown through the house.

Before she knew it, she was sobbing. It seemed like all the fear she'd felt, the horror at hearing Clark rip the cushions from the couch, tear the movies out of the cabinets, shake the books, just came rushing out of her.

"Honey." Her dad wrapped his strong arms around her and held on. Her mom did too, and Kelly had never been more grateful for her parents.

After only a few minutes, she composed herself. "I'm okay," she said. "I am."

Her mother grabbed her hand and squeezed. "You're a strong woman, Kelly."

She wiped her face, but the tears wouldn't stop completely. "Can you go finish the macaroni and cheese? I don't want Finn to see me crying." Her father got a garbage bag, and they worked together to clean up.

Her tears continued, because they were for Squire. But this time, Kelly wasn't upset that she was crying over a man. If there ever was a tear-worthy man, it was the one who came back even after she'd told him to stay away, who snuck through the house, who leapt at her captor and rescued her.

Chapter Sixteen

Squire sat at the police station, listening, but with his thoughts far away. On Kelly. He texted her, but he didn't know if she'd found her phone yet. Or if it would even work. He distinctly remembered it going flying as he wrestled with Clark.

He took a deep breath. *Money first, Kelly second.* Even as he thought it, he knew these kinds of thoughts were what had gotten him into trouble in the first place.

"We're done here," the officer said, and Squire stood as his dad did. They shook hands with the officer and headed outside.

"Where's your truck?" his dad asked.

"Pete's got it." He studied the familiar landscape as his dad headed out of town. He noted the Fourth of July streamers, the storefronts he knew like the back of his hand, the stillness of small-town air.

"Maybe I should go back to Kelly's," he said, more to himself than to his father. She had said to come back soon.

"Let it alone, son. She needs some time."

Squire knew his father was right. He'd seen her face as she sat on the couch, her wrists and ankles bound. Would he always be a reminder of this experience? Just like every time he heard the crack of a whip, he thought of bombs and fire and pain. He hoped not.

When his father pulled into the ranch, Squire asked if he could go for a drive. His dad left the truck idling and climbed out. Squire went back to the main highway and kept going north. When he got to the Texas state line, he pulled over.

He texted his mother that he'd gone for a drive. He wasn't going to leave anyone wondering where he was, and when he'd be back. Not again.

She responded that they had an appointment in Amarillo the next morning, and Squire said he wouldn't be too late.

He missed Benson, who usually settled next to him in the truck. He missed Kelly, who he loved. His heart writhed and withered, and as he watched the stars wink to life, the only thing he could do was hope and pray he hadn't messed up too badly.

Kelly helped Finn get ready for bed, and she was planning to drop onto her mattress immediately afterward. She sent him downstairs to brush his teeth, and just as she was about to stand, her mom turned down the TV.

She'd seen this strategy before, as a teenager. She settled back into the couch. "What's up, Mom?"

She'd been shooting her furtive glances, then turning away as she shook her head. All afternoon. Now she set her book aside. "Are you really going to let him walk away?"

"Who?"

"Oh, come on. Squire."

Kelly threw up her hands in defeat. "I don't know what to do, Mom."

"He loves you."

"He's moving to College Station. I just got a job here. I'm looking at houses. Finn deserves a stable life."

Her mom exchanged a look with her dad, and he glanced at Kelly. "We want you to be happy. And we're glad you're here. But if life takes you somewhere else, well, sometimes you have to be willing to get on the train."

"Honey." Her mom got up and sat on the couch next to her. "It doesn't matter where you live, or what your job is. Those things change like the wind." She tucked Kelly's hair behind her ear. "But love like I've seen in that man's eyes.... That won't change. You could tell him you want to go to Mars, and he'd go with you."

"It's not just about me, Mom. Finn's just starting to be himself again. Dad has been wonderful with him." She'd taken a step, prayed that God would guide her. As she waited for her mother to answer, she realized that God had led her back to Three Rivers at a time when Squire was here.

God had allowed her to find the documents Squire needed. He'd made it possible for him to attend school—and to take Kelly with him.

"Finn needs a wide open space," her mother finally said. "But he can have that here, in College Station, or on the ranch."

"So, what? We just follow Squire to College Station?"

"Squire couldn't be a better father for Finn," her mom said.

"You can let him go, or drive him away, if you want to. You can do anything you *want* to do." She patted Kelly's knee and stood up, leaving Kelly to her thoughts.

Clark's bellowing roars and Squire's heroic rescue haunted her dreams. By the time she got up and stepped into the shower, she was desperate to hear Squire's calming voice, see his rugged face, feel his hand in hers.

She couldn't call him, because her phone had been damaged in the fight. She didn't know if she'd see him at the ranch, and fear pricked her heart every time she thought about coming face-to-face with him, talking to him, and admitting how she felt about him.

God, she prayed. *Do I really get to have a second chance? After messing up so badly last time?*

She didn't have to wait for an answer. A flowing sense of rightness washed over her, and she knew. She had to do what Squire had done: Forgive herself and get out of her own way.

By the time she was ready for work, she felt one breath away from crying. Two away from quitting. She made it into her office with a friendly nod to Tom and a quick smile to the cowboys loitering near the assignment board. None of them seemed like they hadn't slept for the past three nights. None of them seemed like they'd been tied up in their own homes. In fact, none of them seemed like anything about the ranch was different at all.

She hadn't seen Squire's truck when she pulled in, and she had no idea if Frank and Heidi were gone as well. She closed her door behind her, half-expecting the place to be ransacked. But everything seemed exactly as she'd left it on Friday afternoon. As she opened her bottom drawer to put away her lunch and purse, a folded piece of yellow paper caught her eye.

A note. In Squire's handwriting.

Hey Kel,

I'm staying in Amarillo for a few days to get the finances sorted out. My parents want to talk with you when you get in today. Nothing serious. You still have a job at Three Rivers. Just wanted to let you know. I have my phone, but I'm doing a lot and can't always answer or respond right away.

The next part of the letter looked like it had been written and erased several times. But it finally concluded with, *I love you, and I hope to see you soon.*

Love, Squire

She closed her eyes and pressed the paper to her heart. He loved her. And she felt it coursing from his written proclamation and into her heart.

She folded the note and placed it in her purse. Then she headed over to the house to find Heidi and Frank. Strangely, the kitchen was empty. Kelly couldn't even smell the evidence of breakfast.

"Hello?" she called, glancing down the hall in the direction of the bedrooms. A door opened from further inside, and Heidi's delicate footfalls came toward Kelly.

"Kelly," she said, drawing her into a tight hug and holding on. "We don't know how to thank you enough."

"It's not necessary," she said, still being squeezed as if by a python. "Just doing my job."

"Yes, well, Squire wanted to let you know that there's no way we can repay you." Heidi finally released Kelly and stepped back, her eyes moist.

"Have you found any of the money?" Kelly followed Heidi into the living room and sat down on the couch.

"We're waiting for a phone call from Squire," she said. "He's meeting with the manager at a bank in Amarillo this morning."

"Frank didn't go with him?"

"We wanted things on the ranch to be as normal as possible. Without Clark...." She trailed off and focused her attention out the window. "Frank wanted to be here today."

Kelly thought about the letter in her purse. "When did Squire leave?"

"About six. He'll be staying in the city until things get figured out."

"Where is he staying?" Kelly tried to make her voice as casual as possible.

Heidi pinned her with a knowing look. "Why? Thinking of going to see him?"

Kelly set her shoulders. "I want to, yes."

"Thank goodness. That man needs someone to tell him what we can all see."

Kelly's gut pinched. "What's that?"

"That you're in love with him."

"I'm—Is it that obvious?"

Heidi smiled. "Even our most blind cowboy can see it. They keep asking if they'll have to attend the wedding."

"I'm sorry."

"Don't worry about it," Heidi said. "If I couldn't torture my cowhands with the threat of a wedding, what fun would I have?"

Kelly laughed with her. "So about the hotel where Squire is staying...."

"This is a signed affidavit that says the money belongs to Three Rivers Ranch." Squire had been in the bank manager's office for over two hours. Each minute increased his frustration. "I've already proved the name, social security number, and address are bogus. Cynthia Miller with this identification data doesn't even exist. The general controller at Three Rivers stole this money over a five-year period and has been putting it in this account under a fake identity. I have the exact dates, amounts, and receipts."

The bank manager picked up the affidavit. Luckily, Squire had an Army buddy in the reserves who worked as an assistant in the District Attorney's office in Amarillo. He'd been able to discover that the social security number actually belonged to someone who'd died thirty years ago. He'd also examined all the documents and matched the deposit amounts with the sales at Three Rivers.

Clark had gone to great lengths to hide the money, but he hadn't been smart about everything. Deposits in the exact dollar amount matched the sales from several of the auctions. The Assistant DA had determined that the money from those sales were the same deposits into this bogus account.

The bank manager finally set the documents aside. "It certainly seems like what you're saying is true. Would you like to change the name on the account?"

Squire hadn't thought of that. "Who will have access to it?"

"Whomever you determine," he said. "And we'll change the account number, and put maximum security clearance on it, so that you'll know if anyone comes asking about it."

"Let's do it."

It took another two hours to get everything sorted out at the bank, but Squire left with an account in his name, and the name of the ranch. Another company account—which only he could manage. With the interest, the account contained almost two million dollars. He'd talked with his parents after he'd returned home last night, and they'd agreed to pay for veterinarian school, as well as a small allowance for his living expenses.

They should still have more than enough to retire with, and Squire had suggested Tom to replace Clark as the foreman. Squire couldn't help smiling as he slid into his truck and dialed his mom.

"You know, you should check your vehicle before entering it."

Squire yelped and dropped his phone. Kelly sat in his cab, and he hadn't even seen her.

"Kelly," he said, his heart now pounding for a different reason. "What are—? I mean, are you okay?"

She tossed her honey-colored hair over her shoulder and glanced at him. "I can't believe you don't lock your car. We're in the *city*."

"Then I wouldn't have pretty women waiting for me in my truck." He could hardly believe she was here.

"Oh, this happens a lot?" She shifted toward him and scanned him from head to toe. "And you're not even wearing your uniform."

He chuckled. "I found the money. All of it. Plus interest."

Something that looked like fear crossed her face. She wiped it away quickly with one of her dazzling smiles. "Enough for veterinarian school?"

He nodded, unable to convey all he was feeling in words.

"Enough for retirement?"

"Plus some."

She slid a fraction of an inch closer to him. "And your plans are?"

His gaze flickered to her mouth and back to her eyes. "I'm going to help my father hire a new foreman. We're going to start looking for a house in town. I'm going to find them a great financial planner so they don't have to worry about anything."

Her eyebrows slanted into a crease. "But what are *your* plans?"

"I'm going to officially accept the offer from Texas A&M for their veterinary program. I'm going to apply for my GI Bill to help pay for it." A flush rose through his face, but he refused to look anywhere but into her eyes. "I'm going to start looking for a new accountant for Three Rivers, because our current one is hopefully going to be moving to College Station."

He slid closer to her, not too close to crowd but definitely near enough to convey his intentions. "That is, if she'll come. Her, and her cute son, and of course, I'll be taking Benson. You know, all the people I love."

She closed the distance between them, her arms going around his shoulders as she said, "I love you, too, Squire."

As he brought his mouth to hers, he didn't think there were any better words in the world. A moment later, he broke the kiss. "Is that a yes? Will you marry me? Will you and Finn come with me to College Station?"

"Yes." She kissed him again. "And yes."

The End

Read all the books in the Three Rivers Ranch Romance series!

Second Chance Ranch: A Three Rivers Ranch Romance (Book 1): After his deployment, injured and discharged Major Squire Ackerman returns to Three Rivers Ranch, wanting to forgive Kelly for ignoring him a decade ago. He'd like to provide the stable life she needs, but with old wounds opening and a ranch on the brink of financial collapse, it will take patience and faith to make their second chance possible.

Third Time's the Charm: A Three Rivers Ranch Romance (Book 2): First Lieutenant Peter Marshall has a truckload of debt and no way to provide for a family, but Chelsea helps him see past all the obstacles, all the scars. With so many unknowns, can Pete and Chelsea develop the love, acceptance, and faith needed to find their happily ever after?

Read on for a sneak peek at the first chaper of Third Time's the Charm!

Fourth and Long: A Three Rivers Ranch Romance (Book 3):
Commander Brett Murphy goes to Three Rivers Ranch to find
some rest and relaxation with his Army buddies. Having his ex-wife
show up with a seven-year-old she claims is his son is anything but
the R&R he craves. Kate needs to make amends, and Brett needs
to find forgiveness, but are they too late to find their happily ever
after?

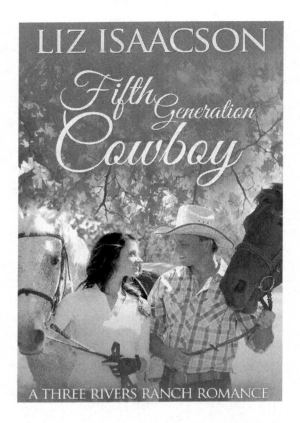

Fifth Generation Cowboy: A Three Rivers Ranch Romance (Book 4): Tom Lovell has watched his friends find their true happiness on Three Rivers Ranch, but everywhere he looks, he only sees friends. Rose Reyes has been bringing her daughter out to the ranch for equine therapy for months, but it doesn't seem to be working. Her challenges with Mari are just as frustrating as ever. Could Tom be exactly what Rose needs? Can he remove his friendship blinders and find love with someone who's been right in front of him all this time?

Sixth Street Love Affair: A Three Rivers Ranch Romance Novella: After losing his wife a few years back, Garth Ahlstrom thinks he's ready for a second chance at love. But Juliette Thompson has a secret that could destroy their budding relationship. Can they find the strength, patience, and faith to make things work?

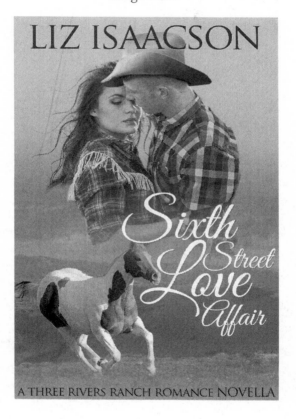

All newsletter subscribers will get this novella for free! The novella will be released on April 25 in an anthology of modern western romances, and individually as a novella on July 15, 2016.

The Seventh Sergeant: A Three Rivers Ranch Romance (Book 5): Discharged from the Army and now with a good job at Courage Reins, Sergeant Reese Sanders has finally found a new version of happiness—until a horrific fall puts him right back where he was years ago: Injured and depressed. Down-on-her luck Carly Watters despises small towns almost as much as she loathes cowboys. But she finds herself faced with both when she gets assigned to Reese's case. Do Reese and Carly have the humility and faith to make their relationship more than professional?

Coming on July 5, 2016!

Read on for a sneak peek at the first chaper of *Third Time's the Charm*, Book 2 in the Three Rivers Ranch Romance series!

Chapter One

The strip of skin on Chelsea Ackerman's ring finger hadn't been so blindingly white before. Of course, the first time she'd been engaged, it had been winter. The second time had been during the previous two months when the Texas sun had been at its pinnacle. This past summer's heat alone could've bronzed her skin while she worked indoors—all except what the diamond had protected.

She stared at that line, taking her attention from the two-lane highway leading her home. Home to a ranch she didn't want. Home to an empty homestead now that her parents were moving into town. Home after her brother and his fiancée had left for College Station so he could finish his veterinarian degree.

A blaring horn caused her to jerk the steering wheel to the right. Since she'd drifted across the middle line, she didn't hit the gravelly shoulder on her side of the road. She skidded to a stop anyway, her pulse bobbing in the back of her throat.

The truck that roared past belonged to Three Rivers, but Chelsea didn't recognize the man who drove it. No surprise there. She hadn't been home since last Christmas, and she certainly didn't keep up with the personnel on her family's cattle ranch.

She glared at the taillights retreating in her rearview mirror, switching her laser-gaze back to the traitorous tan line on her left ring finger. Strong emotion welled where her lungs were, making it impossible to breathe.

Sucking at the air, she fumbled for the door handle, getting a blast of October heat when she spilled from her luxury SUV. She bent over and braced her elbows on her knees, still trying to get enough air, still trying to forget about the circumstances that had led her to this stretch of road in the Texas Panhandle.

As her lungs remembered how to work, she vowed she'd never wear another engagement ring.

Fool me once, shame on you. Fool me twice, shame on me.

There would not be a third time.

Chelsea collected herself, grateful for once for the low population of Three Rivers. She gathered her designer sunglasses from where they'd fallen on the asphalt and returned to the driver's seat. The air-conditioned seats drove away the heat, and when she sealed herself back in the SUV, the air had re-oxygenated itself.

Gripping the steering wheel, she prepared to keep on toward her destination, much as she didn't want to. A sign several yards down the road caught her attention. She inched the car forward until she could read the faded letters.

Three Rivers Ranch, 5 . Five more miles until she met the worst turn her life had taken in the past twenty-eight years.

Beneath the old sign hung a much newer one. One that hadn't been there ten months ago.

Courage Reins Therapeutic Riding. No mileage included. Chelsea puzzled through what the sign could mean. Was this therapeutic riding program at the ranch?

Surely not. Someone would've mentioned as much to her. After all, she was the one taking over the management of the homestead until Squire graduated. The thought of planting and weeding her mother's massive vegetable garden made Chelsea feel twenty pounds heavier.

She pressed on the accelerator and centered the car in the appropriate lane. She'd find out about this Courage Reins in another five miles.

At the turnoff to Three Rivers, she squinted through the dusky sky to see another sign—new, with the same words. *Courage Reins.*

Annoyance sang through her. If the ranch had a new program, she should know about it.

She dismissed the thought. She wasn't in charge of the entire ranch. Her father had made that clear. She was to maintain the homestead—the house and the yard. Tom Lovell was the general controller and he oversaw the cowhands. Her father had hired a new foreman to replace the one who had been stealing money from the ranch for the past five years.

Chelsea sifted through her memories to remember his name. Garth Ahlstrom. He'd been foreman for a cattle ranch in Montana before making the move south. She shouldn't care about what happened once the grass of the homestead turned to the dirt parking lot on the ranch.

She pulled into the driveway leading to the garage, a wash of homesickness hitting her like a cold bucket of water. Which made no sense. She *was* home. This time, for a lot longer than it took to bake a ham and open presents.

She parked the car, but her fingers wouldn't release their grip on the wheel.

"Come on, Chels," she coaxed herself. "Just go in. It's going to be fine."

Fine wasn't quite the word she'd been using on the six-hour drive from Dallas. *Fine* wasn't the word her boss had used when she'd told him she was quitting to babysit a piece of land and a house. *Fine* wasn't the world that came to Chelsea's mind when she got the call from the hospital informing her of her fiancée's "accident."

She pushed away memories and remembrances of her life in Dallas. She didn't have a life in Dallas. Not anymore.

Her open-toed sandals drank up dust as she made her way into the garage. Once there, she scaled the steps to the entrance to the house. She braced herself for the smell of her mother's cooking to hit her upon the opening of the door. Surely her mom had been baking all afternoon in anticipation of Chelsea's arrival.

Sure enough, when she cracked the door, the scent of whole wheat bread slammed into her nostrils, along with the mouth-watering smell of roasting meat. She slipped through the mudroom and loitered in the doorway that led to the kitchen.

The ease with which her mother moved with a knife in her hand only served to remind Chelsea that she'd burned her last microwave meal. She wasn't fit to take care of the homestead, and anyone with one eye knew it.

"Hey, Mom." Chelsea ignored the skittering in her chest and the way her feet had grown roots.

"Chelsea, honey." Her mom set down the knife and moved around the counter for a hug. Chelsea managed to uproot herself and cross the room. "How was the drive?"

"Good," Chelsea lied. "Long." Only because she'd turned around twice, driven for a few miles back toward Dallas before forcing herself north again.

Boxes lined the wall behind the dining room table, which was likewise stacked with packed garment bags, suitcases, and dishware.

"Sorry about the mess," her mom said, returning to the zucchini squash on the cutting board. "But we'll be gone tomorrow, and this place will be yours." Her voice carried too much gravity, breaking at the end.

Chelsea looked away as her mother wept, her own tears pressing so close, so close, so close.

"I'll go look at my room," she said, holding her breath as she clicked across the kitchen tile. Once in the safety of the hall, she released the air, which shuddered on the way out.

She didn't understand why her parents were leaving a house they clearly loved. Squire wouldn't need it for four more years. Chelsea certainly didn't need it now. She could've gone anywhere after the phone call that led to a hospital that led to her wearing black and speaking about Danny like he was the greatest man who'd lived.

A sob shook her shoulders, also knocking something loose inside her chest. Something that felt like her ability to sympathize, forgive, love.

Her mascara smeared when she wiped her eyes, but she didn't care. She wouldn't come out of her room tonight, not even for her mother's goodbye feast.

She didn't go down the hall to her old bedroom. Instead, she slipped downstairs and outside to the patio sheltered by a deck above. She perched on a decorative boulder and let the darkness inside her spread until even her tears felt like tar leaking from her eyes.

"You okay, ma'am?"

Chelsea startled at the masculine tone, wiping again at her face. Her fingers came away stained with black and blue. So much for waterproof makeup.

"I'm fine." She didn't mean for her voice to blow through the space like an arctic wind. She turned toward the man and found a tall specimen with more muscles than she knew could be contained by skin.

The concern in his green eyes frosted at her tone, and as he crossed his arms, Chelsea saw the puckered and pink skin of a burn on his right side. The mark extended under the sleeves of the blue T-shirt he wore and marred all the fingers on his right hand.

"Of course you are," he said. "I regularly cry in a remote place on the ranch because I'm *fine*."

She didn't need this stranger judging her, and she certainly wasn't in the mood for company.

"It's none of your concern." She stood like she'd march away, but realized she didn't have anywhere else to go. Though she wasn't happy to be here, she didn't want to make things harder for her mother.

He saluted her. "If you say so." He ambled to the stone steps he must've come down. She hadn't heard him in her distress.

Her breath hitched and the writhing in her stomach felt like she'd swallowed snakes.

He was leaving, the same way Danny had left.

"What do you do on the ranch?" she called after him, suddenly desperate to keep him there for a few more minutes.

The man twisted back to her but maintained his position on the steps. "I'm opening the new therapeutic riding program."

And she wanted him to leave again. "Courage Reins. I saw the signs on the way in." She reseated herself and flicked an imaginary piece of lint from her leggings. "What is it?"

His gaze gave none of his emotions away. "It's a therapeutic riding program." He spoke slower, like perhaps she didn't understand English.

"What—does—it—do?" She dragged out each word in case his hearing had been affected in whatever accident had given him that burn.

"We take individuals who've been through trauma, and we help them with their rehabilitation."

"So like physical therapy."

"Any kind of trauma," he said.

She swept her gaze meaningfully toward his arm. "Like yours."

His gaze bored into hers, straight past every one of her defenses. "Or yours." He turned and marched up the steps, leaving Chelsea gasping for breath and grasping for something to keep her from drowning under the sudden memories of Danny's death.

Dear Lord, she prayed. *Help me.*

In her distress, she couldn't articulate much more than that.

Pete Marshall stalked away from Squire's sister, the scarred skin covered by his shirt prickling uncomfortably. The princess obviously thought all wounds were physical. Pete knew better, had overheard the Ackerman's say something about their daughter's boyfriend at breakfast a while back.

He'd been so absorbed with getting Courage Reins off the ground, he hadn't paid as much attention as he might have otherwise. All he knew was that she'd quit her job and volunteered to return to Three Rivers so her parents could move into town.

Pete already missed Frank and Heidi and they weren't moving until tomorrow. All their cowhands were helping, Pete included.

He paused outside the horse barn, regret singing through him. He wasn't just opening Courage Reins—he worked the ranch too. And Chelsea was obviously in distress, and she didn't need him exacerbating her condition. He turned around to go back to the house, hoping she'd still be weeping on the downstairs patio. Well, maybe not the crying bit. He had no idea how to deal with weepy women.

The sight of her stomping toward him froze him to the path. Her chestnut brown hair swung in time to her hips as her sandals ate up the distance between them.

"Look," she called from several yards away. "I don't know who you think you are, but I'm going to be taking over the homestead."

"I know, sweetheart."

She stopped a few feet away, flinching as if the lash of his endearment had struck like a backhand to her cheek.

"Who are you?"

"First Lieutenant Peter Marshall." He saluted again, sure she didn't want him touching her if the crossed arms and cocked hip were any indication. Pete had certain skills when it came to reading people, and Chelsea screamed *angry*.

The creases around her eyes softened. "Did you serve with my brother?"

"Twice."

Her eyes flickered to his scars again, and Pete worked hard to keep his expression neutral and the flush down in his chest where she couldn't see it. His injuries belonged to him now, no matter how much he wished they didn't. He'd had a year to get used to the idea, and the past few months of attending church with the Ackerman's had helped him accept God's will.

He was still here, after all. Still alive. And with the concept of Courage Reins getting off the ground, Pete finally felt like he had a *reason* to be here, a purpose for being alive.

"I'm sorry," he said into the gusting silence between them. "I shouldn't have snapped at you back there, what with you crying and all."

"I said I was—"

"Fine, I know." The sun made an appearance behind the

evening clouds. He pushed his cowboy hat lower over his eyes. "You want to go riding anyway? It makes some people feel better."

"I feel fine."

Sure she did. Pete had told himself that for months too, but he also knew she needed time for her own grieving. "Suit yourself. I have a client tomorrow evening, after your parents move, so I need to do a test ride." He hooked his thumb over his shoulder toward the horse barn. "Last chance."

The color drained from Chelsea's face, but it could've been a trick of the fading light. She shook her head, spun on her heel, and hurried away from him like he had a contagious disease.

He saddled Peony and headed along the path he'd mapped out. Past the horse pasture, the bull pens, and out onto the range. His hope was that by bringing people to the ranch they'd find the same comfort, the same peace, the same rehabilitation he'd felt in his body and soul when he'd come to Three Rivers.

The sky turned the color of a deep bruise, and he directed Peony back to the barn. The man coming tomorrow afternoon had suffered some core injuries during his deployment. Working with a horse could provide a bond that would help his self-confidence, and once he learned to ride, he'd be able to work his core muscles as he balanced and directed the horse.

Pete had decided to have Reese start with Peony in the barn first. Brushing, saddling. Then he'd lead her around the arena before Pete would allow him to ride. He had a game of pony ball ready if the veteran could handle it.

The package he'd sold included six weekly sessions of two hours each, and as Pete brushed Peony he let his mind wander to future packages and how he could get the word out about the program to other veterans. Without many new ideas, he closed up the barn for the night and returned to the cabin where he lived alone now that Squire had moved to College Station with his fiancée, Kelly Armstrong.

He flipped open his laptop and searched for information on therapeutic programs for veterans. It wasn't the first time he'd researched other facilities, but just as with the previous few times, the amount of information available became overwhelming after only five minutes.

Pete reached for a pen and scratched out a few more notes to himself. *Research how to join PATH International* and *ask Squire about purchasing land for the facility* got added to his list before he headed over to the homestead for Heidi and Frank's farewell dinner.

As he walked, Chelsea's haunted midnight blue eyes filled his mind. The woman needed help, and as Pete entered the halo of light radiating from the kitchen, he felt certain God wanted him to aid in her rehabilitation.

About Liz

Liz Isaacson writes inspirational romance, usually set in Texas, or Wyoming, or anywhere else horses and cowboys exist. She lives in Utah, where she teaches elementary school, taxis her daughter to dance several times a week, and eats a lot of Ferrero Rocher while writing.

Find her on her website at lizisaacson.blogspot.com.

She also writes as Elana Johnson, who is the author of the young adult *Possession* series, which includes full-length novels POSSESSION, SURRENDER, and ABANDON, and short stories REGRET (ebook only) and RESIST (free). She is also the author of ELEVATED and SOMETHING ABOUT LOVE, which are young adult contemporary romance novels-in-verse, and a new adult futuristic fantasy series that includes ELEMENTAL RUSH, ELEMENTAL HUNGER, and ELEMENTAL RELEASE.

Made in the USA
Lexington, KY
25 July 2017